333 MILES

THIRTY YEARS...
HALFWAY TO NOWHERE...
ALL THE
WAY
TO
VEGAS.

CRAIG BIRK

ACKNOWLEDGEMENTS

Thank you to my parents for providing the love,
support, and environment to create
a life full of opportunity.

Thank you to my gorgeous wife for helping me to
slowly see the real meaning of beauty.

Thank you to my friends for all the good times.
We have been blessed.

Thank you to the three guys who employed
me for a long time. I grew up there in many ways,
and it was a lot of fun.

333 MILES

CHAPTER ONE

Another Friday
Friday, October 13th, 2006 - 1:22 p.m.

"Turn around bitch I got a use for you
Besides, you ain't got nothin' better to do...
And I'm bored"
—*It's So Easy,* Guns N' Roses

ON A WOODEN PARK BENCH, commanding a panoramic view spanning the blue vastness of the Pacific Ocean and the shoreline up to Torrey Pines, stood a healthy four-year-old seagull. The gull had no name. He did have a long, solid, yellow beak with a curved orange stripe toward the end. Despite his general vigor, like many of his fellow Americans, the seagull was visibly overweight.

The gull slowly stretched his neck toward the sky, then shook his head profusely and opened his yellow beak widely four times in rapid succession, but no noise was emitted. He was not enjoying the ocean view. Instead, he was intently focused on a nearby Mexican-American family sitting atop a large diagonally patterned red and yellow blanket.

The family, consisting of a mother, a father, a nine-year-old boy and a five-year-old girl, had just finished a hearty lunch of burgers and fries. The parents, both of whom were significantly more overweight than the seagull, had already consumed the entirety of their food. The small girl, however, had apparently lost interest in the second half of her bag of fries. Herein lay the seagull's primary object of desire.

The bird relied on human interaction for much of his food and had developed very useful stereotypes. Most importantly, the younger, smaller humans were much more likely to mount an attack. But these advances were nearly always harmless and could be ignored or easily evaded. Signs of a physical assault by the larger ones, while rare, should be taken very seriously. He also developed a knack for knowing which humans would stay in one place for a long time and which would change locations more frequently, thereby providing greater access to unattended food. As the gull expected, within minutes, this family had shifted several feet away from the blanket and began kicking a ball back and forth to one another. Lighter-skinned humans usually chose to entertain themselves by passing objects about using their arms, while the darker ones preferred to use their legs. Because of this, the lighter ones tended to be more accurate and dangerous when they threw rocks at the bird, a most annoying and seemingly pointless activity, but an unfortunately common one. All female humans, although they engaged in the throwing of rocks just as often as the males, were essentially harmless. The much darker people, who were quite rare at Ellen Browning Scripps Park in La Jolla, did not usually partake in the passing of objects games and tended to represent a low threat level.

Unlike humans, seagulls do not waste the obvious opportunities life presents. The seagull first used his legs to jump of the bench, and then flapped his wings in three short bursts, achieving an altitude of five feet. From there, he descended quickly, covering the remaining fifteen feet to the red and yellow target in just a few seconds. The gull landed immediately next to the half-eaten bag of fries, grabbed it with his healthy beak and flew back to his bench, careful to ensure the bag remained upright so none of the fries were spilled.

Just beyond the park, below a small cliff, light waves peacefully blanketed a rocky beach, infusing a soundtrack only the ocean is capable of. The air in the park was warm and sweet, with just enough humidity to create a soft, pleasant sense of tangibility. A faint smell of cut grass joined forces amicably with the aroma of seawater. In the middle of a brilliant blue sky, whose shade grew slightly lighter further out toward the horizon, the sun was well positioned to overlook every detail. A few miles up the coast, two medium-sized, puffy white clouds imperceptibly made their way inland. The sense of peace was palpable. It was a very average San Diego afternoon.

Regardless, the seagull did not have the luxury of enjoying a leisurely meal, and he gulped down the remaining fries vengefully. Once finished, undisturbed by humans or other birds, he allowed himself a moment to relax. He again stretched his neck towards the sky, and then settled into a resting position to survey the scene. Thirty seconds later, content with all aspects of life, the seagull again jumped off the bench and took flight. His path led him over the ocean and he looked downwards as he passed over the small cliffs which divided the park and the sea. He lifted his head back up and continued flapping his wings to gain altitude for the next thirty seconds, continuously venturing farther from shore. Once satisfied with his height, the bird banked sharply to the right and began a swooping turn back toward land. At an altitude of forty-five feet, he crossed back over the northeast end of the park and seconds later passed over the Grande Colonial hotel. With no particular destination in mind, the seagull veered to the right again, now peering down at a newly opened restaurant on the site of the old La Jolla Hard Rock Cafe. While doing so, he noticed a slightly uncomfortable feeling in his stomach that was no doubt caused by the greasy fries.

The seagull veered left in a southern direction over Girard Avenue and then made a right over Pearl Street. With minimal effort but significant relief, he paused between flapping his wings and ejected a large quantity of excrement. Like a fighter plane on a bombing run, the gull banked hard back to the right immediately after releasing his payload and headed back to the park to look for more food.

The poop began its descent toward land at a sixty-five degree angle relative to the earth but quickly flattened into a straight downward trajectory. Twenty feet from impact, the poop broke into two pieces, with the smaller piece drifting slightly to the left in the breeze.

At 1:28:13 p.m., Alex Reine was purposefully walking down La Jolla Boulevard. Despite being the fourth most profitable "Financial Advisor" at Pantheon Capital's San Diego branch at only thirty years of age, Alex still did not have a parking spot in the company garage. Parking spots were the final remaining benefit awarded on the basis of seniority rather than profitability. Thus, Alex had to leave the building and walk four blocks to a paid parking lot if he needed something out of his car, usually change to buy Diet Coke from the vending machine. While annoyed about the $180 a month the spot cost him, he liked having an excuse to get outside and take a short walk a few times a day.

Alex wore a grey Joseph Abboud suit with barely noticeable thin blue lines forming a wide checker pattern. It perfectly matched the brown Fratelli Rossetti shoes he bought in Milan last summer, which were currently his favorite pair even though he usually preferred black shoes. Tucked in the back of his violet Thomas Pink tie was an Apple iPod nano. When Alex first saw that they made a tie designed to hold an iPod, he exclaimed to the girl he was with at the time that it was "gay" and wondered, "What are things coming to?" Since then, however, he had come around on the idea and he now owned three ties with the multi-functional design.

It's So Easy, by Guns N' Roses played on the earbuds connected to the iPod at a volume loud enough to enjoy but low enough not to block Alex totally from the outside environment. Observing the world from behind a pair of vintage Wayfarer sunglasses, he quietly sang along:

"It's so easy, easy
When everybody's tryin to
Please me baby
Yeah, it's so easy, easy,
When everybody's tryin to please me

So eaaaasy . . .
But nothing seems to please me"

A minute later, just as *It's So Easy* transitioned into *Nightrain*, Alex arrived at the corner of La Jolla Boulevard and Pearl. On the northeast corner lay the one true fast food chain restaurant in downtown La Jolla – Jack in the Box. He paused for a second on the sidewalk, running his hands through his short, slightly wavy, dark-blondish hair which he once proclaimed to be "like Mark McGrath's." He received so much ridicule for this comment that he never mentioned it again, even though he continued to believe it was a valid comparison.

Alex put a lot of effort into maintaining his looks and was fully aware of the many benefits they afforded him. This was equally true with girls, clients and co-workers. Alex stood barely over six feet tall. However, due to a magnetic personality, frequent use of an engaging fake laugh/smile, and an ability to fully integrate his hands and body into his speech, most people remembered him as taller. Alex was equally as comfortable lunching at the yacht club with retired multi-millionaires as he was playing one-dollar liars dice in a dive bar with the surfer crowd in Pacific Beach. People usually liked Alex largely because he liked himself.

He worked out at least five times a week and was careful what he ate. These efforts, while successful overall, were forced to compete with a robust alcohol intake and frequent Jack in the Box visits. Alex considered if he could justify one now. He remembered he had a salad for dinner the night before and completed a three-mile run before work.

As he deliberated, a small piece of bird poo landed harmlessly in the bushes next to him. Two tenths of a second later, a larger piece landed directly on the left Fratelli Rossetti, covering the brown leather with white and yellowish goo.

Some cultures consider it a good omen to be hit by bird shit, but Alex was unaware of this and would not have agreed in any case. He generally considered himself to be a lucky person and was vexed at his misfortune. "Cock Goblin!" he pronounced loud enough to hear himself over the iPod. Anger overcame surprise and misfortune, but by the time Alex located his assailant, the seagull had began an aggressive descent to the right and was already far out of range of any potential revenge.

The sequence of events left Alex little choice but to enter the Jack in the Box in order to clean his shoe. It would be silly not to enjoy lunch there as well. He reached under his tie with the intention of stopping the iPod, but changed his mind at the last moment and instead turned up the volume and fast forwarded in order to listen to the first thirty seconds of *My Michelle*.

The interior of the Jack in the Box was nearly perfectly square-shaped. The registers were thirty-five feet from the front entrance. Just about everything in the restaurant was red, white, black or yellow. Alex noticed the same was true of In-N-Out, McDonalds (only with more yellow of course), Carl's Jr. (again with more yellow) and Burger King. He wondered if there was something about this color scheme that encouraged burger eating. At one of the half-booth/half-tables on his right, a twenty-three-year-old, slightly overweight, blonde girl was struggling to get her two kids to consume their food items without wiping the condiments all over their Old Navy clothes. There were no other occupied tables, which was strange because it was still within the range of normal lunch hours.

When Alex emerged from the bathroom minutes later, his shoes looking almost newly polished, two registers were open. An obese lady (crazy, gigantic fat actually), wearing some kind of huge denim skirt with a black shirt, and who may have been about thirty-five years of age, was ordering at the one on the right.

The left register was empty. From the opposite side of the restaurant, a fortyish man with some type of muscular disability, wearing acid-washed jeans and a classic wife-beater shirt, was lurching heavily toward it. The man was about fifteen to twenty feet away from the available register and was making steady progress despite his handicap. Alex broke into a medium-speed trot and successfully overtook him, gaining the front spot and feeling somewhat relieved he would not have to wait for anyone else to order before him. He was completely oblivious to the fat lady observing him with a disgusted look on her face, her stringy brown bangs held out of her face with one of her pudgy hands.

The cashier working Alex's register was a short Mexican male in his late twenties. His name was Jose, according to the red and white name tag attached to his uniform. Though the Jack in the Box employee English as a Second Language program, Jose had become a fluent English speaker over the past two years. In another six months, he would be promoted to shift manager and make more money per month than he ever imagined when he lived just over the border in Tecate, Mexico. So much money, in fact, that it would exceed what Alex earned in a typical day.

At restaurants, Alex always made an effort to be courteous and to make eye contact with the servers. This practice was the result of a date he had when he was twenty-six in which the girl told him that one of her primary ways to judge a guy was to see how he treated the help. "Because that is probably how he is going to treat me in five years," she explained cheerfully between bites of a papaya salad.

The comment stuck with Alex, but he did not afford the same respect to fast food cashiers. "Two-tacos-and-a-sour-dough-Jack-with-no-mayo-and-a-medium-Diet-Coke please," Alex requested in rapid speech, all while leaning back and staring at the black menu with little white letters and numbers and pictures of various meal combinations above the cashier's head. The words ran together, taking only two seconds to come out of his mouth.

Nine highly satisfying minutes later, Alex sucked down the last sip of the Diet Coke and re-read for the fourteenth time the paper insert inside the red tray his food was served on. He was by now vaguely aware of its message: it seemed Jack (a tall guy wearing a suit who possessed an abnormally big, round, white head) felt there was a valid comparison between the restaurant's new sandwiches and those served in the cafes in Saint-Tropez. Alex made a weak mental note that he should try to see Saint-Tropez before he turned thirty-five and would be too old to really enjoy it. Realizing that one probably needs a yacht to do that particular trip properly, he cursed himself lightly for not making more money. Then he made a mental note to try and make more money. This thought led to the realization that he should probably go back to work.

"Donkey Punch," he thought to himself.

After checking his Tag Heuer watch (he had one with a blue face like the one in the Tiger Woods ad, though he really only wanted one after he saw Maria Sharapova promote the women's version) he sat back in his red plastic chair and exhaled deeply. He subconsciously Al Bundied his right hand halfway into his pants, the lower part of his palm resting on his stomach outside of his Armani dress shirt. He scanned the interior of the Jack in the Box and focused in on the fat lady from the register. She was struggling to scoop out the last of the fries from her jumbo-sized container because her hand did not fit cleanly inside of it. He noticed with some revulsion that it appeared she had already eaten one Jumbo Jack and still had a Sourdough Jack waiting on deck. All of this was being washed down with a large vanilla shake.

Alex simultaneously grimaced and said quietly aloud to himself, "Gross." He sat up and exited the restaurant. Energized by the meal and invigorated by the sunshine, Alex found himself in a very good mood, feeling pleased with himself and his life and no longer bothered by the unfortunate seagull incident. He checked the Tag Heuer again, which now showed that it was 1:40 p.m. Most of the more successful brokers took Friday afternoons off to play golf or drink beers. Alex usually worked diligently until at least five o'clock, finding that this was a good time to get ahead on things without being bothered much. Today, however, he distinctly did not feel like being back in the office.

He retrieved his Motorola Razr cell phone out of his pants pocket, hit the contacts button and scrolled down to "Deez Nutz," which was sandwiched between "Danielle" and "Dianna." Danielle he had gone out with three times, fucked once, and then took on an ill-fated trip to Rosarito where they both got food poisoning from the taco shop outside of the hotel and took turns using the bathroom for the next twenty-four hours. They did not go out together again. He had no idea who Dianna was. "Deez Nutz" was really Mike Bochner, Alex's best friend from college. Alex pressed the green Send button.

CHAPTER TWO

The Cubicle

1:41 p.m.

"So I was sitting in my cubicle today,
and I realized, ever since I started working,
every single day of my life has been worse
than the day before it. So that means that
every single day that you see me, that's
on the worst day of my life."

—Peter Gibbons, *Office Space*

WHEN THE PHONE RANG, Mike Bochner was sitting in his cubicle on the third floor of the nondescript beige Qualcomm headquarters building in Mira Mesa, about fifteen miles north of downtown San Diego. He was subtly picking his nose with his left hand and playing a miniature golf video game embedded into a popup Orbitz ad with his right hand. Though the ceiling of the room was eleven feet high, his cubicle was exactly six feet by six feet by six feet. He sometimes wondered, because of this, if the devil had anything to do with his confinement to corporate prison/hell. He often wished the grey "sound-proof" walls were higher because he was sick of hearing the incessant pseudo-drama from the girl in the cube next to his (a short, blonde girl from Ohio named Molly). Molly had been married for two years and was upset that her husband was getting fat. Apparently, since the wedding he spent most of his time playing X-Box online and drinking Sierra Nevada. Mike often wondered if she realized this may be related to the fact she too had gained about twenty pounds since the wedding and was so fucking annoying to begin with that putting on headphones and cyber-joining some geeks in the Midwest to help kill a bunch of space aliens (or Germans on Thursdays) was probably the best alternative the poor guy had. It puzzled Mike that, although he genuinely disliked Molly and found her utterly unattractive, he frequently fantasized about her while jerking off.

Unlike most of his co-workers, who behaved as though their cubicle was a college dorm, Mike's cube was sparsely decorated. He had a Padres season schedule to the left of the computer and, though he considered himself to be a staunch Republican, an autographed picture of Chelsea Clinton to the right. Three-inch-tall plastic figures of Beavis and Butt-head stood at opposing ends of the base of his seventeen-inch flat-screen monitor. On the rear wall was a bookshelf whose contents resembled the software programming section at Borders.

While generally good-looking, Mike was probably about as plain as the cubicle. At about 5'11," 185 pounds, he was not a small guy, but he could blend in pretty well just about everywhere. He had short brown hair and was not exactly balding but had what Alex annoyingly liked to describe as "major league power alleys." He mostly wore Dockers' pants and Banana Republic button-up shirts to work. Every time Qualcomm stock dropped more than fifteen percent, there would be increased talk of requiring people to wear ties, but thankfully, that policy had not yet become official. Mike thought that would be the thing that would finally make him quit, but he had also thought that about a lot of other things. All in all, he knew it was a pretty good job, and it paid fairly well. Because he started with the company in 2001, he missed out on the boom years of stock option rewards during the bubble and had nowhere near the kind of money many of his older co-workers, now frequently referred to as "volunteers", had. Nearly daily, Mike fantasized about moving up to Silicon Valley to join a dot-com or some other start-up, but at the end of the day he knew he wasn't a big risk taker and was fairly comfortable where he was. This didn't mean he didn't bitch a lot.

Mike snapped up the phone quickly: "Good afternoon, this is Mike Bochner."

Alex's response came immediately: "Whattup douche-bag! Happy Friday."

Mike replied with neither enthusiasm nor annoyance: "Hello Alex."

Alex: "Hey big man."

Mike: "What's up?"

Alex: "I am sure you are busy, so let me get right to it. I was thinking…going to bars tonight, getting drunk and trying to trick ourselves that we are still twenty-six doesn't sound terribly appealing at the moment. There is more to life …greater things can be accomplished. And as much as I would enjoy staying home and spanking your ass all night in Madden, there is an even better option. You deserve more, and so do I. You work hard, right?"

Mike was by now used to Alex using leading questions and largely ignored them: "Sure."

Alex: "And that is why we are going to Vegas instead."

Mike: "Vegas? Tonight? The two of us? I don't think so, dude."

Alex (assuming his closing voice): "Yes. That's right. Tonight. It will be fantastic. Make it happen for us, Mike. Let's do it together."

Mike missed a one-and-a-half-inch putt in the Orbitz game and cursed beneath his breath. He finished the three-hole course with a two-under-par seven, about average but nowhere near as good as his record, a very lucky four. He hit the Try Again button to resume another game.

Mike: "I don't know, dude. I mean if we want to gamble, maybe it would be easier just to go out to the Injin casino."

Alex: "Fuck that, the Injin casino sucks and you know it. I think you are forgetting I grew up in Reno and there is a reason I left. I am talking Vegas here. Anyway, I don't really want to gamble that much. I want us to go party together."

Mike: "Dude, your family lived in Reno for like ten months so save the sob story. Plus, I heard they have a new attraction where there's a drunk Indian in a tent or a tee-pee or something out behind the bingo room. He sits on a stool and for twenty bucks you get a shot of whiskey and a pair boxing gloves and you can take a swing and hit him as hard as you can."

Alex: "Bullshit."

Mike: "No, I'm serious. It is called the Drunken Indian Booth."

Alex: "Can you hit him in the face?"

Mike: "I think so, yeah."

Alex: "Does he get a shot of whiskey also?"

Mike: "I'm not sure, I guess probably if you buy one for him. Apparently, it's pretty hard to knock him off the stool even though he is totally wasted. I think if you do you get a free bingo card or an entry into a slot tournament or something."

Alex: "You are so full of shit it is unbelievable."

Mike: "No, I swear to God. I saw a thing on it on Channel Nine last night. Some of the activist groups are like, um, all pissed off about it and stuff."

Alex (wrinkling his nose in thought): "Interesting. Is it at Viejas or Barona?"

Mike: "Viejas."

Alex: "Hmmm. Well...I mean that sounds cool and all, but even so, I want to do Vegas. We can check out the drunken Injin next week."

Mike (laughing): "Jesus, you are stupid. There is no drunken Indian booth. But anyway, I don't know about Vegas. It sounds like a hassle and I don't think I want to blow the cash."

Alex: "Come on. Sack up. I don't want to go back to work and I am bored. If I can get Roger and G-Balls to come, are you in?"

Mike: "Yeah, right. Good luck. The Rodge is for sure dead broke, and I don't think Gary has been out of the house since, like, they had the kid."

Alex: "I think Roger hit a four-teamer last weekend so he should be good. Anyway, let me worry about them. It will be good for you. And it will be like the good ol' days. Come on. Just say yes."

Mike, like most people, for some reason or another usually went along with what Alex wanted to do. "Fine, but only if everyone is in, which will never happen," he said.

Then, after a pause in which neither said anything, he asked, "Are we flying or driving?"

Alex: "I'll drive. It will be cheaper. Can you leave work at three?"

Mike: "Yeah probably, but like I said, I am only in if everyone is in. And I am not sharing a bed with The Rodge."

Alex: "That's the spirit. You won't regret it. I'll call you back. Tell that slap-dick boss of yours you are leaving at three."

CHAPTER THREE

The Blair Project
1:53 p.m.

*"Behind every good man there is a woman,
and that woman was Martha Washington,
man, and everyday George would come home,
she would have a big fat bowl waiting for him,
man, when he come in the door, man. She was
a hip, hip, hip lady, man."*

—Slater, *Dazed and Confused*

WHEN ALEX CALLED, BLAIR Williams was sitting at the
kitchen table with her three-year-old daughter, Sarah. They
were playing a Fisher Price game that helped kids learn
European geography. Usually kid's toys bored the hell out of
Blair, but she found she was learning quite a bit with this one.
Also, it allowed her to indulge her favorite fantasy about trav-
eling to Paris with her husband Gary (usually she pictured
Gary), driving through Bordeaux for a few days and then
renting a villa high above the French Riviera. In these visions,
her hair was a very dark brown (just like Penelope Cruz) and

her body looked like it did before Sarah was born (sort of like Penelope Cruz).

Her real house was not a French villa but instead a perfectly nice three-bedroom, two-and-a-half bath home located in University City, about ten minutes northeast of downtown La Jolla. Though a stereotypical, peaceful, middle-class suburban neighborhood, it maintained a vibrant, young feel to it. Gary had lived in a similar house just around the corner when he was in college. In fact, a few of their current neighbors were college students renting houses. Blair usually thought this was cool, but was less happy about it when the girls renting across the street would wash their cars or water the lawn in outfits she thought more appropriate for a Britney Spears video. She had noticed the girls' outdoor household chores often seemed to coincide with a rare decision by Gary to do some lawn maintenance.

Still, it was a nice neighborhood and she felt secure. The two hundred thousand dollars or so the house had appreciated in the few years since they purchased it didn't bother her either. At twenty-eight years old, Blair considered her life a success so far. She had a good marriage, a beautiful daughter, and owned a nice home. What more could a woman ask for? Well, maybe the Gucci bag she had her eye on. And that trip to France.

Blair put down a piece of the geography game identifying Ljubljana as the capital of Slovenia and moved to pick up the cordless phone. "Hold on one minute, sweetie," she said to Sarah cheerfully before answering. She wouldn't be in as good of a mood in five minutes.

Alex was now sitting on a bus stop bench a half a block from the Jack in the Box. The bench was enclosed by two large advertisements and a small plastic roof. On his right side was a beautiful blonde girl photographed in black and white advertising Guess jeans. On the left was an unhappy-looking woman who was also photographed in black and white. This second display appeared to be advocating against domestic violence but Alex was not immediately sure because it was in Spanish and he was focusing on making a phone call rather than studying bus stop advertisements. His call was answered on the fourth ring.

Alex: "Hey Blair, this is Alex. How are you?"

Blair's eyes instinctively narrowed at the sound of his voice: "Hi Alex. Gary is still at work."

Alex: "Yeah, I know. Actually I wanted to talk to you about something."

Blair: "Really? What is it?"

Alex: "Well, I want to ask a favor, but it isn't for me. I'll spare you the details, but the bottom line is that Mike met a girl and yada, yada...something crazy happened, and they are getting married next month. It is totally nuts. Really wacky stuff. I can barely believe it. Anyway, we want to give him a bachelor party and there are conflicts for the other weekends left, so this is the only possible time. A few of us are taking him out to Vegas tonight for a real quick weekend trip and I know it would mean a lot of Gary could come."

"Mike is getting married?" Blair asked incredulously. Somehow in her mind this cheapened the whole institution of marriage.

Alex: "Yeah, it's unreal. I can't believe it either."

Blair: "Why doesn't Gary ask me himself if he wants to go to Vegas?"

Alex: "Well, Gary doesn't even know yet. The whole thing just happened in the last few days. My guess is the booze outsmarted Mike and he just proposed in a moment of drunken inspiration, but really I don't even know all the details myself. But I do know it would mean the world if G-Ball, I mean if Gary, could be there for this weekend. Since its so last minute I wanted to be in touch with you first, because I am sure you guys have plans already."

Blair: "Yes, we are supposed to buy a new table for the dining room. Also new plates and steak knives for the kitchen."

Alex: "Well there you go. See, I knew it. But the thing is you only get married once (laughs), though in Mike's case the over/under is at two and a half. But seriously, it would mean a lot. Anyway, I will let Gary talk about it with you, but I just wanted to let you know the situation first so you know it isn't his fault for the late notice."

Blair: "Gee, that is sweet Alex. Okay listen, Gary can go, but make sure he stops by here first."

Alex: "You're the best Blair. Mike will really appreciate it."

Blair: "Bye, Alex."

Alex: "Thanks Blair. Say hello to Sarah for me. Talk at you later. Bye."

CHAPTER FOUR

The Rodge
2:00 p.m.

"You got to know when to hold em,
know when to fold em,
Know when to walk away and
know when to run.
You never count your money when
you're sittin at the table.
There'll be time enough for countin
when the dealin's done."

– *The Gambler*, Kenny Rogers

ROGER WALKED OUT OF Moondoggies in Pacific Beach at exactly 2:00 p.m. wearing black slacks and a wrinkled blue short-sleeved Hawaiian tee shirt. For having only worked three hours on a lunch shift, he was relatively pleased to have ninety-five dollars in his pocket. He was not pleased that he forgot his sunglasses at home and he recoiled sharply when he hit the sunlight. He briefly put his left arm in front of his face to shield the light, then ran his hand through his full head of closely cut brown hair. After, he raised his right arm to take a sip out of a twenty-ounce plastic bottle of regular Coke.

It was a very pleasant day, but the sun radiated off of the heavy concentration of cement and asphalt on Garnet Street, pushing the temperature into the slightly uncomfortable range. The usual Friday afternoon crowd was milling about the streets. It featured about half college chicks shopping at the various boutiques and surf shops, a handful of college dudes doing basically nothing, scattered military guys starting the weekend beer drinking marathon early, and a few middle-aged people who probably had some kind of job, though it really didn't seem like it. After orienting himself to the light and remembering where he parked, Roger began to walk down the street. After about thirty feet, he untucked the Hawaiian shirt, placed the Coke bottle in his mouth so he could hold it with his teeth, and dug into his pockets with both hands, ultimately locating his objective in the left pocket. He pulled out a one-third full, silver and green can of Kodiak wintergreen chewing tobacco.

Roger looked around and spotted a bus stop about forty feet farther up the road. He walked over, took a seat on one of the benches, set the Coke on the ground, and began packing the can of chew, subconsciously scanning the street to see if there were any hot chicks he could be looking at.

He opened the can, glanced inside to ensure it was adequately packed, and took inventory of how much remained. He squeezed a medium-sized pinch of Kodiak between his right thumb and forefinger and placed it in his lower lip. Despite his frequent use of the product, he still felt the soft pleasing burning sensation the tobacco caused in its first few seconds. He grabbed a few more grains out of the can and added them to the amount already in his mouth.

Then he used his tongue to marry the new addition into the old one. Satisfied with his chew, Roger reached down to grab the Coke and proceeded to pour the remaining contents onto the sidewalk. While doing so, he noticed a colony of ants crawling around by his right foot. He used the last two ounces to attempt to drown as many of them as possible. At least fifteen of the small black creatures were engulfed in the brown foamy liquid and began squirming helplessly.

Roger pressed the chew further down into his lip with his tongue and then spit once into the now empty Coke bottle. He then reached into his right pocket and removed his cell phone. After pressing the button for Cingular web service, he hit the # key and then the 1 key for "favorite #1," which was ESPN.com. After waiting about ten seconds, he realized he didn't have reception in this area. "Fucking Cingular," he muttered to himself for what seemed like the millionth time.

Roger spit again, this time adding his tobacco-filled saliva to the brown mixture on the ground and further thinning the ants' chances for survival. He rose to cross the street, breaking into a slow jog at one point to avoid an oncoming lime-green Volkswagen Beetle driven by a small Asian guy wearing a Dallas Cowboys hat and who had selected a violet tulip for the little holder built into the dashboard.

Roger arrived at the corresponding bus stop on the other side of the street and took a seat. Almost immediately after he sat down, an attractive girl walked by. She looked to be about twenty-three, had medium-length brown hair, and long, firm, well-tanned, shapely legs that disappeared into a short denim miniskirt. The skirt was complemented by a white half-shirt that read, in neon pink letters, simply, "Billabong." About ten feet past him, the girl stopped and bent down to re-tie the laces on one of her white Vans sneakers. Much to Roger's delight, this caused her skirt to hike up in the back, revealing the bottom of a pair of light yellow cotton panties. Roger instinctively leaned forward and tilted his head to get a better viewing angle, spitting into the Coke bottle again on the way down. Unnoticed at this point, to his left, a large man of about thirty years of age stopped walking to concentrate on Roger. The man wore brown lace-up boots, camouflage pants and a black Slayer rock tee shirt that covered a bulky upper body most likely achieved with the help of steroids. He had Oakley sunglasses on, clearly had not shaved in a few days, and had spiky black hair.

"Hey asshole," the Rocker Guy said loudly to Roger who looked up at him startled, "Did you get a good look?"

"Um, no I was just…um,…So, um…do you know her?" Roger asked, nodding his head in the leggy girl's direction.

Rocker Guy walked closer so he was standing right above Roger. "Yeah, you could say that," he said.

"Girlfriend?" Roger asked.

"Wife," Rocker Guy answered and held up his left hand, displaying a traditional gold band. Then he waved his fingers around before closing them into a fist.

Roger began talking quickly, "Oh, well hey, sorry. I um, I didn't mean anything by it."

"Yeah, I bet you didn't," Rocker Guy said. Then after lingering a moment he started to walk away and muttered to himself, "Fucking joke."

After the Rocker Guy had moved about ten feet away and caught up with his wife, Roger spoke again, "Hey, bro?" he asked.

The rocker guy turned around, "Yeah, what?"

Roger spit into his bottle, then asked, "You don't happen to know the final on the Ohio State game from last night, do you?"

"What the fuck do you want?" the Rocker Guy asked, pronouncing the word *fuck* a lot more slowly and a bit more loudly than the other words. He started walking back in Roger's direction.

Roger immediately changed strategy, "Never mind. It's cool. Sorry," he said.

Just then, Roger's cell phone broke out in song, producing the familiar tunes of Jay-Z's *Big Pimpin'*. This meant Alex was calling.

Roger looked quickly at the phone, then back up at the Rocker Guy. "Oh, hey, I've got a call so, um, you know. Have a good one," he said. Roger waved first at the guy, then smiled and waved at the girl. Then he flipped open the phone and answered all in one motion, "Yo, Alex, what's up?"

Alex, who as far as he could recall had never ridden a municipal bus in his life, was still sitting on his bus stop bench in La Jolla, about five miles away. "Hey dude, what are you doing?" he asked.

Roger: "Just got off a lunch shift. Hey, I had the over on Ohio State last night and have not been able to check it. Do you have any idea where it came in?"

Alex: "35-24 Ohio. You should be good."

Roger: "Talk to Daddy! All I need is Stanford with the points tonight to pop a nice three-teamer."

Alex: "Dude, you have issues. Anyway, I have something I think you will like – you up for Vegas?" With Roger, there was no need to do much promotion when it came to Nevada trips.

Roger: "Oooohhhh. When?"

Alex: "Today. I can pick you up in two hours. G-Balls and Mike are in."

Roger: "Shit, no way. Mmmmm. Look I really want to, but I was up until six last night banging one of the regulars and am fucking beat. And I have to work a double tomorrow."

Alex: "Get it covered. You can sleep in the car."

Roger: "Well, the other thing is if Stanford comes in it is all good, but otherwise I have no funds. The shift this morning sucked. I only made ninety-five bucks."

Alex: "I thought you hit a four-teamer on Sunday?"

Roger: "Yeah but I had some errands I needed to do and I still owed some rent."

Alex: "Jesus, Rodge. All right, listen, don't tell the other guys, but I'll underwrite your share of the room and your vodka when we go out. Also, I am driving so don't worry about gas or anything. All you need to pay for is what you gamble. And you can bring some Kodiak for me."

Roger: "Thanks, cool. You know I'll get you back. I just need to make sure I can get my shifts covered for tomorrow."

Alex: "All right buddy. Make it happen."

Roger: "Nice, see you."

Alex: "I'll talk at you."

CHAPTER FIVE

Good Oral Hygiene
3:28 p.m.

"If you can't take the heat get
yo' ass out the kitchen
We on a mission
Come along and ride on a fantastic voyage
Slide slide slippity-slide"

– *Fantastic Voyage*, Coolio

ALEX'S BLACK 2006 BMW 550i, which he paid cash for the previous January after receiving his year-end bonus, needed only a fraction of its 4.8 liter, 360 horsepower engine to smoothly approach the back entrance of the Wind and Sea apartment complex just north of Pacific Beach. The car had a black leather interior, incredibly soft to the touch, but which got annoyingly hot when left in the sun. Even so, it tended to cool off remarkably quickly once the air conditioner was turned on. Also, temperature controls built directly into the seats helped speed things along if desired. The windows were just cracked open, making Jay-Z's *Girls, Girls, Girls* barely audible outside of the car. Gary Williams was sitting in the front seat with a silly half-smile on his face, still not quite believing that he was headed for a weekend in Vegas with the boys. Just forty-five minutes ago he was doing a final proof-reading of an adjusted SEC filing for a client who had to delay their quarterly numbers because it turned out the CFO had spent over three million dollars on yacht rentals and private jet flights to the Caribbean for himself and various "companions." Unfortunately, it was challenging to justify these as "marketing expenses" as the company had been doing.

Gary was sporting a fashionable haircut he got in the Gaslamp quarter last week for sixty-five dollars. Surprisingly, his wife Blair thought this was a very worthwhile use of money, even though she was upset about the six-dollar Tony Gwynn talking bottle opener he purchased the same day. The haircut, while nice, was conservative. It nicely complemented his khaki pants and a tucked-in white short-sleeved collared golf shirt. The pants were Banana Republic, the shirt by Greg Norman.

Alex was in the driver's seat singing quietly along to Jay-Z …

"…Got this indian squaw
The day that I met her
Asked her what tribe she with, red dot or feather?
She said all you need to know is I'm not a ho
And to get with me you better be Chief Lots-a-Dough..."

Alex had changed clothes and was now wearing shiny black Nike sweat pants, black and brown Louis Vuitton leather sandals, vintage Wayfarer sunglasses and a white tee shirt that read, "I Just Did It" with the Nike swoosh logo in the shape of a smile underneath it. Both he and Gary were wearing the same blue-faced Tag Heuer watch.

As the car came to a stop, Gary rolled down his window further and deeply inhaled the soft San Diego air. He grabbed the roof of the car with his fingertips, resting his elbow on the open door window and let out a small laugh, turning toward Alex. "This is fucking insane. I can't believe he is really getting married," he said.

Alex (pausing briefly): "Um, well, yeah. It is insane."

Gary: "Where did he meet this girl again?"

Alex: "I don't even really know all the details. Listen, don't drill him too much on it. He is still kind of shy about it."

Gary: "It's like a Russian bride or something? Did he knock someone up?"

Alex: "I don't think so. I'm sure it will all come out, though. Hold on a sec."

Alex flipped open his Razr and hit the auto-dial button for "The Rodge." Roger picked up on the second ring and Alex let him know they were outside waiting for him. Then he flipped the phone shut and shoved it back in the front pocket of the Nike sweats.

Gary started talking again while tapping the roof of the car in synchrony with 2Pac's *Shorty Wanna B A Thug*, which was now playing on the stereo. "Well, this is crazy, but it comes at a good time for me. It will be good to get away for a few days and get nice and fucked up," he said, then added, "though I was looking forward to getting those new steak knives."

Alex resisted the urge to ask what the big deal was about the steak knives and simply replied, "I am glad to hear you say that. And I agree a hundred percent."

Gary: "And plus, I have been working my balls off the last few months."

Alex: "Yeah, I know. Hey, we can't have G-Balls with no balls. You deserve this. Look, there's The Rodge."

Roger busted through the metal pedestrian entrance gate for the Wind and Sea. He was wearing black shorts, blue Adidas flip-flops, a short-sleeved blue and white bowling shirt, and imitation Gucci sunglasses. He approached the BMW and gave Gary a high five through the open window, profoundly expressing, "Ahhh yeahhhh, bitches."

Behind the fake Gucci's, Roger was sporting bloodshot red eyes from lack of sleep, but it was with genuine enthusiasm that he asked, "Which one of you dirty sluts wants to go to Vegas?"

Alex leaned toward the passenger side of the car and looked out the window eying Roger suspiciously. "Where's your shit?" he asked.

Roger pulled a toothbrush out of the left pocket of his shorts and waived it around. Then he pulled a fresh can of Kodiak and what was now eighty-seven dollars out of the right pocket. "I'm ready, baby," he exclaimed.

Alex: "No way, dude. We have table reservations both nights and I want everyone to be there. Go back and pack some decent clothes. Jesus Christ."

Roger: "I don't really care that much about going to clubs to try and ramp a bunch of dumb hoes from L.A."

Alex: "Rodge, just give Gary the toothbrush and go back and grab some clothes."

Roger: "All right, tough guy, but you're paying for the bottles."

He passed the toothbrush to Gary through the car window, then turned around and started back toward the apartment in a slow trot. Gary put the toothbrush in the glove compartment, careful not to touch the well-worn bristles.

Gary (shaking his head): "God bless that guy. He is amazing."

Alex: "No fucking doubt."

Gary: "Sometimes I think maybe he has it all figured out. He definitely has a chill lifestyle. I'm getting up before dawn every day and wrapping a tie around my neck and he is sleeping in and getting paid to hang out in a sports bar."

Alex: "And he gets to sleep with the customers."

Gary: "Don't forget the hostess."

Alex: "Oh yeah. Yeah, you might be right. Maybe he does have it all figured out. Either way, at least we know he puts a high priority on oral hygiene."

They both laughed.

INTERLUDE ONE

Gary (.00000001)

GARY'S MOTHER, MELINDA JOHNSON, met his father, Timothy Williams, after a football game at the University of Minnesota in 1968. The whole thing was really about as "America and Apple Pie" as it gets except for the fact that the Vietnam situation made it hard for anyone to have a good time without feeling guilty about it, especially after the Tet Offensive earlier in the year had effectively proved the optimists wrong.

Melinda was a psychology major starting her junior year. She was starting to get nervous because she still didn't have a steady boyfriend and her two best friends had already secured promise rings. Given that she was already on the wrong side of twenty, she was starting to feel she may be left behind. As everyone knew, if you were not married by twenty-four, you were likely destined to end up alone in a houseful of cats. Besides, she had already had sex with two guys and would consider herself a total slut if she didn't settle down soon. The whole summer of love thing took a slower pace in Minnesota.

Nevertheless, on this evening she was enjoying herself, especially because it was another month before the below-zero weather would kick in. Even so, she had a few shots of bourbon during the game to keep warm. The Golden Gophers put on a seventeen point ass-kicking of Iowa State.

Melinda didn't care much about the game, but the result seemed to put everyone else in a good mood so she was happy about it.

She first noticed Tim toward the end of the first half. Actually, it was her friend Barbara who noticed and pointed him out to her. Tim was sitting in her row, one section to the right. It was not until after the game, when they ended up at the same off-campus party, that she was able to talk to him. Tim made her laugh, didn't get obnoxiously drunk like most guys, and had similar views on most political topics. He was wishy-washy enough about Vietnam that it didn't create any reason for her not to see him again (she was adamantly opposed).

Despite her best efforts to be good, Tim became number three before the next home game, a disappointing thirteen-point loss to Notre Dame. But his efforts in bed were not at all disappointing and by the time the thermometer dropped below freezing they were in love. Of course at that age love and lust were indistinguishable. With little incentive to go out in the cold, sex was a frequent activity. By spring they had done it a hundred and seventy-nine times, though no one was counting. But all of these, even the first, paled in comparison to number nine hundred and sixty-two. Included somewhere between number one seventy-nine and number nine sixty-two were a lot of condoms, a wedding ceremony, first jobs, more condoms, a brief stint on the pill, more condoms, and then a miracle.

In the early morning of July 18th, 1974, one of Timothy Williams' microscopic little sperm achieved its primary objective while heading up Melinda Williams' vaginal canal. Roughly nine months later, on April 20th, 1975, Gary Williams achieved his primary objective of the day, heading back out the other way. While he would generally be a quiet

kid, he was crying like all hell when he came out. Still, everyone involved agreed it was a marvelous day. A healthy baby
boy arrived who would get to experience all the great highs
and lows and achievements (hopefully) that his father did
before him. And what could be better than that?

As for Gary himself, he didn't have much of an opinion
on that day. For the most part, his undeveloped little brain
was just trying to figure out what the fuck was going on. And
he cried. And then he got food. And then he pooped. And so
life started for Gary "G-Balls" Williams.

CHAPTER SIX

The Ruse
4:01 p.m.

"I don't appreciate your ruse ma'am....
Your ruse. Your cunning attempt to trick me."
—Randal Graves, *Clerks*

ROGER REQUIRED FOUR MINUTES to pack to Alex's satisfaction. Twenty minutes later, Mike was successfully assimilated into the driver's side back seat and the crew was officially on US Interstate 15 northbound, just past Scripps Ranch and advancing toward Las Vegas. Unfortunately, there was heavy traffic and progress was slow. Madonna's *American Life* played on the Harmon Kardon stereo. Roger and Mike simultaneously declared the music selection to be "really gay," but they were overruled by Alex and Gary who had joint control of Alex's iPod which was hooked up to the car's auxiliary connection.

Mike was now wearing a Ken Caminiti Padres jersey that his younger brother bought him last month for his thirtieth birthday. It complemented blue Nike shorts and white Nike sneakers. Other than the sporty outfit, he looked a bit like Chandler from *Friends*, though as one girl once told him after several glasses of wine, "not as cute and funny...but still cool in that bitter kind of way."

After a slight lull in the conversation during which Alex was trying to decipher what Madonna was saying about a double latte, Gary broke the silence, turning fully around in his seat to talk to Mike. "All right, dude, I gotta hear about it. First of all, congratulations," he said.

Mike: "Oh, thanks man. Yeah, I am pretty pumped about the whole thing."

This comment elicited Alex to glance back in the rearview mirror, eyebrows slightly raised.

Gary: "So tell me about it. Where did you find her?"

Mike: "Well, you know, it was pretty much the standard procedure. I just got an agent and looked at a bunch of options and picked the best one I could afford."

Gary: "No shit. Is there a large range in the prices?"

Mike: "Of course. Some of the really nice ones are just ridiculously expensive, but there were some really attractive choices that were within my limits."

Gary: "Did you look at pictures online?"

Mike: "Of course, but ultimately you need to go in person and really get a feel for each one. It's a huge commitment so you need to make sure you take the time to examine all the details and kick the tires and check under the hood, so to speak. A lot of the choices that look good at first actually have big flaws that only reveal themselves after a thorough investigation. Actually, I really enjoyed the whole process. It is more interesting than I thought."

Gary (laughing): "Of course, I can imagine. That sounds sweet. Was the agent Russian?"

Mike: "Um…No. It was your typical twenty-eight-year-old blond chick who lost a dotcom job up north after the bubble and moved down here. Standard stuff."

Gary: "So she was American?"

Mike: "Yeah, from Chicago I think."

Gary: "That's strange. I wouldn't have thought they would be open to letting Americans get into the business."

Mike: "What do you mean? I think she even went to State down here. Didn't really make it in San Francisco but has her shit together and is good at sales. You know the type. Typical real estate agent."

Gary: "Okay. I am confused. I thought we are talking about the people who found the girl you are marrying. What are you talking about?"

Alex chose this moment to re-enter the conversation: "Hey guys, do you want to hit a strip club tonight, or wait until tomorrow during the afternoon to kill some time? I heard a rumor that Crazy Horse Too may be closing because it got too skanky, but maybe the Rhino or Club Paradise?"

Mike: "Sure, whatever, Alex. Marrying, Gary? What are you talking about? I haven't even been on a date in nearly four months."

Gary, whom Blair often accused of being too trusting, finally smelled the rat. "Mike, are you, or are you not, getting married? Is this or is it not a bachelor party trip?" he asked in a deliberate and deep tone.

Mike laughed heartily. "Married? Shit, I'm all for it if you can find me a nice bitch this weekend with big tits and maybe a trust fund. Maybe we will run into Britney Spears at Ghostbar and she will want to give it another try. But I wasn't planning on it. I just closed on a new house in Del Mar. I thought that is what you were asking about."

An awkward silence dominated the car for the next several seconds. Somehow the fact that they were only going twenty-seven miles an hour made the situation even worse. Madonna was complicit in letting the moment sink in. She ended her song and paused lengthily before *Hollywood* began to play.

Gary was the first to speak. He looked directly at Alex. "Alex, you mother fucking, mother fucker. This is not cool. You called Blair and lied directly to my wife. Basically that means I have now lied to her about this whole trip as well. This is fucked. We are fucked. I am fucked."

Alex tried to sound calm: "Okay, I knew we would have to deal with this at some point, so I just have to say, I really think you are focusing too much on the negative here."

Gary: "The negative? The negative? What is the positive? You are out of your mind. This is a very bad situation. Just turn the car around."

Alex: "It is cool. Nothing is fucked here. We are just normal Americans trying to have a good time. Everything will work out fine. Just watch."

Gary: "What the fuck are you talking about? What does this have to do with being American? This has to do with me being married. Turn the car around at the next exit."

Alex: "Okay, but let's think about this for a moment first. Just hear me out. Listen, this was the only way I could get you to come with us. And you know that is true. I only told Blair that Mike was getting married for you – so you could enjoy this weekend with us. We are going to have a great time and when we get back, we can just wait a week or so and then just tell her that the engagement broke off cuz, like, um...I don't know...maybe Mike fucked the stripper we got him or something. Maybe he even caught a disease or something. It will be cool."

Mike, who had not planned on further participation in this conversation, chimed in at this point: "Hey, Alex – usually I don't care what kind of shit you pull, but I don't want to come off like the asshole to my friend's wife. Did you think of that in your little scenario?"

Alex: "Okay, sorry buddy. You're right. And I don't have all the details worked out right now, but it will be okay. No strippers. I am the asshole here; you don't have to be."

Mike: "And I don't want any diseases either."

This elicited a chuckle from Roger, who up until now was also pretending to ignore the whole situation and was instead trying to get updated football lines on his cell phone.

Alex: "You're right, Chief. Bad story."

Mike: "I mean, at least not without really getting laid."

Everyone turned toward Mike, equal parts confused and disappointed.

Gary got them back on topic: "Just get off the next exit and take me back. We aren't fucking moving anyway."

Roger suddenly realized he had a vested interest in the outcome: "Dudes, I got a double shift covered on a Saturday for this, so someone better still be taking me to Vegas."

Alex: "See, The Rodge is the voice of reason. Fantastic. Okay, Gary, how about this - we get to Barstow, you call Blair and tell her that I made the whole thing up and you had no idea until then. But at that point there is really no way you can come back. And I am the asshole."

Gary: "So, what, the topic just didn't come up for two hours?"

Alex thought for only a moment: "Right, because I told you and Roger not to mention anything until we got to Vegas because Mike told me he didn't want the trip to be considered a bachelor party because he didn't want strippers because his fiancé would be pissed and he wouldn't go if it was a bachelor party. Therefore, he would only go if you and Roger didn't know about the engagement until the second night of the trip."

Gary: "But there is no engagement?"

Alex: "This is true, but if I lied to you and Roger separately then no one's the wiser and no one is talking about any engagements. We are all just going to Vegas. But then somehow you caught on to my ruse and immediately call Blair. However, by then we are in Barstow and everyone else still wants to go and there is nothing you can reasonably do. I am the only asshole. We go to Vegas and have a blast."

Gary: "She is going to be pissed and is going to make me get on a bus and get my ass back to San Diego no matter what you douche-bags are doing."

Alex: "I don't think so, Gary. I don't know too much about married chicks, but the one thing I know about women is they all want to seem "cooler" than other girls. If the word got out that she made you come back on a Greyhound from Barstow, she would appear as a bitch and decidedly un-cool. She won't want that."

Gary thought about this for a moment: "You are a clever asshole sometimes. You don't care that my wife hates you?"

Alex switched from his sales voice to his compassionate voice: "I do care, G-Balls. I like Blair and I am happy for the two of you. But the truth of the matter is, I have seen you in person maybe twice in the last year anyway, so I don't think this is going to, like, fuck up the great situation we have now or anything."

Gary knew that it was a problem that he very rarely saw friends who didn't also have kids anymore. "I'm still pissed," he said, but the conviction in his voice was gone.

Alex: "I know. Look, I am sorry. Really. I just wanted all of us to go to Vegas and have a good time together. I mean, for me, personally, these days it is kind of a bummer. Five years ago all you had to do was send out an email with the subject "Vegas" and within thirty minutes eight guys had booked flights. Now I am lucky if I can get The Rodge to come with me."

Roger: "What is that supposed to mean?"

Alex: "Sorry, dude. You know I love charging Vegas with you. I just mean that it doesn't take much for you to want to go to Nevada, which is a good thing. Look, the point is just that we never get to do anything as the four of us anymore. I know it was fucked up to lie to your wife and I know you were going to buy new steak knives and all that this weekend, so I am sorry. But how about if we move on and have a great weekend?"

Gary: "Jesus, man. You are a fucking dickhead sometimes. Total fucking dickhead." He paused. "Fine, let's go. But I am still pissed. Are you paying for dinner?"

Alex: "Absolutely. N9NE at the Palms tomorrow. Steaks and martinis are on me."

Gary: "Fucking dickhead."

Roger, now content that the trip was still on, lost interest in the conversation and made a statement: "Okay, if we are all still friends, I am going to pass out now. One of us was up all night having sex."

Mike (with more than a tinge of jealousy): "You are not still killing it with the hostess are you?"

Roger: "No, no. It's one of the regulars. She is like forty and just got divorced. Crazy in bed. Fucking brilliant."

With that Roger slouched into the corner of the car and pulled out a Viejas Indian Casino hat and pulled it down over his face. He lifted an empty twenty-ounce bottle of Coke until it disappeared under the cap, spit into it, and issued his parting words for the moment: "Okay, you double-headed-dildos, I'll see you later. Wake me up when the Stanford game comes on the radio."

Roger (5)

MOST OF WHAT ROGER KEMP remembered from his childhood about his father, Jack Kemp, was him arguing with his mother in the kitchen or behind a closed door in the bedroom. The house they lived in, just outside of Sacramento, California, only had two bedrooms and a small living room, so there were not many alternatives.

If the discussion was in the kitchen, then Jack usually had at least four empty Budweisers in front of him, though never more than six. Roger didn't think about this until much later. In his twenties, and now a bartender by profession, Roger had the opportunity to observe firsthand many people's drinking habits. Most people either didn't drink at all, only had one or two drinks, or kept drinking as long and as much as the situation allowed. It was very rare for someone to actually just have four to six drinks, but that was his dad's routine.

Anyway, Jack did his arguing with his wife much like he did his drinking, frequently but never too out of control. So he and Sheryl, Roger's mom, never seemed to reach the breaking point because both would raise their voices but never quite yell and there was never any physical violence. It was as if they preferred slow torture.

There were a fair amount of good times in the Kemp household as well. In fact, the week before the day that would spell the end of the marriage, the three of them enjoyed a lovely vacation to Tahoe where five-year-old Roger played in the lake and got sick eating too many tacos.

But in the end, things unraveled very quickly, for two reasons. Jack was a typical scumbag guy, and Roger never slept well as a kid or an adult. So, on a Saturday night in March of 1979, Roger woke up and went into the kitchen to get some apple juice. He remembered to bring his cup with him from the bedroom and felt he was well prepared. He was not well prepared for what he saw next. His baby sitter, Jessica, who was a student at the local community college, was bent over the kitchen table and his daddy was behind her. They were both naked. Roger had no idea why, but he knew this was a bad thing and was not something he was supposed to see. To this day, the most vivid part of the memory was the hideous orange and red wallpaper in the kitchen. He was eternally grateful to that wallpaper for muting out the rest of the vision in his mind.

No longer interested in apple juice, Roger ran back to his room and wished his mother was there, but she was visiting his grandparents in Arizona. Roger began to wonder if he should mention this to his mother at all. In the end, he didn't have to because Jack told her what happened when she returned. Sheryl Kemp could put up with a lot of things, but for whatever reason, infidelity was not one of them. She filed for divorce the next week.

Roger's dad ended up moving to New York by the end of the year. From then on, Roger lived with his mom, and it was just the two of them until he was in high school and his mom remarried with a man who owned a medium-sized contracting business. His stepdad, Howard, was also divorced, though Roger never heard the story about why. He didn't really care why, and was just glad that his mom had found someone who made her happy and secure. Howard was a good husband and a good father. There were rarely any arguments and Roger was too old to have another babysitter to mess things up, so everything seemed to work out.

Roger didn't often think about fate or the meaning of life, but one day when he was twenty, enjoying a Kodiak after a few whiskeys, he realized that while society deemed his parents' marriage a failure, from his perspective it worked out perfectly. If his dad had not married his mom, he wouldn't exist. If his parents had got along well enough to stay together, they would have been moderately unhappy all of these years and his mom would not have Howard, who truly did make her happy.

CHAPTER SEVEN

Work
4:27 p.m.

*"You see that building? I bought that building
ten years ago. My first real estate deal.
Sold it two years later, made an $800,000
profit. It was better than sex. At the time
I thought that was all the money in the
world. Now it's a day's pay."*
– Gordon Gekko, Wall Street

TWENTY MINUTES AFTER ROGER passed out in the back seat, the mood in the car was better, though still somewhat subdued. Traffic had thinned and Alex noted with satisfaction that the needle on the speedometer was slowly creeping past the orange 80.

It turned out that during the disagreement, traffic had cleared, and they had made decent progress. The group was now just a few miles from Temecula, where Gary had almost bought a house while he and Blair were engaged. Just five years ago, they would have been able to afford a four-bedroom place in Temecula with a pool in the back and a nice view of the hills. Today, the same house would cost nearly

$400,000 more. Blair occasionally brought this up during arguments because she had been the one who wanted to buy the house rather than waiting until they could afford something closer to the city. Few things pissed Gary off more, because he was the one who would have had to deal with the ninety-minute commute every day. So while he occasionally regretted missing out on some of the gains in the housing market over the past few years, he knew that it was worth waiting because he probably would have gone crazy and lost his marriage if they had lived in Temecula. And financially they were still doing fine with their current house.

Entering the city, a large sign declared Temecula to be a place of "Old Traditions, New Opportunities." As they passed through the suburb, Gary noticed that while it still seemed like a fairly nice place, the negatives of sprawl from Los Angeles and San Diego were starting to show. There were occasional patches of graffiti on the brick walls lining the freeway and a few patches of shitty-looking townhouses and condos had appeared. The graffiti on this particular stretch consisted of one XIV in huge black letters and, to the right, in red, a rhetorical question, "Bush, WTF?" He also noticed a new Del Taco, which he considered a welcome addition to any neighborhood.

Alex broke the silence, or at least spoke over Avril Lavine who was singing about stealing a skater boy from a prissy chick. "Hey Mike," he asked, making eye contact with him in the rearview mirror, "how's work going?"

Mike: "Fine. How about you?"

Alex: "Cool, man. They keep paying me anyway. G-Balls?"

Gary turned back from staring out the window and thinking about how much Del Taco he would eat if he did live in Temecula: "Oh, its good. We have a big case and if it goes well and then I work four more years of seventy-plus-hour weeks I may have a good chance for Junior Partner."

Neither Alex nor Mike had any idea if he was being serious or sarcastic. They responded in unison: "Cool."

INTERLUDE THREE

Alex (5)

ALEX REINE'S FAMILY, WHICH consisted of father Edward, mother Cynthia, and older sister Samantha, moved a lot when he was young. Edward was a project manager for a consulting firm focused on complex computer programming. The company's primary client was the military. Most projects lasted roughly two years. Then it was time to pack up and go. The family owned a home in Florida, but Alex only lived in it for the first year of his life. Normally, they resided in rented houses.

When Alex was five, it was an oceanfront ranch house on the East side of Oahu, Hawaii. In the backyard, Edward taught Alex to surf on the days when the waves were not too large. In Honolulu, on the other side of the H3 tunnel, Alex was enrolled in a private kindergarten where he was expected to improve his very simple reading and math skills and hone his abilities to interact with other children.

Probably because his family had moved three times by his fifth birthday, Alex had never had the time to develop a true best friend like most children had. Still, he was good with other kids and usually gained acceptance into any group he chose.

On the first day of the new school, Cynthia had worried that little Alex would be upset to leave his mother. On the contrary, he was so eager to join his new classmates that she found herself fighting an emotion of rejection.

Alex had no reason to be afraid. In his brief life he had always been treated like a king. His parents probably over-compensated for their guilt at moving so much, and he won over most strangers by learning how to look cute. With other kids, he already understood the tactic of gaining acceptance by sharing and taking an interest in others.

So, during the first recess at his new school, Alex did not fret when he found himself playing alone on a tire swing in the playground. When a new child came to join him after a few minutes, in this case a larger seven-year-old from the adjoining elementary school, Alex found it natural to climb off the tire and offer it to the other child. The bigger kid grabbed the tire and pulled it back, but did not climb on it. Instead, he paused, looking at Alex who was watching expec-tantly, not saying a word. The other child then threw the tire in Alex's direction with as much force as he could muster. There was no mistaking the fact that the intent was to inflict pain. The tire struck Alex squarely in the chest, knocking him back a few inches but not down to the ground.

Alex took inventory of his body and realized that he was not meaningfully injured. Unsure what to do, he simply stared at the other boy, trying to comprehend why he did what he did.

CHAPTER EIGHT

Sex
4:42 p.m.

*"Yeah, you're not hurting it. You're just kinda
gently batting the bunny around, you know
what I mean? And the bunny is scared, Mike,
the bunny is scared of you, shivering.*

*...And you got these fucking claws and these
fangs, man! And you're looking at your claws
and you're looking at your fangs. And you're
thinking to yourself, you don't know what to
do, man. "I don't know how to kill the bunny."
With* **this** *you don't know how to kill the
bunny. Do you know what I mean?"*

—Trent, *Swingers*

WITH ROGER SLEEPING SOUNDLY in the back seat, Temecula
was now in the rearview mirror and *Superman* by Eminem
had replaced Avril on the stereo.

"Put anthrax on a Tampax
And slap you till you can't stand
Girl you just blew your chance
Don't mean to ruin your plans
But I do know one thing though
Bitches they come they go"

Alex: "I had a dream last night that I was A. C. Slater from *Saved by the Bell*."

Gary: "Were you doing it with Jessie Spano?"

Alex: "Who?"

Gary: "You know. Jessie, Elizabeth Berkeley's character."

Alex: "Oh, right. No. She wasn't in it."

Gary: "What about Screech?"

Alex: "Was I doing it with Screech?"

Gary: "No. Just was he in the dream?"

Alex: "Oh. No. Zack was in it briefly, but he didn't have any meaningful role."

Gary: "So what were you doing as A. C. Slater?"

Alex: "I had made this chair and attached a bunch of helium balloons to the bottom it. I was bouncing up and down on the chair and was going higher every time. I was next to a large swimming pool so my objective was to go about ten meters high and then jump off the chair into the pool. But somehow I didn't jump in time and the chair kept going higher and higher and I couldn't get off and couldn't get the chair to go back down. Mr. Belding was screaming at me to just jump already, but I was paralyzed. Then I woke up."

Gary: "Yeah, I used to have one like that too sometimes, only without the *Saved by the Bell* part."

The BMW followed its lane in a sweeping curve to the right, revealing the valley holding the city of Corona. A thick blanket of smog had floated in from greater Los Angeles and created a ceiling above the town. Alex had no more desire to analyze his dreams and switched topics.

Alex: "So you've been married like three years, right?"

Gary: "Five."

Alex: "No shit. Time flies. Five years? Wow, it seems like your wedding was just yesterday. So, like, how often do you boff after five years of marriage?"

Gary: "You are asking how often do Blair and I have sex?"

Alex: "Yep."

Gary: "Well, before Sarah was born it was about twice a week, but now I would say more like once a week. Usually it is once a week. Sometimes once a week anyways. I think. Maybe, anyway. I don't know. Actually, I don't even remember what is normal before being married. What about your latest chick?"

Alex: "The one from Dallas?"

Gary: "Yeah, what is her name?"

Alex: "Courtney. Well, it's hard to say because when we are together it's like minimum three times a day, but I tend to only see her like once every few weeks. Angela was the last real girlfriend I had who lived in San Diego. With her it was a solid once a day program, but we didn't see each other every day either. But, I think, you know, after five years of marriage, once a week sounds like you're doing pretty well."

Mike: "Once a week sounds great to me."

Gary: "Dry spell?"

Mike: "Mojave desert."

Alex: "Are you on official hiatus clock?"

Mike: "Yeah, a few months deep."

Gary: "What is the hiatus clock?"

Alex: "Dude, you have been married too long. Any time you hit three months from last intercourse, you are officially on a hiatus. It can be quite scary."

Mike: "Tell me about it. The thing is, once I get on hiatus I notice I start doing shit I wouldn't otherwise do. It's like, if I had sex the night before, and then I meet Anna Kournikova at the beach, I would want to determine if she has a good personality before I am willing to even hang out with her. But after a few months on the hiatus clock I find myself at Rodge's bar trying to ramp up some fat bitch who works at a Mervyn's."

Gary: "Maybe she could get you a discount on a Maytag for the new pad."

Alex: "Or some candlesticks for the dining room. You should just get over yourself and join Match. A bunch of my buddies at work do it and they say it makes getting laid like shooting fish in a barrel."

Mike: "Maybe you are right. I just feel so stupid doing it for some reason. It seems so desperate, but maybe I am desperate so it doesn't matter. Anyway, it is starting to make sense. Going out just doesn't seem worth the hassle anymore, especially at this age. You want to hook up, so you go out, but lately I just feel old."

Alex: "Dude, we are not that old."

Mike: "Lately I feel pretty geriatric when we go out. I mean, I don't want to be that guy."

Alex: "We are not that old."

Mike: "We aren't young."

Alex: "Fair, but we are not that old either."

Mike: "It's like, you know, when you go to Vegas and see George Maloof out partying, and he just looks so, just fucking old. And it's sad."

Alex: "Yeah, you're right. You are sitting at home on your couch with a forty-ouncer watching a Die-Hard rerun on USA and he is sitting in the club partying with Paris Hilton and Tara Reid. I don't feel that bad for him. Give my apologies to Bruce Willis, but there is not even a comparison."

Mike: "All I am saying is, it is getting tired and I almost never meet anyone anyway, so there isn't much point."

"Yippee Kay-Yeah, Mother-Fucker!" Alex nearly shouted, then continued in a more serious tone, "You are so negative. Come on, it's really not that bad."

Mike: "Easy for you to say."

Alex: "Dude, I've had my share of dry spells. Plus, I am sick of all the bullshit too. I would love to settle down with one chick."

Gary: "Be careful, Alex. Your credibility is already on thin ice today."

Alex: "No, I'm serious."

Gary: "Actually, to be truthful, it had been once a week, but for the last couple months I have been pretty much cut off completely."

Alex: "Are you talking about Blair again?"

Gary: "Yeah."

Alex: "Oh. Why, what happened?"

Gary: "You know, sometimes outside factors interfere. It's just temporary. I think it will blow over soon."

Mike: "Like what outside factors?"

Gary: "Well, if you must know, Blair found my porn stash and she wasn't at all happy about it. She has been applying sexual sanctions ever since."

Mike: "Sanctions never work. Just look at North Korea."

Gary: "Well, in this case I would have to say they are pretty effective."

Mike: "No, it is stupid. It's just going to drive you to cheat."

Alex: "Anyway, that sounds like bullshit. I mean there isn't anything wrong with having some porn. It's a hell of a lot better than most of the dirt-bags out there looking for the real thing."

Gary: "That was my point, but she didn't exactly see it that way."

Alex: "I mean, I could understand if it was something super-pervy like *Tiny White Holes and Huge Black Cocks* or *Barely Legal* or something like that, but otherwise where's the harm?"

Gary paused. A few seconds later he said softly, "Well, yeah, that was sort of the thing."

Alex, excited, raised his eyebrows and turned his head to the right toward Gary. "*Huge Black Cocks?*" he asked, sounding like a five-year-old shyly asking if he was going to get a puppy for Christmas.

Gary: "No, closer to the *Barely Legal*, but let's just leave it at that."

Mike: "Dude, I didn't know you were a pederast."

Gary: "Let's just forget it. It wasn't kiddy porn or anything."

Mike: "Eight year olds, dude!"

Gary: "Very funny, Mike."

Just then Nick Lachey's *What's Left of Me* started to play in the car, providing Gary with a welcome exit from the conversation.

Mike: "What the fuck is this?"

Alex immediately reached down and fumbled with the iPod, hitting fast forward as quickly as possible, thankful to hear Too $hort's *Good Life* start.

Gary: "Take it easy on him, Mike. Alex can't help it if he secretly wants to be Nick Lachey."

Alex had little choice but to give himself a jab to end the conversation: "Pre or post Jessica?"

The comment elicited mild chuckles, and Gary looped back to the previous conversation from before his rather unfortunate porn admission. "So, do you think things might get serious with Courtney?" he asked Alex.

Alex: "No. I doubt it. She is cool, but I don't really feel like it has legs. Also, there is this weird thing with her where it seems her head is always facing a bit to the left. It bugs me. Perhaps the chick who came down last month from San Francisco. She was pretty incredible, but we have not been able to schedule another time to meet."

Mike: "Megan?"

Alex: "Um...yeah, Megan. G-Balls, check this out. I met this chick last year at Bay to Breakers when I was wearing my Super Dave Osborne costume. I had not seen her since then, but we emailed occasionally. Last month she flew down to see me but paid for her own flight. I pick her up at the airport and we go straight back to my place and boff all night. We spent the whole next day at the beach but were running late so all we had time to eat for lunch was Taco Bell. She has two Mexi-melts and a Nacho-Supreme with no beans and a Diet Coke. Probably about $4.75. For dinner we went to The Cove but, get this, she paid. After, we go home and watch *Top Gun* on DVD but end up getting naked on the couch before Kelly McGillis does in the movie. Her return flight was early in the morning and then she's gone. It was unreal. My CPL was about a buck fifty which is simply unheard of."

Gary: "CPL?"

Alex: "Cost Per Load, dude. I mean, usually, I am well into the triple digits. Lately it is even worse sometimes. This was brilliant. I mean, a dollar fifty? She may has well have paid me."

Gary: "So you define the potential for a long-term relationship based on how little it takes to get your rocks off? You could go to Tijuana and probably find plenty of girls to help you out for a few bucks."

Alex: "No, that isn't what I meant. She was really cool. She has a lot of other great qualities also. I mean, not even counting her body. I just wanted to point it out because I thought it was unique."

Gary: "Well, it sounds like you are still having fun with the single life."

Alex: "It is okay. Sometimes it is a lot of fun. Sometimes I wake up hung over next to a girl I wish was something she isn't and it feels very empty. To be fair to Mike's point, the whole going out and getting wasted thing may be close to running its course, though I maintain we are not that old."

Gary: "Okay, I think we can agree we are no longer young, but are not old either."

Alex: "Fair enough. I don't know, man. I mean, a lot of times I feel like my life should have some other direction or focus. Maybe something real? But I just have absolutely no idea…what it could be."

Gary: "You will, when it is right. You just need to be open for it."

Alex: "Thanks. I hope so."

Gary: "Suddenly, hanging with you two, marriage doesn't seem so bad. No hiatus and no CPL to worry about."

Alex took his eyes off the road and looked straight at Gary with a serious expression on his face: "No, no. You've got to be careful with that shit. I'm serious, dude. Mother-fucking alimony. It's the super-highway straight to a six-figure CPL. No shit, I've seen it happen."

This gave Gary a laugh: "I'm not too worried about it. Listen, let me ask you guys a question. Do you ever, you know, bottom out?"

Mike: "What do you mean?"

Gary: "Well, in certain positions, I run out of room. I can't get it all the way in. I am just wondering if this is normal. I can't really remember having this issue when I was single."

Alex: "Now this is interesting. Are you talking regular positions, or kinky weird shit?"

Gary: "No, just regular. Blair's idea of kinky is leaving the lights on."

Alex: "In that case, dude, no, I don't think it's normal."

Gary: "Hmmm."

Mike: "What are you saying, like you've got a huge fuck-stick or something?"

Gary: "No, no, it's not that...I think maybe Blair has a shallow dish."

CHAPTER NINE

Games Part I
5:02 p.m.

"Do you believe in miracles? Yes!!!"
—Al Michaels, *1980 Winter Olympics*

IT WAS STILL EARLY IN THE trip, but the group was making solid progress and had just passed through Corona, California. Despite the fact that the Stanford game had not yet started, Mike woke Roger up several miles back because he was snoring and they were starting a game of categories. Nirvana's *Smells Like Teen Spirit* was playing lightly on the stereo. Roger yawned and stretched his arms, straightening them into the front seat, one on each side of Gary's head. In the driver's seat, Alex was trying to crack his left knee but was struggling because there was not enough room to fully extend it. Behind him, Mike rearranged his balls with the hand in his right pocket.

Roger: "Alex, do you mind if I have a dip in here?"

Alex: "You mean another one? No, not as long as you give me one. Just don't spill. Hundred dollar penalty you spill. Plus I beat the shit out of you."

Roger agreed to these terms. "Done and done," he said. He grabbed the Kodiak can off the floor, and packed and inserted a dip within five seconds. "When have I ever spilled?" he asked through a mouthful of tobacco grains, handing the can up to Alex who had put his right hand awkwardly into the back seat but kept his eyes on the road.

The question was directed at Alex, but it was Gary who answered, "Oh, I don't know. Maybe like the time when you got drunk and tried to hide your open spitter inside Blair's new Dior bag."

Because this elicited no response from anyone, Gary got back to the game at hand. "Okay, the scores are Alex three, me two, Rodge four and Mike three. If Roger loses here, I win and Alex gets his money back. And the category is…either World Series winning teams or league MVPs – you need the team or the player and the year. I will start with the '86 Mets."

Roger: "So a World Series winner or a regular season MVP?"

Gary: "Yes, and you need the year."

Roger: "Okay, Bonds, 2004."

Mike: "Bonds, 2003."

Alex: "In that case, Bonds 2002."

Gary: "Bonds, 2001."

Roger: "Yeah, that guy sucks, Bonds, '93."

Mike: "Bonds, '92."

Alex: "Bonds, '90. Next?"

Gary: "Okay, I guess that is done. How about Kevin Mitchell, 1999?"

Roger: "Ooooh – nice one. I will go with Sosa, '98."

Mike: "Caminiti Baby. 1996."

Alex: "Mike, you really are gay. The guy is a juiced-up crack-head. And a dead one at that. Whatever. Okay, I can do World Series, right? 2005, White Sox."

Mike: "Have some fucking respect. The dude won the MVP and led the Pads to the World Series. Who are you to judge his private life?"

Alex: "Okay, fair enough. Take it easy."

Gary: "2004, Red Sox."

Roger: "2002, Angels."

Alex: "Those bastards."

Mike: "Larry Walker, 1997."

Alex: "Pujols, oh-five."

Gary: "Yastrzemski, 1967."

Roger: "Good one, last triple crown winner. Okay, if we are going old school, Bob Gibson, 1968."

Mike: "He won the Cy Young and MVP?"

Roger: "Yep."

Gary: "Yeah, that's right. He did."

Mike: "Okay, 1989, Oakland A's."

Alex: "1955, Brooklyn Dodgers."

Gary: "Yes. I will go with the Marlins in 2003."

Roger: "George Brett, 1980."

Mike: "2001, Yankees."

Alex, Gary and Roger immediately sounded the buzzer sound in unison: "Aaahhhhhhhhhhhhhhhhhhh."

Roger: "Sorry, buddy, Yanks won 1998 through 2000. Womack singled off Rivera to beat them in 2001."

Mike: "That's what I meant, 2000."

Gary: "Sorry, dude, no take-backs. New score Gary two, Alex three, Rodge four, Mike four. Rodge, your category."

Roger: "Okay, we're gonna go with, in honor of lover boy driving the car, actresses who Tom Cruise has boffed in a movie. I will start with Renee Zelweiger in *Jerry McGuire*."

Mike: "You fags are daydreaming about who sleeps with Tom Cruise and you call me gay? Okay, whatever...um, Nicole Kidman in *Eyes Wide Shut*."

Alex: "Rebecca Demornay, *Risky Business*."

Gary: "Cameron Diaz, *Vanilla Sky*."

Roger: "Demi Moore, *A Few Good Men*."

Mike: "Wait, did they actually fuck in that movie?"

Roger: "Come on, they must have."

Mike: "Does anyone else remember?"

Alex: "No, I don't."

Gary: "I don't either. I think we have to give it to him, though. They must have at some point."

Mike: "So you won't let me change the Yankees but this is okay?"

Alex: "Just fucking go."

Mike: "Fine. Kelly McGillis, *Top Gun*."

Alex: "Shit, how did that last this long. Okay, E-liz-a-beth Shue. *Cocktail*."

Gary: "Good one. Nicole Kidman, *Far and Away*."

Alex: "You actually saw that?"

Gary: "No, I just remember the preview."

Roger: "Jeanne Tripplehorn, *The Firm*."

Mike: "Okay, give me a minute...Didn't he fuck Brad Pitt in *Interview With a Vampire*?"

Alex: "No dude, I don't think we can give you that one."

Gary (eagerly): "Is that a loss?"

Alex: "Yes, unless Mikey can come up with another one in five seconds."

Mike: "What about the six-year-old girl in the vampire movie?"

Alex: "Christ. What's wrong with you? No."

Mike: "That's all I got. This is bullshit."

Gary: "Ah very nice, that means I take the pot and Alex gets second."

Mike: "Great, so I'm already down twenty bucks and we are not even to Nevada yet?"

Gary: "Shit, we're not even to Barstow yet. You are in for a world of hurt."

Mike: "This is bullshit."

Alex: "Jesus, chill out, Sourpuss."

Roger: "I really need Stanford to hit. Let's play another game for double the stakes."

INTERLUDE FOUR

Mike (9)

IT WAS A PICTURE-PERFECT DAY at Scripps Ranch, twenty miles northeast of downtown San Diego. A slight wind carried the smell of the sea air, and random puffy white clouds floating overhead provided periodic respite from the warm sun. Much to the delight of the kids, as well as the parents, an occasional F-14 Tomcat from Miramar Marine Air Station buzzed over the field on its way back to base.

The weather was ideal, and so was the baseball diamond hosting the day's Little League game between the Mets and the Royals. One of the fathers from the Cubs (one of the other teams in the league) had started a bio-tech firm that was bought out by Genentech. This particular dad had a fetish for baseball diamonds and dropped $475,000 into turning the Scripps Ranch Little League diamond into one of the finest places to play baseball on the West Coast. It was complete with sunken dugouts, a padded home run fence, bullpens, an electronic scoreboard, and seating for up to five hundred people. The field itself was brilliantly manicured. People joked that it was better than Jack Murphy Stadium where the Padres played. Somewhat unfortunately, the dad's name was Schtupp, so the complex was officially renamed Schtupp Field. There were still plenty of errors made on

Schtupp Field, but here, unlike most youth leagues around the country, bad hops were rarely the cause of any of them.

Mike Bochner showed up this particular day expecting to play third base and hit sixth in the lineup, as he usually did. Mr. Schtupp also funded an official league score-keeper who printed out a stats sheet for the league, called Schtupp's Stats. Years later, in college, Mike would joke with some of his childhood buddies about what their Schtupp stats were with the ladies, but at the time they took their baseball numbers very seriously. Some of the parents felt that displaying all of the kids' statistics for everyone to see was inappropriate and unhealthy for those who had very low batting averages or high ERAs. Already showing signs of being the conservative Republican he would become years later, Mike found these parents to be "pussies" (a newly learned word he thoroughly enjoyed using) and felt they needed to deal with reality and quit being so politically correct. He astutely observed that most of the parents who objected happened to be the ones whose kids tended to suck. Mike was hitting a respectable .315 at the time.

Five minutes before the game, Walter Chen, one of the kids who had a very low batting average, was practicing his swing in left field. He neglected to look behind him and his follow-through hit Tyler Jones, the Mets' best pitcher (arguably the best in the whole league), squarely in the jaw. Tyler dropped to the ground as blood sprayed out in every direction. Some of it went farther than just about anything else Walter hit that year. Though Tyler's jaw would hurt every time he opened his mouth for the next six months, he was quite lucky because the bat hit just under his teeth, which remained intact. He was taken immediately to the hospital where it was determined that his jaw was not broken, which the doctor also said was very lucky.

With Tyler out for the day, this meant Willy Christensen would start the game on the mound for the Mets. Willy usually pitched the second half of the game, after Tyler, and was usually pretty good. This day, however, he just didn't have it. The game started twenty-five minutes late due to the time it took to get Tyler off the field and on his way to the hospital. When the umpire finally said, "Play ball," Mike watched Willy's first pitch sail four feet above the catcher, batter and umpire. Pitch number two was equally as short as the first one was high. Number three drilled the leadoff batter in the wrist, at which point the child dropped the bat, grabbed his wrist and promptly started to cry.

"Jesus, what a pussy," nine-year-old Mike thought to himself while smoothing out the dirt in front of third base.

Willy's luck with the second batter wasn't much better. He walked him on four pitches. He was more efficient with the third batter, hitting him in the head on the first pitch. The ball struck near the top of the batter's helmet and bounced harmlessly up into the air toward the backstop. The child was unfazed and took off in a trot toward first base.

One of the parents from the other team was not happy about two of the first three batters being hit. "Hey, get this guy out of here. He's terrible and he is going to hurt the kids," he yelled.

Willy's dad, who was a home-building contractor and could rarely attend games, happened to be at this one. Mr. Christensen was a former marine who stood about 6'4" and didn't take shit from anyone. He didn't intend to let anyone insult his kid on the field. "Stick a cork in it," he instructed the other vocal parent.

Everyone assumed that would be the end of it, but it turned out Mr. Protective Parent was a cop and didn't like being told what to do. He immediately stood and walked right up to Mr. Christensen and reiterated that if his son couldn't throw strikes then he shouldn't be in the game and was a danger. Other parents started slowly backing away as it seemed a physical confrontation was all but inevitable.

Sixteen-year-old Ryan Sackson, who was acting as home plate umpire for this game for the tidy sum of $18, had other ideas. For a high school kid, he took impressive control of the situation. Ryan walked immediately back to the backstop and, just as Willy's dad was sticking his finger in the other parent's face, he began to shout. "You two – you are both out of here. This is a little league game, for God's sake. You should be embarrassed. Pack up your stuff and go home."

The two adrenaline-fueled men looked at sixteen-year-old Ryan and realized his point was valid. They also realized he had given them a face-saving out that wouldn't require fighting in front of their kids. Without saying a word, they turned away from each other and began gathering their stuff to leave. Pretty much everyone in the place had forgotten the kids on the field, but Willy was not happy about his dad getting thrown out of the first game he had come to see that year.

"Hey, fuck you, Blue, you can't throw my dad out of the game," he yelled at Ryan from the mound.

Willy got thrown out of the game as well. Four minutes later, he and his dad were walking out toward the car together. Mr. Christensen was proud of his son and gave him a pat on the back. "How about if we go to McDonalds and hang out for a while and not tell your mom about this?" he asked. "Sure, dad," Willy agreed.

Fifteen minutes later, still with no outs on the board, the Mets coach put Mike on the hill to pitch. Mike had only thrown three innings the whole year, but he had a good arm and was as anxious as anyone to get this game moving. He struck out the first batter on three pitches, the second on four pitches and got the third to pop up to first base. The inning was over, and no runs had scored.

Because of all the commotion earlier in the day, when Mike breezed through the fourth inning, no one had quite realized yet that the Mets had a no-hitter going. By the sixth (the last inning in little league), however, with the Mets up 4-0, everyone was very aware of it. Mike got the leadoff hitter to ground out to third and then struck out the second hitter on a curveball that was just as sharp as it was in the first inning. The only thing standing between Mike and Scripps Ranch Little League history was Bobby DelFavro who entered the day hitting .421 according to Schtupp's stats. Mike started him off with a fastball down in the zone that DefFavro took for a strike. The second pitch was a curveball that DefFavro hit well, but he was out in front of it and pulled it foul. Mike nervously took the sign, realizing he was just one pitch away.

He looked into the catcher for the sign and then scratched his balls and spit as he had seen the pros do. He delivered a fastball that was supposed to be outside, but it went right down the middle of the plate. DelFavro hit it well and drove it deep into right field. Mike's heart sank as he saw Willy Chen turn his back to the field and start running toward the fence. Willy's defense was equally as futile as his hitting. The ball began to descend near the warning track and Willy had still not turned his head back toward the infield. Mike was sure the ball was going to actually hit Willy in the head. But at the last minute his neck rotated about half way back toward the infield and his gloved left hand stretched out from his body. Only a full two seconds after the ball settled into Willy's glove did the crowd erupt into cheers and Mike started jumping up and down on the mound before running to hug the catcher.

Mike would go on to have a mediocre high school baseball career, but his all-time highlight was pitching a no-hitter on Schtupp Field that Saturday.

CHAPTER TEN

In N' Out
5:36 p.m.

*"Well, if you like burgers give 'em a try
sometime. I can't usually get 'em myself
because my girlfriend's a vegetarian which
pretty much makes me a vegetarian.
But I do love the taste of a good burger."*
—Jules, *Pulp Fiction*

THE BMW WAS HURTLING UP Highway 15 northbound somewhere northeast of Los Angeles at about eighty-three miles
per hour. On the right side of the road was a sign alerting
drivers that the exit for Highway 40 to Needles was
approaching. Inside the car Roger was asleep again and the
other three guys were conducting meaningless conversation.
Snoop Dogg's *Gin n' Juice* played lightly in the background.

Gary: "Did you guys know Snoopy's cousin lives in
Needles?"

Alex: "Snoop Dogg?"

Gary: "No. Who gives shit where Snoop Dogg's cousin lives? I am talking about Snoopy the dog from Charlie Brown."

Alex: "No, sorry, I didn't realize Snoopy the dog had a cousin in Needles."

Mike: "Fucking fascinating."

Gary: "Hey man, Snoopy kicks ass."

Mike: "I guess so. Is anyone else getting hungry?"

Alex: "Yeah, a bit. What do you guys want?"

Gary: "Taco Bell would be good."

Mike: "How about McDonalds?"

Alex: "No, I'll do anywhere but McDonalds."

Mike: "Panda Express?"

Alex: "Nah, no Panda either. I don't trust those fuckers."

Mike: "Who?"

Alex: "You know. Them."

Mike: "Them, meaning Asians?"

Alex: "Sure. Whatever."

Mike: "You eat sushi all the time."

Alex: "Let's just find something other than Panda."

Gary: "J-Box?"

Alex: "No, can't do that either. Had it for lunch. I think if we can hold out for another fifteen minutes there is an In-N-Out in Rancho Cucamonga."

Gary: "Good call. Anyway, any trip is more complete if it includes a stop in Rancho Cucamonga."

Mike: "Yeah, definitely In-N-Out."

Roger was also inspired: "Fuckin' A," he chimed in from the back seat, apparently less asleep than he appeared.

Seventeen miles later, Alex pulled into the right lane and pulled off onto Foothill Boulevard, Rancho Cucamonga.

Immediately on the right, in the parking lot of a nondescript strip-mall, a relatively modern-looking stand-alone In-N-Out Burger beckoned. There was an open parking spot right by the front door and Alex eased into it. Roger seized the opportunity to rip a loud fart just as the car came to a stop.

Alex was not amused: "Dude, fucking prick. You couldn't wait another ten seconds?"

Roger was clearly pleased with himself: "I just thought you guys would want a little appetizer."

All four doors opened and three of the guys rapidly exited the car. Alex reached toward the sky and simultaneously got up on his tippy-toes trying to stretch out from the first part of the drive. Gary had to pee and broke into a slow jog, entered the restaurant and immediately turned right once inside the doors. Though he had not been there for a few years, his brain recalled a detailed knowledge of the layout of this particular In-N-Out.

The other three slowly walked toward the front door, happy to be out of the car, and looking forward to eating. There were only four people in line for food. By the time Gary rejoined them, Alex had reached the register. Somewhere between the car and the entrance, Alex had swapped his Ray Bans for wrap-around silver Elvis sunglasses which he donned inside the restaurant.

Much to his delight, the girl working the register was extremely attractive. She looked to be about twenty-four, with long brown hair, large breasts that snuggled perfectly inside her white In-N-Out crested blouse, and beautiful big brown eyes that sparkled as if they possessed their own energy source. She looked like a fairy tale character that had been accidentally transported into a fast food restaurant. With a perfect smile, she asked, for the two hundred and fourteenth time that day, "Welcome to In-N-Out. What can I help you with today?"

Alex resisted the urge to reply with his first instinct, instead scanning the menu and then looking down at the girl's chest to read her nametag. Tara, it said. She was wearing the In-N-Out uniform, but not the paper hat that the rest of the crew had. He also noticed that she smelled nice, similar to the standard vanilla-strawberry stripper scent, only more elegant. Curiously, it blended well with the omnipresent cow meat and fried potato aroma permeating the establishment.

Alex: "Hi Tara. Today, I would like a double-double with no mayo, mustard, ketchup or sauce of any kind. And also fries and a large Diet Coke."

Tara informed him the cost would be $6.15. Alex pulled his wallet from the front pocket of his sweat pants and opened it up. After rifling through a stack of bills and unable to find something small, he peeled off a hundred dollar bill and handed it too her.

She checked it for authenticity, then counted out his change and handed him a receipt. "Here you go, you are number twenty-nine. Your order will be out in about fifteen minutes," she informed him.

Alex was puzzled. "Fifteen minutes, what's the deal with that?" he asked, though his tone was more flirty than truly annoyed.

"We don't make it until you order it sir," Tara replied.

Alex looked back up at the menu, trying to see if he missed something the first time. Nothing had changed. The only items were the three burger choices, fries and a selection of beverages. He looked back at Tara and removed the Elvis glasses. "Did I catch you guys off-guard by ordering a burger?" he asked.

Tara was not used to getting attitude from the customers and was annoyed. "I am sorry sir, please just wait for your order," she requested while giving him another smile, fake this time.

"As you wish," Alex said, stepping aside.

Mike was next at the counter, "Sorry about Elvis Timberlake. We picked him up hitchhiking back in Poway. I really don't know him," he said.

Tara laughed, this time legitimately. "That's okay, don't worry about it. What can I get you?" she asked.

"Double-double, no sauce, fries and a large Diet Coke, please," he replied.

Tara laughed at this also. "Okay, that's gonna be $6.15 and about fifteen minutes." Mike gave her a five, a one, and a quarter. She gave him back a dime and a receipt, and looked directly into his eyes. "Here you go. You are number thirty. I hope you enjoy it," she said as her head tilted slightly to the right.

The food actually took only twelve minutes. The group had selected a booth by the window where they could see the car. They simultaneously began unwrapping their burgers. Alex quickly scanned the restaurant to see if there may be any other hot chicks inside, but there were not. He instinctively glanced at Tara before taking a bite of his burger.

Meanwhile, Roger was inspecting Gary's order. "G-Balls, what's the deal? A single burger and no fries? Are you on a diet?" he asked.

Gary: "Yeah, I guess. Blair and I are both working out and trying to lose some weight."

Alex: "I always thought the reason to get married is so you can let yourself go and don't have to worry about being fat anymore."

Gary: "Well, believe it or not, you still won't want to be fat. Plus, if you get fat, that pretty much gives her a free pass to get fat also, and you really don't want that."

Roger: "That makes sense, but you don't look fat."

Gary: "Thanks, but I'm not so sure. The other day I was at Macy's buying some clothes and I was in the dressing room. They've got like six mirrors in there. So there I am in nothing but my boxers looking at myself from six different angles. It was not a pretty picture."

Mike: "Ah, Macy's syndrome. Typical."

They sat quietly for a moment pondering this. Then each took a bite of their burgers.

Mike broke the silence: "You didn't have to be a dick to the girl working the register."

Alex: "Me? Was I?"

Mike: "Yeah, you were."

Alex: "Oh. Sorry. Well I love this place, but I don't know why it is such a shock when someone orders a burger."

Mike: "It isn't her fault."

Gary: "Aw, how cute. Somebody has a crush on the In-N-Out chick."

Mike: "I don't have a crush. I am just saying there is no reason to be rude."

Alex: "Okay, I am sorry if I was insulting. She was pretty hot actually. You should go ask for her number. She seemed to like you."

Mike: "Totally. That will work out great for the next time I am in the middle of the fucking desert."

Alex: "Well, whatever then, let's finish these and get back on the road."

Mike: "Shotgun."

Gary: "Dude, you can't call shotgun before we are headed toward the car. Everyone knows that."

Alex: "He's right."

Roger: "Yep."

Mike: "Whatever. Jesus. Fuckers."

INTERLUDE FIVE

Alex (10)

MIDWAY THROUGH FOURTH GRADE, Alex's family moved from New Mexico to Seattle. Usually, Alex despised moving, but he never much liked New Mexico and immediately felt more comfortable in the lush green surroundings of Washington. He liked the new school as well. The only immediate obstacle was that the social dynamics were radically different. Most importantly, boys and girls at this school were paired up together and were considered to be "going out," whereas in Albuquerque girls were generally to be ignored and actual physical contact with one was cause for embarrassment and ridicule.

Alex's dilemma was not with the principle of the idea, since he liked being around girls. However, all of the ones cute enough for him to consider socially acceptable were already taken upon his transfer. Alex was still unaware that the average fourth grade relationship lasts somewhere around three weeks and a bit of patience would go a long way. Instead, he settled into a courtship with the most attractive remaining choice, Tiffany Monrose. Tiffany was very shy and their relationship was for appearances only, something like a high society Manhattan marriage without the charity balls, affairs and cocaine habits. Instead, their interaction consisted of passing a note back and forth in class once or twice a day.

The notes typically discussed classroom gossip or debated who was better, Duran Duran or Prince.

Due to his lack of enthusiasm for Tiffany, Alex was easy prey to succumb to a scheme devised by Peter Dunn, who was probably the most popular kid in the class. One Friday during the lunch recess, Peter and a few of the other boys convinced Alex that he should approach Jessica Kempinski and tell her he would like to go out with her instead of Tiffany. Jessica was a bit fat and tended to smell like stale bacon, the fault of living in her parent's house which reeked of various cooked meats.

On Monday, after Jessica would proudly announce her new boyfriend to the other kids, Alex would announce that he was actually going out with Julie Simpson, who Peter had arranged would break up with her current boyfriend Jimmy Everth. Alex would further declare that his conversation with Jessica was actually a friendly act in which he helped her to pair up with Billy Massey, a spectacled kid with a strange fascination for frogs, whom no girl wanted anything to do with. The plan was cruelly genius in its ability to humiliate Jessica, Tiffany, Jimmy and Billy all at once. Also, it was entirely plausible because many couples began official courtship through a third-party intermediary.

Alex at first resisted the idea and had no interest in hurting the more vulnerable kids. Even so, he was eager to fit in at the new school and eventually went along with it. Wearing white Reebok tennis shoes, blue Gotcha shorts and a white Seattle Mariners tee shirt, he approached Jessica and followed through with the first part of the plan toward the end of lunch. She was, of course, ecstatic.

Over the weekend, Alex began to have even more serious reservations about the operation, but at this point he saw no clear way out. Sure enough, on Monday during the morning recess, once Jessica had bragged sufficiently of her pairing with Alex, Peter and Alex jointly revealed the actual status of things. Peter took extra care to reveal just how crazy Jessica must have been to believe Alex intended to be associated with her. The humiliation succeeded beyond Peter's expectations. After recess, Jessica broke into a crying fit so severe her mother had to be called in from work to pick her up and take her home. Tiffany was also visibly upset. Jimmy was simply confused. Billy, who was by now largely used to such attacks, ignored the spectacle Jessica caused in class. During the delay, he sat at his desk happily drawing a frog. The dark green frog was holding a sub-machinegun and was happily mowing down some children in the distance. Three of the children were standing and screaming while four of them were depicted in a prone position, surrounded by growing pools of red blood.

Alex felt awful about the whole thing and wished he had never listened to Peter. He wanted to take it all back, but this was impossible. He refrained from crying until he was home alone after school.

CHAPTER ELEVEN

Breakups
6:08 p.m.

"Then we're through. And you're fired!"
—Jerry Seinfeld, *Seinfeld*

MIKE FORGOT TO CALL SHOTGUN on the way out of the restaurant, and the seating arrangements remained unchanged from the first leg of the trip. Alex followed the signs back on to Highway 15 north toward Barstow. He briefly rolled the windows down, as the inside of the BMW had become quite hot while they were inside the restaurant, even though the sun was now hanging low in the sky. As they pulled onto the freeway a blue Aston Martin flew by in the fast lane. A plastic-looking hot blonde was sitting in the front seat. Alex, Mike and Gary were all thinking some variation of jealous curses directed at the guy driving the car. Roger didn't notice and was happily packing a dip in the back seat. After Roger was done, Alex decided to take one also. He always found a Kodiak most enjoyable right after a meal, especially a nice greasy one. He readied the empty In-N-Out cup he had kept for a spitter and rolled up the windows, satisfied that the air conditioner was now sufficiently working.

Mike thought about throwing in a dip but decided against it because it sometimes made him queasy. "That girl at the In-N-Out really was cute, wasn't she?" he remarked.

Alex agreed, "Yes, little Tara was quite a biscuit. You really should have asked for her number."

Gary switched the topic. "You know what I have always wanted to do?" he asked rhetorically. No one acknowledged him, but he provided the answer anyways. "I have always wanted to fuck a girl wearing one of those Hot Dog on a Stick uniforms," he announced decisively.

Roger found this humorous and almost coughed up a mouthful of chew spit. "Nice, G-Balls. That would be hot. Then afterwards you could share a corndog and lemonade together."

Mike did not find any of this amusing. "I am glad hot dogs excite you morons sexually," he said.

A thought entered Alex's mind. His eyebrows furrowed and he looked to his right toward Gary. "Dude, I just realized, aren't most girls who work at Hot Dog on a Stick like fifteen years old? I think you really might have a problem."

"Save it," was the only response he got.

Without thinking, Gary stuck his hand down his pants and scratched his balls, then remembered something. "Hey Alex, didn't you date a chick who worked at one of those street-side hot dog stands?" he asked.

Alex: "Um, oh yeah. No, no – it was a one-dollar taco truck. She was a hot little Mexican number. I think she was the only Mexican chick I have ever been with."

Mike: "Must be, considering you don't have any kids yet."

Alex: "Very funny, jackass."

Gary: "Seriously, Alex, you must actually care sometimes. Have you had any breakups that hurt?"

Alex: "Well the other night I had a dream that I was double-teaming Kournikova and Sharapova and then I woke up. That was a pretty painful dose of reality."

Mike: "Are you sure that wasn't Roddick and Federrer?"

No one laughed because it was a stupid comment. After a ten-second pause Alex began to speak again. "Seriously though, when Stephanie and I broke up, I was pretty messed up for a while."

Mike: "Oh yeah, I remember that. You were deep into the Jim Beam for a good six months."

Gary: "Six months isn't bad. Isn't the general rule that it takes half the amount of time you go out to recover? You guys went out for almost two years, right?"

Alex: "Yeah, just over two. She was a good one."

Gary: "I forget. Why did you guys break up, anyway?"

Alex: "My cock was too big. I kept bottoming out."

Gary: "Asshole."

Alex: "Seriously, I don't really know what the problem was. I think it just got to the point where we had to take the next step and we were both too scared to do it so we just broke up."

Mike: "Time to shit or get off the pot."

Roger: "More like Alex realized he may have to deal with only one pussy for the rest of his life and ran to the hills."

Alex: "No. It really wasn't like that."

Gary: "How so?"

Alex: "Well, I don't know. She was awesome, but I just don't know. Something else wasn't right."

Gary: "Like what?"

Alex: "I don't know. One thing I do know is about two weeks after we broke up she took off to Europe with some other dude. She said it was just a friend and all, but really, who goes to Europe with a friend of the opposite sex?"

Gary: "You think she was cheating on you?"

Alex: "No. Well, I don't know. Probably, I guess. It just seemed really weird. I don't know. I still think about her sometimes, but I am pretty sure I am better off that it didn't work out. It was too soon and I wouldn't have wanted to miss out on everything else."

Mike: "That's the thing about bitches. They are all just monkeys. They don't let go of one branch until they have a firm grip on another one."

Notorious B.I.G. took over the conversation through the speakers and let everyone know,

"I love it when you call me big pop-pa
Throw your hands in the air, if youse a true player I love it
when you call me big pop-pa
To the honies gettin money playin niggaz like dummies
I love it when you call me big pop-pa
If you got a gun up in your waist please don't shoot up the
place
Cause I see some ladies tonight who should be havin my
baby...
Bay-bee"

Roger interrupted the deceased rapper: "Can we check if the Stanford game is on?"

Alex ignored the request. "In any case, at a certain point it is usually better to move on anyway," he said as he picked a small booger out of his nose with his left hand. He rolled the booger between his left thumb and forefinger and then dropped it on the floor between his legs.

Gary: "At some point you are going to need to quit being such a pussy."

Alex: "I am a pussy because I like to get pussy?"

Gary: "Basically, yes. You are just scared to commit. Don't get me wrong, I can see the benefits of being single, but even you admitted something is missing."

Alex: "You may be right, but, no offense, being married just seems stupid. I mean, what is the point of making a legal commitment that doesn't really change anything except that you can be fucked out of half of your money? Why can't people just commit to each other in their hearts instead of depending on the government to tell them it is official?"

Mike: "Wow, you really are a romantic."

Alex: "Seriously though, what are the benefits?"

Gary: "It is okay. I mean in some ways it is nice to have the comfort of just knowing that you are with someone and you will always be connected."

Mike: "Okay, that is pretty much bullshit. Almost everyone cheats and you never know when your significant other will deem you insignificant, regardless of your marital status."

Gary: "The statistics say only one in four married people actually end up cheating."

Mike: "That is like saying only one in every million boys will grow up to be in the NBA. It isn't because they don't want to play for the Lakers. It is because they can't. Did you ever notice how almost every movie star or athlete ends up cheating eventually. It is because they can."

Gary: "So, what, you have to be famous for someone to want to sleep with you?"

Mike: "No, but it makes it a lot easier. Of course most people can find someone to have sex with, but it isn't going to be anyone good looking so there probably isn't much point."

Gary: "Well, I can't opine on people's hypothetical affairs, but the bottom line is marriage gives you a permanent stability."

Mike: "Tell that to the fifty-plus percent of the people who get divorced."

Gary: "Yeah, that is a good point. But even so, if you want a decent chick to commit to you and to have kids with you, then she needs to have some assurance that you are going to stick around. Marriage gives her that. All I am saying is from the girl's perspective, they can't take the risk of having some dude impregnate them and then bail on them and leave them broke with the kids."

Alex: "Fair enough, but what about all the times the dude gets fucked? I think marriage is a relic of a time when it made more sense. In the old days, the rich people had to marry to join forces with other families of power to stay on top. The peasantry couldn't finance a decent single lifestyle anyway, so there really was no reason not to get married. Nowadays, it is a scary proposition. I have seen some awful situations at work. One of my buddies there, who is only thirty-five but has a huge book, married his college sweetheart. Really romantic, right? Except when they were twenty-eight and he was pulling close to a mil a year the chick realizes she could take half of what he makes and also half of what they saved. So suddenly this broad, who had not even worked in a few years, decides she wants to live in Paris and be an artist. The dude tried to be supportive and got her an apartment in Paris to do the long distance thing, but of course this was doomed. After a few months she started fucking the waiter from the corner café and filed for divorce. Got six hundred grand in cash plus half of his salary for four years. The dude did nothing wrong."

Roger: "Sometimes I wish I was a chick. I wouldn't mind marrying some dude and sticking it out for a few years and then just chilling."

Gary: "Good plan, Rodge. Yeah, look, these things happen. I am scared all the time that I am going to come home and find Blair with the gardener, but you can't let fear prevent you from moving forward. Sometimes you have to trust."

Alex: "Yeah, maybe, but this doesn't seem smart. Divorce is a big fucking problem that I don't want to deal with. It makes people crazy. Another guy from work got in this huge battle over assets and they got insane. He had some old vintage Ferrari that was his favorite thing in the world so the chick told her lawyer to go after the car. Anyway, every cent was fought over and the chick ended up getting the house, the Ferrari, and some amount of cash. She even got custody of the dog, one of those fluffy white Maltese things. So this is where it gets wacky. The rumor is, and I don't know for sure if it is true or not, but what people say, is that the guy kidnapped the dog, took it home and killed it. Then he barbecued it and ate it with a side of asparagus and a two-hundred-dollar bottle of Barolo. He hated his wife so much that he waited until he took a shit, and then shit in a new Prada bag he had bought for the occasion. He went to her new apartment and told his ex that she could keep the Ferrari and the dog and that he even bought her a new bag. Then he presented her with the Prada with the shit in it."

Mike: "That's got to be bullshit, right?"

Alex: "I don't know. People swear it is true. The guy is a bit strange so it is possible. All I know for sure is, marriage is a crazy risk and I still have not figured out what the reward is."

Gary: "Whatever, someday you guys will all be married and you will understand. Maybe one or two of us will get divorced, maybe not. But however you feel now, there will be a time when you will not only concede to get married, but you will really want it. And later, believe it or not, you will realize you have ended up with something more valuable than money or anything else. Don't get me wrong, marriage is more work than your job, but it can be more rewarding also."

Mike: "Well, maybe you are right. But until then, let's go to Vegas and find some hoes."

Alex: "Amen."

Roger: "Amen. Can we check the Stanford score?"

CHAPTER TWELVE

Barstow
6:25 p.m.

"Well, all I'm saying is that I want to look back and say that I did the best I could while I was stuck in this place. Had as much fun as I could while I was stuck in this place. Played as hard as I could while I was stuck in this place...Dogged as many girls as I could while I was stuck in this place."
—Dawson, *Dazed and Confused*

ANYONE WHO HAS EVER DRIVEN to Las Vegas from Los Angeles or San Diego knows that a certain amount of anticipation builds to get to Barstow, California. Not because there is anything remotely redeeming about Barstow, but because it is a milestone which marks the fact that you are halfway to Vegas. It is otherwise difficult to get excited about a city of just over twenty-one thousand on the outskirts of the Mojave desert which ranks as one of the ten poorest in California with over twenty percent of its citizens below the poverty line.

Many people stop at one of the seemingly infinite fast food choices, though if one was feeling particularly fancy, he may choose to hold out for gyros at The Mad Greek sixty miles away in Baker. Since the guys just had In-N-Out a half an hour ago, and Roger was fully loaded up on Kodiak, there was no reason to stop now. Alex blew through Barstow at eighty-two miles an hour as 2Pac sang about the merits of living and dying in Los Angeles. Out here, Los Angeles was already another universe. The sky behind them had evolved into a collage of purples and oranges as the sun prepared to relinquish her role for the day.

Alex looked out the side window and noticed a new housing complex going up at the edge of town. "You could be home now!" a billboard promoting the complex announced. "Yeah, fucking great," Alex said mostly to himself, wondering where one would likely be coming home from.

"Can we turn the game on?" Roger asked.

Alex complied and hit a button on the steering wheel which changed the audio from auxiliary to AM preset. After a few minutes of a stalled Stanford drive resulting in a punt, the score was announced. The Cardinal was down 13-3 midway through the first half.

Roger combined his displeasure and motivational speech into one concise statement: "Come on – pull it together, you fucking cum-guzzling fucks!"

With that the group passed the last cluster of fast food joints on the eastern edge of the town. This one included a Carl's Jr. (with a Green Burrito add-on), Jack in the Box, Burger King and Taco Bell. Immediately past the exit was a green sign indicating that Baker was fifty-nine miles away and Las Vegas was now a hundred and fifty-two miles away.

"Rock n' roll," Alex said.

In the back seat, Mike decided to bum a Kodiak from Roger after all. He clumsily packed it as a Stanford corner-back intercepted a pass and returned it sixty-seven yards for a touchdown, eliciting a round of applause from Roger. Mike pulled his lip out and inserted the tobacco, spilling about a third of the grains down the front of his Caminiti Padres jersey. As the extra point was kicked, he spit once in his In-N-Out cup and brushed the spilt chew off his chest and stomach and onto the leather seat between him and Roger.

INTERLUDE SIX

Gary (14)

MIDWAY THROUGH THE SUMMER of 1987, in Thousand Oaks, California, Gary was feeling like quite the stud. At thirteen years old, he had already been to second base with a girl. Although it only happened once, and the girl, Millie Adams, had kind of freaked out afterwards and said they could not do it again, he was quite sure that he liked it and was also pretty sure that she would change her mind. If not, he also had a sense that Susan Andrews from his social studies class would let him try it also.

By July 26th, the night of his friend Casey Wilson's big sleepover party, school had been out for over six weeks and seemed like a distant memory. Eighth grade didn't start for another five weeks, so Gary's only concerns were summer baseball and trying to get his hands back on Millie's boobs. Because he had no source of transportation and there were no social events involving girls, the boobs were becoming less and less important.

On this particular night, neither baseball nor boobs mattered much. This was the second annual big sleepover at Casey's, whose parents were usually drunk by ten o'clock and really didn't care what the kids upstairs were doing as long as they were not too loud and did not leave the house. One of the other guys at the party, who was seriously named Larry

Hagman, had promised to bring a case of beer, but did not deliver. Some of the guys were disappointed, but Gary, who had never had a beer in his life, was glad and was looking forward to a fun night without alcohol.

His vision involved the guys watching a movie (maybe one with some decent nudity) until Casey's parents were asleep. Then there would be a round of pillow fights before settling into a serious Nintendo RBI baseball tournament. Gary was nearly unhittable if he got to play with the Mets, who had Dwight Gooden and Bob Ojeda as starters with Roger McDowell and submarine-throwing Jesse Orosco in the pen. He took it for granted that he would win the RBI tournament. He was eliminated early in the pillow fighting last year, however, and was anxious to fare better this time.

Things were going very much according to plan until about forty-five minutes into the pillow fights. Gary already had two victories. Each match consisted of one round of five minutes. The winner was determined by vote among the spectators, unless one person chose to surrender early. Knocking your opponent to the ground twice was considered a victory by technical knockout. Getting hit once with a pillow is not a big deal, but being struck repeatedly in the head could make one quite dizzy.

Gary had a long pillow case with a small hard pillow bunched up in the end of it. This meant it was significantly less maneuverable and it took longer to get the pillow head moving. Gary was forced to take big, long swings. However, due to the greater centrifugal force and extra mass at the end, his pillow allowed for a much greater impact if he could connect. His first fight was against a kid named Ryan who was not very athletic and was an easy pushover. Actually, Gary was surprised Ryan was even invited to the party to begin with.

Gary kept his swings to short circles by choking up on the pillow case and repeatedly connected with blows to Ryan's stomach, occasionally mixing it up and going for the head. Meanwhile, Ryan was playing more defense than anything and only took a few offensive swings the whole five minutes. Gary probably could have forced a knockout if he really tried, but was satisfied to advance with an easy victory by decision and avoid Ryan the embarrassment of getting knocked down. It was not a challenge.

The second match, against Casey, was more difficult. Casey was a well-skilled pillow fighter. For most of the five-minute match, Casey was able to back away from Gary's long swings and then step in and deliver quick blows to Gary's head with his Chicago Bears pillow-cased pillow (Casey and his parents originally were from Chicago).

However, with a minute left in the round, Gary swung his pillow from the left side of his body to his right, missing Casey by a good two feet. Casey didn't realize this was an intentional miss and that the pillow would be quickly be returning from the other direction, this time with the full force of Gary's stronger right arm driving it. Casey stepped in to try to connect with a short swing of his own.

Gary's bunched-up pillow connected squarely with the left side of Casey's head. It was enough to cause Casey to stumble backward, slightly dazed. Gary did not miss the opportunity. He quickly swung his pillow around his left side and over his head, bringing it back down on the top of Casey's head with an axe-chopping motion, driving Casey's head down between his knees. Gary then choked up and swung repeatedly from his right side, delivering rapid blows. Casey was able to block most of these shots with his pillow, but the damage was done. Though the outcome was not a knockout, Gary was easily determined to be the winner.

This only left Larry, who had won the event last year. Gary expected a two- or three-minute break before the final battle. However, during these next few minutes the course of the night took an unexpected turn.

"As much as I would like to kick Gary's ass and win pillow fighting again this year, I think we should do something a bit more grown-up," Larry announced.

All of the other nine boys gathered at the event stared at him in silence, wondering where this was going. "I am sorry I didn't score the beers like I hoped to," Larry went on, "but since we can't get drunk, we should at least go toilet paper someone's house and fuck it up," he finished, with a smile on his face.

To win support of the idea, Larry also announced that he and Casey had found a dead raccoon in the backyard and they would set it on fire on the front doorstep of the house being attacked.

Casey acknowledged that his parents had three huge cases of toilet paper from Costco in the garage and probably would not notice if one was missing. Also, Casey mentioned that they could take the twelve eggs in the fridge if they made one of the frying pans dirty to make it look like they cooked them for a late snack.

Gary was not happy with this plan. He was looking forward to his chance to defeat Larry in pillow fighting and then kicking everyone's ass in RBI. He also knew he could probably talk everyone into throwing one or two dollars into a pool for the RBI tournament. He figured if he won ten bucks he could add twenty percent to his current net worth, most of which was safely hidden at home under the sweater of his stuffed Winnie the Pooh doll.

Gary tried to steer the night back toward his original design, and even went so far as to call Larry a pussy for trying to avoid finishing the pillow fight tournament. It did not work. The toilet-papering idea had an unstoppable momentum. This being America, a quick vote was taken. It was seven to three in favor of toilet-papering. The decision was final.

One important choice remained. Whose house to hit? After about three minutes of discussion, a target was identified.

Patrick Zell was a sophomore at the local high school. At the end of the last school year he had hooked up with Casey's seventh-grade girlfriend, Mindy Stewart. It was widely known that Mindy had sucked his dick, but this tidbit was not mentioned among the group of young adventurers planning their mission from Casey Wilson's bedroom.

The next thing Gary knew, he and Larry were rifling through Casey's dresser drawers trying to find dark clothes to wear. Within minutes they were entirely clad in black, looking something like pre-teen versions of Joe Pesci in *Home Alone*.

The ten boys took great care to sneak out of the house quietly. Casey's bedroom was a loft-like structure above the garage. Once armed to their satisfaction, the group exited out the window. One at a time, they climbed down a steeply slanted section of the roof onto a fence that divided the front yard from the back yard before dropping six feet into the soft bushes in the front. Casey explained that this was important because it allowed the group to silently enter the front yard without having to open the very noisy gate. While this was true, the the group just as easily could have walked out the front door. Casey's parents had mowed through three one-liter bottles of Fetzer White Zinfandel before passing out around 11:15 p.m. They were in no position to hear, or care, who was entering or leaving the property.

Gary touched down in the bushes last and quickly scanned the horizon, searching for the rest of the platoon which was now huddled behind a big oak tree in the front of the yard. It took a few moments to find them because everyone was wearing black and it was a dark, moonless night. Casey lived in one of the original developments of Thousand Oaks and this section of the city did not have street lights.

Gary waited for his eyes to adjust to the darkness, noticing how much cooler it had become at night. The temperature had dropped over thirty-five degrees from its peak of ninety-four in the afternoon. A slight wind caused the trees to rustle and created the feeling of being in the wilderness instead of upper-middle-class Los Angeles suburbia. Gary thought he heard a wolf howl in the distance but was not sure if it was real or if he simply imagined it. He felt a stab of fear before reminding himself the whole thing was no big deal. He blinked his eyes a few times and then jogged over to the other guys.

Larry and Casey assumed leadership of the operation and whispered instructions. The group was to maintain zero visual contact with potential civilians. This meant that if any cars came, everyone should meld into the darkness and remain still until the threat passed. If they were spotted by a cop, instructions were to hide if possible. If not, the order was to scatter and avoid capture by any means. The meeting point was back at the house but only after you were sure you were not being followed. Larry reminded the group that Thousand Oaks cops were "a bunch of lazy fucking pigs" so this pretty much just meant you had to hop over a few backyard fences to get away. Casey solemnly reminded the participants that anyone caught was on their own and could in no way

implicate the rest of the group. Larry threatened serious physical harm to anyone who snitched and held up the plastic bag
holding the dead raccoon to emphasize the point. In the darkness, Gary rolled his eyes at the overdramatic approach.

After a few more minutes of babble, Larry and Casey got
to the interesting part of the plan, what they would actually
do when they got there. Casey took the lead here, and it finally occurred to Gary that this was a well-planned event and
not a spur-of-the-moment idea in the middle of the pillow
fight tournament. It seemed Casey was more upset about the
Patrick Zell situation than he had let on.

Casey announced the battle plan: "All right guys, each of
you is armed with three rolls of TP. Additionally, Dave has a
bag of confetti for the yard, Larry has a dozen eggs and I have
a baseball bat for the mailbox. When we get there, split into
groups of two and start the TP process. One guy throws over
trees or branches and the other guy tries to catch. Then tear
and re-throw. Try to get it as high up as possible and don't
worry about the bushes at eye-level that are easy to clean up.
While you are doing this, Larry and I will sneak into the
backyard and use half of the eggs on high-level targets.
We will then come around and hit the car and the front of the
house with eggs. They have a BMW they usually leave in the
driveway. At this point, Dave will confetti the yard. Finally, if
we still have cover and no one is coming out, I will place the
raccoon on the welcome mat and light it on fire. Once the fire
is lit, Gary takes out the mailbox with the bat and I will ring
the doorbell. Then we run like hell. Avoid the expressway on
the way home and cut through the Turnburry's yard and
across the creek instead."

Gary could see that Casey was quite proud of his plan,
but he still had a few questions about the wisdom of this mission: "Hey guys, I realize Zell is a dweeb, but don't you think

this is a little much? I mean, it is probably just the parents who will have to clean everything up, not him."

Larry: "Gary, quit being such a pussy."

Casey: "Yeah."

No one had further questions, so the unit got underway. Larry quickly ran out from behind the tree and headed north on Hummingbird Lane. He maintained a crouched position as if avoiding enemy fire. Each man followed in a single line, with Ryan bringing up the rear and Gary just in front of him.

The boys returned to base in Casey's bedroom seventy-three minutes later and debriefed about the mission. All targets were hit. Twenty-four rolls of TP were now hanging from the trees in the yard, the lawn was heavily laced with confetti, the mailbox was destroyed, eggs were splattered all about, and a smoldering pile of raccoon remains lay on what was the welcome mat.

They encountered no police and only a small number of civilian drive-bys. The boys felt confident they were unsighted and congratulated themselves on a job well done. Casey went to the garage and brought back a six-pack of root beer and a six-pack of Coke to celebrate with.

It would not be for another four days that they would learn that Casey got the address wrong and they actually attacked the house of Pamela Boardman, an innocent girl in the class below them. The Boardmans had a long talk with their daughter about who would want to do something like this to them. They were very concerned about her associating with such disgusting kids. No one considered any connection to the actual assailants, and the attack went unsolved.

Perhaps some good did come from the event, however. Much to his own surprise, Larry felt extremely guilty about what happened. A few days later he walked over to the Boardmans with the intention of confessing and offering to help clean up, but he chickened out at the last minute. While he never accepted responsibility, he did learn an important lesson about the value of good intelligence.

Years later, Larry was part of another group, this one flying F-17s over Iraq. His job was to guide five-hundred pound bombs to their targets, regardless of what they may be. Larry didn't mind killing people. Actually, he felt pretty darned good about it when he did his job well. But he cared passionately about the quality of his work and he understood the costs of error. One fall day in 2004, Larry disobeyed an order to bomb a small camp of tents outside of Basra because he felt the intelligence was suspect and something seemed wrong. He probably would have been severely punished had it not turned out in debriefing that the target in question was part of a British field hospital.

CHAPTER THIRTEEN

Porn + Games Part II
6:38 p.m.

"Truckin', like the do-dah man.
Once told me, "You've got to play your hand"
Sometimes the cards ain't worth a damn, if
you don't lay 'em down,
Sometimes the light's all shinin' on me;
Other times I can barely see.
Lately it occurs to me, what a long,
strange trip it's been"
—*Truckin'*, The Greatful Dead

TEN MILES BEYOND THE OFFICIAL Barstow city limit, Alex, Mike and Gary outvoted Roger three to one and switched off the Stanford game, promising to put it back on for the second half. Gary cycled through the iPod in the front seat and announced he would start things off with a vintage beat. Moments later, Skid Row's *I Remember You* began to play.

Alex and Gary sang along in the front seat, "We spent the summer with the top rolled down," while Mike turned toward Roger in the back and simulated shooting himself in the head. A lack of enthusiasm for the vocals emanating from the front wasn't the only thing contributing to Mike's lack of appreciation for life at the moment. His stomach was churning in a way that had morphed from annoying to painful. He now regretted the Kodiak.

Mike rolled the window down. At the current speed of eighty-four miles per hour, the noise from the wind mostly drowned out Sebastian Bach and his newfound chorus. He firmly pinched the chew with his left hand, reached out the window and flipped it into the nothingness on the side of Interstate 15. Alex tried to look in rearview mirror to make sure Mike wasn't making a mess in the car, but the sun was now directly behind them, a fireball resting on the horizon rendering the mirror useless.

"That better not be all over the car out there," Alex said sternly.

"Don't worry, there is none on the outside of the car," Mike said, smiling to himself.

Roger had been trying to go back to sleep for the past few minutes, but the burst of air from Mike's window left him completely awake, and bored. "Can we pull over and get some beers and maybe play a drinking game or something? Even better, let's play something where I can take some of you bitches' money."

Alex did not want to stop for beers. His vision involved getting to Vegas as soon as possible, perhaps allowing for time to relax with a few drinks in the room before going out. Also, he knew if the other guys started drinking now it would have the following negative effects on him:

- At least three additional piss breaks prior to arrival
- Small jealousy factor that everyone else was drinking

- Higher likelihood the one or more of the other guys would end up too drunk by midnight to enjoy the whole night
- Risk of spilling in the car
- Legal risk if they get pulled over

Alex: "Let's just make it to Vegas and you can drink all you want there."

Mike: "A few beers would be nice to take the edge off."

Gary: "I agree, let's hit the next store and grab a twelver."

Alex realized he would not get his way on this one. Five miles later they pulled off on an exit containing a Shell station with a twenty-four hour mini-mart. Though he still had a third of a tank of gas, Alex got out of the car and began to fill up, first inserting a Southwest Airlines Visa card in the pump and then entering his zip code. Meanwhile, Gary headed toward the store to get the beers. The sky was now dark blue with the last reminders of daylight coming from the west and a sliver of a moon starting to assert itself from the north. Gary broke into a slow jog because the temperature had dropped significantly in the brief time since they left the In-N-Out and a brisk wind had picked up.

Mike was happy that Gary had proactively taken the initiative to go in and buy the beers because he knew Gary wouldn't ask him to chip in, but he felt his stomach really starting to turn and wondered if he should try to use the bathroom in the Shell. The thought of taking a shit in a gas station sounded entirely unappealing, however, and Mike decided to hold out for a few hours until they got to the hotel in Vegas. Also, should the situation deteriorate, he knew there would be more bathroom stops before too long if they were going to start drinking beers.

Four minutes later the Beemer was fully fueled and Gary was getting back in the front seat, placing a large brown bag on the floor between his legs.

"What've you got in there?" Mike asked.

"Oh, it's a Bag O' Tricks," Gary answered excitedly.

Alex accelerated aggressively up the onramp, demonstrating the power of the BMW's engine and hitting seventy-five miles per hour well before entering the right lane of Highway 15. Gary instinctively fastened his seatbelt before opening the bag. On the stereo, Gwen Stefani was explaining what she would do if she was a rich girl, which always bothered Mike considering she was, in fact, a rich girl. Gary pulled out one of the two six-packs of Budweiser tall boys in the bag and quickly ripped off two beers. Without looking back, he reached behind his head and offered them to the back seat. They were removed from his hands instantly.

He put one more in the cup holder next to his seat and returned the remaining half of the six-pack to the bag. When his hand re-emerged, it was holding a pack of Bicycle playing cards, which he also handed to Roger in the back seat. Next he pulled out one of the four Slim Jims in the bag and handed it to Alex.

"Thought you might want to slip into a Slim Jim since you can't join us in a beer," he suggested, before adding, "Rodge, why don't you shuffle up the cards and we can start a game of High/Low, Red/Black?"

Alex accepted the synthetic beef stick, grateful for a friend like Gary who was compassionate enough to alleviate the difficulties of being unable to drink by providing a desirable savory snack. His admiration only grew when Gary then produced a twenty-ounce plastic Diet Coke and placed it in Alex's cup-holder.

In the back seat, Roger opened the deck of cards and began shuffling them, using his left hand only. It was a trick that he thought was incredibly cool, but for some reason most women did not share his enthusiasm. Gary again stuck his hand in the bag, this time pulling out a copy of the latest *Club* adult magazine. It was wrapped in a bright pink cellophane packaging which prevented one from seeing most of the front cover. Gary hungrily tore off the packaging to see what it revealed. It featured Tera Patrick sitting on top of what appeared to be an antique wooden kitchen table. She was leaning back, her legs spread and knees raised, naked except for a small white lace apron which covered part of her stomach but left her breasts and everything below the waist exposed. Behind her was an attractive blonde who was kneeling on the table and leaning over Tera's right side. The blond had one hand on Tera's shoulder and was looking down toward her stomach. Her other hand was looped under Tera's knee and was holding a baby-blue colored dildo. Gary suspected that the other end of the dildo was a few inches inside Tera's vagina, but it would forever remain a mystery because there was a bright yellow star covering this particular part of the picture. According to the headline (also in bright yellow) next to the blonde's head, more information could be found starting on page thirty-four under the story, "French Country Lesbo Chefs Cook up Something Hot!" Other noteworthy items included "Janitor's Closet Orgy!," "Young Tennis Star Bares All on the Court!," and, simply, "Bobby does Nikki." Gary noted that this was the only article that in the opinion of the cover editor did not warrant an exclamation point. The remaining contents of the magazine fell under the umbrella statement, "More Filth and Nastiness Than You Can Handle!"

Gary felt a twinge of guilt at buying porn, given the cause of his recent arguments with Blair and the fact that he probably should not even be on this trip to begin with. Nevertheless, he couldn't help but flip to "Young Tennis Star Bares All on the Court!" It featured a girl who looked enough like Maria Sharapova to make the obvious connection. Most of the pictures were kind of lame, but on the third page of the article he found one of the girl (named Maria, of course) bent over a tennis net with her little white skirt pulled up over her waist. She was holding a Wilson tennis racket in one hand and was using the other to lightly pull apart her butt-cheeks in order to reveal more of her pussy and asshole. She was looking backward over her shoulder, bright red lips slightly parted, heavy blue and black mascara surrounding closed eyes.

"Game, set and match," Gary mumbled to himself while reading the all-too-obvious commentary on the sides of the pictures about "playing with balls" and "ground strokes."

"That's enough for you, pederast. Unless there is an underage burger flipper in there, let me take a look," Mike demanded.

Gary conceded and tossed the magazine back to Mike while Mary J. Blidge declared that there would be no more drama in her life.

Roger, now finished shuffling, cracked his beer and took a healthy sip. "Damn, that's good," he declared. "You can't beat the King of Beers."

"Congratulations, I am happy for you," Alex said through a mouthful of Slim Jim. Internally, he began justification for the acceptability of having a beer during the last forty minutes of the trip, once they crossed the state line into Nevada.

Roger ignored Alex and announced the rules of the game. "Okay bitches, Red/Black, High/Low is the game. The stakes are a quarter a point and ties pay double. Someone find a pen."

Gary searched the glove compartment, pushing aside the registration for the BMW and an assortment of somewhat crumpled currency notes which looked to amount to about a hundred and thirty Euros, thirty-five British Pounds, fourteen hundred Japanese Yen and a hundred Czech Koruna. In the very back he found a blue and white pen advertising Barclay's Global Capital. Meanwhile, Mike tore out a page of "Bobby does Nikki." It featured her blowing him on a lounge chair, but also provided a lot of empty space to use as a scorecard. He handed it to Gary, who briefly checked out the other side of the page for exciting pictures, but it contained only a host of uninspiring phone sex advertisements. He flipped it back over and made a score sheet in the upper right portion of the page, writing R   M   A   G along the top.

Roger declared he would go first. He held out the deck of cards to Mike who cut them roughly in half. Roger put the bottom half on top and buried the top card, a six of spades. He then flipped over the next card which was a ten of hearts.

"Low," he said and flipped another card, this time a three of spades. Predictably, he guessed the next card would be higher, but a two of diamonds appeared. "Sons of bitches," he exclaimed and flipped over another card to start the process again. After two more failed attempts, he got two in a row correct and passed to Mike, netting a score of negative two. Mike correctly guessed the next card would be red, passed to Alex, and began inspecting the rest of the magazine.

When the cards came back around to him, Mike correctly guessed "high," racking up seven points, then made an important realization.

Mike: "Have you guys noticed how much better porn is now than even, like, four years ago?"

Roger: "What are you talking about?"

Mike: "Well, the obvious difference is they didn't used to show penetration. Now they have close-ups of a guy's cock buried in there. Sometimes a bit too close-up, I am afraid. But more importantly, now they show you the pictures you actually want to see. Take this, for instance…"

Mike held up the magazine opened to the Tera Patrick spread. Tera looked as though she was about to spank the blond girl from the cover with a wooden cooking spoon. Meanwhile, the blond girl was bent over the antique table with her legs spread so you could clearly see the entirety of her ass and pussy. The red high-heels covering her feet were about eighteen inches apart. She was looking back over her shoulder, with her lips forming a bright red O shape and her eyes closed. The other guys took a look and nodded appreciatively.

Mike continued: "See, this is what you want to see. You want to see a direct shot from behind of a chick bent over with another hot chick with big tits right next to her. Now, a few years ago you would not have had this picture. It would have been some side angle and they would have maybe been playing with each other's tits and laughing or something. It used to be all very Playboyish, trying to be art or something. But this is what you want. It is tremendous progress."

Alex agreed: "The evolution of smut. Capitalism at its finest. Competition and innovation."

Gary: "I am not sure Mike's opinion of spank mags qualifies as betterment of society and validates the free market experiment."

Alex: "I think it does. It is a great example. For instance, a 2006 Honda Accord is probably a better and nicer car than a 2000 BMW 5-series. In 2010, the Accord will probably be nicer than this car is now. This is all because of competition. And as with cars, porn will continue to evolve as well. Probably it is because of the Internet that the magazines had to get better and you see so much positive change so quickly."

Gary: "So you don't think the communists had good porn?"

Alex: "I am guessing not. But I don't think the communists had much good of anything."

Gary: "So maybe in fifteen years there will be, like, virtual 3-D porn?"

Alex: "Yeah, probably something like that."

Mike: "If they can make a virtual chick who will suck my cock and then cook my dinner, it will be a better world."

With that, the topic was exhausted. Over the next twenty minutes the score sheet slowly filled itself. Roger initially took a big lead, but then got greedy with a four showing and fourteen points on the board. He caught another four and gave up most of his advantage. Still he ended the session up $25 on Mike and $7 on Alex. Gary, who was hoping to win back the money spent on the Bag 'O Tricks, broke even.

In Palo Alto, Stanford's kicker hit a field goal to tie the game at thirteen.

Roger (15)

IN HIS TWENTIES, ROGER USUALLY had little interest in the news, other than the sports section. There was one other type of story that always attracted his attention. It was any type of accusation of statutory rape, especially where it was a female being charged. Roger found it curious that the women in these cases were almost always attractive. The same could definitely be said of his tenth-grade history teacher who claimed his virginity.

Ms. Peters was thirty-two years old and was widely agreed among the student body of Parker High School to be the hottest of the female teachers. Therefore, Roger didn't terribly mind when he failed a test on the American Revolution and was asked by Ms. Peters to meet her after school to discuss his poor performance. Roger was so woefully prepared for the test because he expected to be given the answers during brunch recess from a friend who had the same class for first period. The plan went awry when the girl was called home for a family emergency during second period and was nowhere to be found for the exchange of information.

Roger showed up for the teacher-student meeting, as instructed, at 3:15 p.m., completely unsure what to expect. He had always been a decent student, but he never took school all that seriously. He wasn't the Ivy League-bound type of kid who would raise red flags by failing one test. He hoped Ms. Peters would try to teach him personally about the founding of the country, but assumed there was a greater chance he would get a lecture. He didn't think anything of it when Ms. Peters closed and locked the door to the classroom.

Ms. Peters: "Thanks for coming, Roger. You know, I was a bit concerned about your performance on the test yesterday."

Roger: "Yes, Ms. Peters. Sorry about that. I knew we had the test, I just sort of forgot to study, you know? I will make sure to study for the rest of them."

Ms. Peters: "Maybe there is a way we can improve your grade for this one as well."

Roger: "Yeah, okay. That would be great."

Ms. Peters: "Why do you think the Founding Fathers were so insistent on declaring independence from the British?"

Roger: "Um. Well, they believed in liberty and justice for all?"

Ms. Peters: "Well, it is good to see you remember the Pledge of Allegiance, Roger. That is basically exactly right. To say it another way, they believed in the idea that people should not submit to silly rules and over-burdensome taxes, would you agree?"

Roger: "Um. Yeah, that sounds right."

Ms. Peters: "And the Founding Fathers were brave enough to explore new ideas and fight for what they wanted, even if others considered it wrong. Am I correct?"

Roger: "Uh. Yes, of course."

At this point, Ms. Peters got up from behind her desk and walked around to the front of it, leaning against it so she was half sitting and half standing. She was wearing a simple black dress that covered her knees and shoulders but it was ambiguous enough to be used for a fancy dinner date or a trip to the grocery store. While still leaning against the table, she moved her left foot to the side, so her legs were spread to the maximum amount allowed by the dress.

Ms. Peters: "Would you like to explore new things also, Roger?"

Roger was by now thoroughly confused. He was fairly sure Ms. Peters was hitting on him, but everything was happening so fast he did not have time to properly process it. Part of him desperately wanted to touch her body. Another part of him, already fearing punishment for the failed cheating endeavor, just wanted to get the hell out of there. He felt like he was six years old. All he could think to say was, "I guess so."

Ms. Peters sensed his hesitation and confusion. She was slightly annoyed but mostly amused by it. She attempted to clarify things for him. "How would you like it if I walk over there and get down on my knees and suck your cock?" she asked seductively. This helped Roger considerably and his lust conquered his fear. His only remaining doubt was if he was dreaming or not. Either way, his answer was the same.

Despite his willingness to participate, Roger was too shocked to move, never mind undress, so he simply swiveled in his chair, where Ms. Peters pulled off his shorts and delivered on her promise. This was a quantum leap for Roger's sex life which, other than rampant masturbation, had previously consisted mostly of making out and the occasional boob grab. Twice he had stuck his hand down Karen Anderson's pants, but both times the angle was awkward and each event yielded little new information or pleasure for him, and almost certainly not for her either, he guessed. In contrast, the feeling of the blowjob was exquisite, far and away more

pleasurable than he had previously fathomed. He contentedly watched his penis disappear in and out of Ms. Peters'
mouth, not wanting the moment to ever end, but it did.
Ms. Peters stood up, gave him a quick peck on the cheek,
walked back over to her desk and hopped up on it so she was
facing him. She spread her legs, hitched her dress up above
her hips, and leaned back so much of her weight was on her
hands. Roger was delighted to see she was not wearing
panties. "Now, come over here and fuck me. Teach me
a lesson," she commanded in the very same tone she used
earlier in the day to describe the circumstances of the Boston
Tea Party.

Roger complied, though based on her subsequent
instruction not to come inside her, he was only able to partake for about ninety seconds before he pulled out, at which
point she jerked him off onto the classroom carpet.

Roger went straight home and locked himself in his room
to think about what happened. He was not immediately sure
how he felt. He felt somewhat used and somehow dirty.
He took a shower to cleanse himself but ended up mastur-
bating in the shower, reliving the event in his mind. By the
time he toweled off, his mind had reconciled the situation
and he simply felt happy. He now saw only good in the
events of the day. The next day in history class, he sat in his
seat with a half-grin on his face for the whole period. He had
to restrain an outright smile when he saw the faint outline of
the stain he left on the brown carpet. Two days later,
Ms. Peters asked him to meet her after school again.
She swore him to absolute secrecy about their meetings and
then had sex with him again. This time Roger lasted four
whole minutes. The affair ended six weeks later, coinciding
with the conclusion of Roger's sophomore year. Remarkably,
the whole time Roger told no one but Gary, and Gary

managed not to tell anyone until college started. There were rumors about Ms. Peters and other boys the next year, but nothing ever came of it and she moved out of state during Roger's senior year.

Looking back years later, Roger wasn't sure how he should feel about the way he lost his virginity. He came to understand that he was supposed to feel somehow victimized, but the truth was that he treasured the whole experience and wouldn't have changed a thing. Maybe it would have been nice to have lasted a little longer.

When he was twenty-five, he heard that the male biology teacher at his old high school was convicted of having sex with some of the female students, including the younger sister of a friend of his. He was outraged. Gary was the first person he discussed it with.

Roger: "I hope his corn-hole gets stretched out one inch in prison for every high school girl he fucked."

Gary: "You don't think that is a double standard, given your history?"

Roger: "There is no such thing as a double standard. There is simply right and wrong. If it is discrimination, people know it. We can disagree about what is right or not, and sometimes there are shades of grey. Maybe Ms. Peters was wrong, maybe not. But this scumbag was just plain wrong."

CHAPTER FOURTEEN

Death & Outhouses
6:58 p.m.

"All our times have come
Here but now they're gone
Seasons don't fear the reaper
Nor do the wind, the sun or the rain.
We can be like they are
Come on baby...don't fear the reaper"
—(Don't Fear) The Reaper, Blue Oyster Cult

WITH BARSTOW NOTHING BUT a fading memory, the guys hurtled toward Vegas and away from the last vestiges of day and light at eighty-six miles an hour.

For rabbits living in the desert, night was a blessing. During the day, it could be hot as hell. Also, nasty mean birds could see you running around and swoop down to make a lunch out of you. One particular rabbit, who made his home east of Barstow and lived in a hole that didn't require a mortgage and didn't have a sign saying, "You could be home now," headed out for the evening a few minutes earlier than usual.

This rabbit had soft, fluffy light brown fur with a large white patch on his left side and a smaller one on top of his head. He also had cute little whiskers that bounced up and down when he tried to sniff out food or danger. This particular rabbit, who had no name, usually went left out of his hole, but today decided he would search for food to the right. Eighty yards later he found himself on the edge of northbound US Interstate Highway 15. The rabbit did not understand that it was a freeway and did not understand how the cars on the freeway burned gasoline to propel several thousand pounds of metal forward at relatively high speeds.

The rabbit also did not appreciate how quickly things moved at what was now eighty-seven miles per hour. He was curious about the different terrain of the pavement and hopped off the desert sand and onto the outer edge of the freeway. Encouraged by the warmth of the asphalt and its solid feel, the rabbit scampered about, zigging and zagging with amusement until he reached the fast-lane.

Inside Alex's BMW, Alice Cooper was very excited that school was out for summer. Mike was still removing the remains of the Kodiak, which he now very much regretted putting in, from his mouth. He reached into his lip with his forefinger and scooped out several more grains which stubbornly remained behind. Mike gagged but did not puke. He spit into his In-N-Out cup several more times and announced, "I've got to take a shit," followed by, "please pull over."

Because he thought it would be highly amusing, Alex started to probe Mike to see if the situation was bad enough that he would consider shitting on the side of the road if he pulled over immediately. Mike said it was not, so Alex offered him $50 to do it. The negotiation, which was going nowhere, was suddenly interrupted when the lower right corner of the front bumper of the BMW struck the upper left part of the rabbit's head. The rabbit's skull shattered instantly and its brain flew outward like a shotgun blast with a slightly downward trajectory. The rabbit never knew what hit him and died instantly and without pain. Alex also never knew what he had hit, but because he was still alive and was concerned about his car, he was more curious. "What the fuck was that?" he asked no one in particular.

Though the rabbit only weighed twelve pounds, he embedded a golf ball-sized dent into the bumper. This turned out to be his lasting legacy.

The rabbit's demise was quickly forgotten inside the car, especially by Mike whose attention returned to his previous concern. He had arrived to the point where he had waves requiring him to forcibly clench his ass to keep from going in his pants. Based on that way in which one just knows in these situations, he estimated he had about fifteen minutes left before the inevitable. "Dude, I've really got to take a shit. Please pull over at the next gas station," he pleaded.

Alex was not happy about having to pull over again so quickly and was getting anxious to be in Vegas. He was tempted to keep going on the small chance that Mike actually did shit his pants, which he would have found hilarious had it not been his car they were driving. But it was his car, and there seemed to be little choice, so three miles later he took the first available exit. The area was fairly barren. The only signs of civilization were a Chevron station and, strangely, what appeared to be a yoga studio.

The problem was that both were closed, though the automated gas pumps were working and there were two other cars filling up. Mike was not amused. "You've got to be fucking kidding me!" he declared. Alex asked if he could make it to the next exit and Mike replied that he didn't think so.

Alex began to smile: "Well, it looks like you are just going to have to go behind the yoga studio. I've got some paper towel in the trunk."

Mike: "No fucking way."

Alex: "There doesn't seem to be much alternative, is there?"

Roger shared Alex's perspective of the situation and was by now laughing and poking Mike in the side alternately with both hands: "Go behind the yoga shop. That will give them something to meditate about."

It was then that Gary noticed three port-o-potties about fifty yards past the yoga shop where it appeared someone was considering constructing another building. He pointed them out to Mike, who had never been so happy to have the opportunity to use an outhouse. He opened the car door and started waddling briskly toward the port-o-potties.

Gary, Roger and Alex had a nice chuckle about this and Alex decided to use the time to top off the gas tank even though they had only burned a few gallons. Just as he was maneuvering the car to line up with the pump, his phone vibrated in his pocket. He checked the ID display on the outside and was pleased to see it was Cindy, a girl from Georgia whom he had hooked up with a few times last year.

Alex opened his car door and flipped open his cell phone at the same time. "Hey. How is my sexy peach?" he said into the phone.

Cindy sounded like she had already had a few drinks and was being very friendly. After the requisite small talk she asked Alex, "Do you know what I really want for you to do?"

Alex did not know, so he inserted the gasoline pump into the opening of the tank, squeezed the trigger, and simply responded, "No. What?"

It turned out Cindy was in San Diego for a few days for a family event and she wanted to meet up later that night at around midnight. Alex explained that he would be in Vegas, which disappointed Cindy. "Nooo, that sucks, sweetie," she cooed. "I want you to be with me tonight."

Alex concluded the call quickly before she started going into any more detail about her desires. He was pleased to realize that he was not at all upset about missing Cindy in San Diego. As the gas flowed, he again pondered the fact that physical encounters with random girls were not as rewarding as they used to be. Frequently it even led to something closer to regret than satisfaction. He wondered if he should avoid trying to hook up in Vegas altogether. Then he smiled and shook his head, chiding himself for having such an utterly stupid idea.

Another six Southwest miles earned, Alex quickly replaced the gas pump, indicated that he did not want a receipt, and returned to the warmth of the car. "Let's go fuck with Sourpuss," he suggested. He started the car and slowly drove over to the large blue plastic portable toilets. As they pulled within fifteen feet he asked Gary, "Which one do you think he is in?"

Gary reluctantly put down the *Club* magazine and leaned forward, squinting at the toilets. "He is in the one on the right," Gary declared with confidence.

Alex: "How do you know?"

Gary: "It is the only one with the red occupied signal on the door. He is in there. The other two are green."

Alex: "Oh yeah, good call."

Alex lifted his foot off the brake and turned the wheel slightly toward the right. "Watch this," he said. Two seconds later the front of the BMW impacted the targeted outhouse at about five miles per hour. The force was significant enough to move the whole facility about two inches backward.

In the back seat, Roger was delighted. He took out the can of Kodiak and instinctively started to open it. Between bouts of laughter he suggested, "Hit him again."

Alex put the car in reverse and backed up about ten feet. Then he flashed the brights a few times, gave the horn a few light taps and accelerated forward into the outhouse again. This time he hit it at seven miles per hour, causing it to rotate slightly in a clockwise direction. Alex was not sure, but he thought he heard a sloshing sound coming from inside the structure. Additionally, the front door was now pinned shut by the car so it could not be opened.

A banging noise began from inside the outhouse and the front door started to bend slightly outwards as the occupant tried desperately to get out. This was too much for Alex, Gary and Roger to take. All three were now laughing uncontrollably, Roger trying to put in a dip at the same time. Alex had tears rolling down his cheeks and tried to ask a question between bursts of laughter. "Jesus, you don't think anything splashed up on him, do you?" he finally managed to ask before tapping on the horn a few more times.

Gary indicated that he didn't know. "How long should we keep him in there?" he asked, starting to feel guilty.

Roger: "I don't know, but I just put in a freshy so I don't mind waiting a bit."

Alex: "Let's just let him soak up the ambiance for another thirty seconds. If we leave him in there too long he will be way too bitter the whole weekend."

Alex wiped the tears from his face and spoke again, "God, this is way too funny." Just then, Gary glanced in the passenger side rearview mirror. Then he rapidly swung around in his seat to look out the back window.

"Oh shit, there's Caminiti!" he nearly shouted.

Alex pivoted around and saw Mike leisurely walking toward the car from the direction of the Chevron station. "What the fuck?" Alex wanted to know. This was followed up by a quick, "Oh, shit!"

Alex put the car in reverse and quickly backed it in Mike's direction. At the same time he rolled down his window and yelled, "Quick, get in the car. Just get in the car."

Mike slightly increased his pace, then opened the door and hopped in the car behind Alex. Alex put the car in drive and rapidly accelerated back toward the direction of the freeway onramp.

"What's the rush?" Mike wanted to know.

Alex replied hurriedly, "Oh nothing. We just pinned some random person in the shitter so we need to get the fuck out of here. Where did you go? Did you use the outhouse?"

Mike explained that he intended to, but on the way over he saw someone working inside the closed mini-mart of the Chevron and they had let him in to use the store bathroom. None of the other guys had noticed.

It was quiet for a few seconds as the BMW sped down the onramp.

Then Gary excitedly exclaimed, "No fucking way! Who do you think was in there?"

"Probably whoever was driving the Acura at the other pump. Someone who is probably scared shitless right now," Alex replied, adding, "literally." Laughter dominated the next two miles of the drive. With a renewed sense of energy and purpose, Alex slowly brought the BMW up to ninety miles per hour to continue its quest to Las Vegas.

CHAPTER EIGHT

Roger (20)

IN THE SUMMER OF 1994, just after Curt Cobain blew his head off, Nirvana was, unsurprisingly, rapidly losing influence. It was nearly three years after Guns N' Roses released the *Illusions* albums, and there was a lull in any kind of musical leadership. In mid-July, the albums on the top of the charts included Green Day, Soundgarden and Oasis. It created a perfect window for a good, but not great, rock band like Stone Temple Pilots to be considered pretty huge. So Roger was quite enthusiastic about having tenth-row tickets to their show along with three of his buddies whom he worked with at the TGI Friday's next to the Long Beach State campus.

Roger was in the middle of a three-month self-imposed gambling hiatus and was flush with cash from his bartending job at Friday's. Therefore, he had splurged on a twelve pack of Corona to share for the pre-party instead of Meister Brau or Natural Light, which were his standard choices purely for fiscal reasons. After finishing two beers each in the parking lot during the opening act, each of the four shoved one of the remaining bottles into the waistbands of their shorts and prepared to enter the arena.

Once inside, and both needing to pee quite badly, Roger and Steve—a nineteen-year-old busboy at Friday's who happened to be black—headed immediately to the left where a sign indicated the nearest restrooms were located. About halfway there, they encountered a troubling situation. Seven black men in their early twenties had formed a ring around a pretty black girl who looked to be about seventeen and was wearing jeans and a pink GAP sweatshirt. They were shoving her lightly back and forth around the inside of the ring and raining insults on her. Each of her futile efforts to escape was blocked, and she was returned to the middle.

Roger had always felt comfortable around people of all races. He generally found black people to have a good sense of humor, and that summer he counted as many blacks as whites among his better friends. He stopped to try and better understand what was going on.

At this point, the treatment of the girl became markedly rougher. One of the guys in the circle caught the girl on the perimeter, grabbed her shoulders, then spun her around to face inward and wrapped his arms around her tightly. "You should learn to think, you dumb bitch," he said loudly into her ear before releasing her and pushing her as hard as he could into the open space. She flew forward and was intercepted by another guy on the other side who stepped forward, lowered his shoulder, and drove it into the upper body of the oncoming girl. Outweighed by at least sixty pounds, she dropped to the ground like a quarterback who never saw the hit coming. Once down, her body curled slightly but she did not move much. The circle started to open with a few of the guys bending down and pointing at her, wanting to add one last comment.

Roger instinctively moved in and lifted the girl up, asking her if she was all right. She wrapped an arm around him weakly and began to walk slowly. They had only advanced a few feet when the guy who threw her the last time stepped in front of them.

"Who the fuck are you, bitch?" he demanded of Roger.

"Just leave her alone. She needs some air," Roger said, at this point still not overly concerned about his own safety.

"She got what she needed. Maybe you should think about what you need, bitch," the guy said, moving his face closer to Roger's.

At this point, rage at the whole situation took over Roger's actions. "Why? Are you tired of beating up girls?" he asked loudly. The comment elicited a round of laughs from the rest of the group. The largest of them was the most audible. He was slightly overweight, very muscular, nearly six and half feet tall, and was wearing a black oversized Dr. Dre tee shirt over Air Jordan shorts. A massive gold chain distracted attention from the rest of the outfit.

"Ah, shit. He clowned you big time, Chris-dog," the big guy said, laughing.

Chris-dog didn't think it was very funny. "You think you are some type of hero, bitch? What the fuck do you know? You think you are right and we are just a bunch of dumb niggers? Is that it?"

Roger did not have time for a reply. Chris swung with his right hand. Roger, who was nearly unbeatable at ping-pong, always had quick reflexes. He was able to move away from the girl and block the punch with his arm. Before Chris had a chance to swing again one of the other members of the group came from behind and connected with a roundhouse that landed on the back of Roger's head and bent him forward. Chris then hit him on the side of the jaw with a weak left that was just enough to send Roger to the ground. The next blow came from the side and was an unhindered kick to the ribs that partially knocked the wind out of Roger and rotated him so he was flat on his back.

From head to toe, fists and shoes began pummeling him from every direction. Roger instinctively curled into a fetal position, using his arms to protect his head. The Corona bottle, still wedged into his pants, stuck into his abdomen and produced a sharp pain before falling to the side and rolling away, unbroken. He wet himself a little. The remainder of the beating only lasted nine seconds, but it seemed much longer.

"That's enough!" a deep voice boomed from above. The blows immediately ceased. Roger looked up between his elbows to see where this divine intervention came from. It was the biggest of the group, who obviously held authority and had apparently refrained from participating in the beating. It occurred to Roger later that if this man had chosen to join in, or had not stopped things when he did, that he may not have walked away from the incident without serious permanent damage.

No one moved for about ten seconds. Roger looked from the big guy to his friend Steve who stood about fifteen feet away and was completely frozen with a look of shock on his face. Chris-dog saw who Roger was looking at and took a step in Steve's direction. "What are you looking at, nigger?" he shouted.

At this point, eight concert security guards wearing ridiculous yellow jackets arrived on the scene along with six baton-wielding members of the Los Angeles Police Department. The police shouted for everyone to lie face down on the ground and put their hands behind their back. Their instructions were barely issued when they began using the batons, relying on their training to beat anything black, including Steve, until it was on the ground and motionless. They faced little resistance. Roger watched as two officers beat down the big guy in the Dre shirt who had saved him. The big guy stood as long as he could, his own way of protesting, but he did not hit back. Roger's thoughts were still overwhelmed by rage and adrenaline and he found himself hoping the police would continue to pound on the other six, but they stopped as soon as all were handcuffed.

Once back in a normal state of mind, it took him five minutes to convince the police to uncuff Steve. He tried and failed to persuade them to also uncuff the big guy, who he told them did not participate in the assault.

Roger refused to see a doctor and insisted to the police that he was all right. Because of the adrenaline, it was not until several hours later that he was able to sum up the extent of his injuries – one black eye, three large bruised bumps on his head, a fat and bloody lip, a loose tooth, a cracked rib, and numerous bruises on his body and legs including a deep blue circle where the Corona had tried to penetrate his stomach.

It took a few weeks for his body to completely erase all signs of the incident, but from that night he would never again live his life among his fellow humans in a color-blind manner. If anything, he became more acutely aware of the extent of the racism in the world and in his country, and more convinced of the ignorance of its roots. But he no longer imagined a world where it would be fully overcome because he realized that in some way it would now always be alive inside him.

CHAPTER FIFTEEN

Breakin' The Law
7:18 p.m.

"Breakin' the law, breakin' the law..."
—Beavis, *Beavis & Butt-head*

WITH THE PORT-O-POTTY INCIDENT now safely a dozen miles behind them, the moon began to assert itself in the sky to the north of the freeway. On this night, however, it appeared as a sliver of its entirety, only dimly lighting the vast expanse of cacti and dirt below.

Inside the BMW, Alex had agreed to put the Stanford game back on. Roger and Mike were sitting quietly in the back listening while Alex and Gary discussed who they would rather have, Jennifer Anniston or Angelina Jolie. Both quickly agreed they would rather fuck Angelina but would rather marry Jennifer. A consensus was also reached that Brad Pitt was stupid to leave Jennifer Anniston even if Angelina was more desirable sexually. Gary referred to him as a douche-bag, but agreed with Alex's positive reviews of his performances in *True Romance* and *Fight Club*.

Conversation halted for the next few minutes because Stanford had taken the ball inside the three-yard line after a forty-eight-yard gain on a broken tackle on a screen play. The Cardinal tried to run it straight in on first and second down but managed to gain just a yard on both efforts. However, on third and two, the Stanford quarterback drew one of the linebackers in too far on a play action fake and then spun and hit his tight end in the back of the end zone for a touchdown and a six-point lead.

Roger's parlay was looking better and everyone was happy for it, especially Roger.

"I think we are in for a prosperous weekend, fellas," he exclaimed while mentally figuring which NFL games he could bet on Sunday. "Hot-Damn! I feel lucky. Very lucky," he added.

As if to punctuate his statement the car suddenly exploded in bright blue light. A loud siren pierced the air.

Alex's widened eyes shot downward to the needle on the speedometer, which had secretly crept just to the right of the 100 figure. "Fuck me," he exclaimed as his foot flew from the gas pedal to the brake. The BMW slowed from one hundred and two to sixty-six in the same one-point-eight seconds it took for Stanford to successfully add the extra point.

Alex quickly made an appeal to God that the California Highway Patrol car would pass him and pursue other business, but instead it turned off the siren and settled in just twenty feet behind him with its side lights still flashing. It maintained this posture as Alex moved to the right lane and then slowly onto the shoulder, decelerating until the BMW reached a full stop. During the process, Gary, Roger and Mike frantically tried to hide their beers. The task was complicated by a very bright white light emanating from the patrol car.

To avoid it, Mike slouched down below the top of the back seat and tilted his head back while chugging the remaining four ounces left in his Budweiser can. He then shoved the empty receptacle under the seat in front of him, causing a crunching sound as another empty already there put up a futile resistance.

Roger's beer was still half-full and he did not think he could rapidly finish it. He saw Mike's sweatshirt lying between them and tucked his beer under it in a position he hoped would not spill too much. With the beer now basically out of sight, he reached over his right shoulder and pulled the seatbelt strap over his chest while trying not to move his head or shoulders.

Alex once heard from an old high school friend who became a cop that the best way to get out of a speeding ticket is to be firm but polite and also to have your license and registration ready to hand to the officer when he arrived at your car. The other choices were to act like you had a really bad stutter or were slightly retarded, but Alex didn't feel confident he could get away with either of these in the current situation. He pulled the registration out of the glove box and his wallet out of the front pocket of his sweat pants.

"Make sure the booze is hidden," he commanded, suddenly very glad he had chosen not to commence drinking with the guys.

With that, he saw that both of the officers in the patrol car were approaching the BMW. He began rolling down the driver's side window as one officer arrived at the front of the car. The cold air struck him in the face and filled the car almost instantly. Alex extended his hand out the window, offering his drivers license and car registration. The CHP officer was tall, his uniform immaculately pressed. He was also wearing one of those goofy police hats that were like cowboy hats but with the perfectly straight brim. Alex thought only park rangers or Smokey the Bear should wear these, but he didn't say this. He noted that the officer looked quite a lot like Jeff Kent, longtime second baseman for the New York Mets, San Francisco Giants, Houston Astros and Los Angeles Dodgers, and the National League MVP award winner in 2000. The look included a neatly groomed mustache that wasn't quite blonde and wasn't quite brown. "Good evening, officer," he said as he exchanged his documents.

The Jeff Kent cop took the papers while keeping his eyes firmly on Alex and Gary. Meanwhile, officer number two approached the back right of the vehicle where Roger was sitting. He rapped on the window by Roger's head. Roger responded by rolling down his window as well. Lacking creativity, he said, "Good evening, sir."

Officer number two spoke first while officer number one finally took a look at Alex's license. "Generally, we recommend you fasten your seatbelt before getting pulled over," said officer number two. "Please hand me your identification," he added.

As Roger and Mike were fumbling for their wallets in the back seat, officer number one shined his flashlight into Alex's face and asked him if he had been drinking. Alex indicated that he had not. He was then asked if anyone else in the car had been drinking. Alex could not remember what the potential penalty was for having open containers in the car but he really did not want to find out.

"No, I don't think so," he responded stupidly.

"You don't think so?" Kent-cop asked.

"Well, no, I mean, not that I know of."

With this, Kent-cop shined his flashlight toward Gary's feet. Alex followed the beam of light and was happy to see that there was no evidence of any beer, though he wasn't sure the illuminated display of two women about to engage in lesbian sex was helping the situation. He guessed not, due to the cop's complete lack of reaction.

Kent-cop: "Do you know how fast you were going?"

Alex: "No, sorry. Perhaps it was a little too fast. Maybe eighty-five?"

Kent-cop: "Yes, perhaps. Actually, we got you at one-oh-two. It took us five minutes just to catch up with you."

Alex: "Oh jeez, are you sure? I don't think we were going that fast."

Kent-cop: "Yes, son. I am quite sure. Technically, this is considered reckless driving, meaning you put yourselves, other drivers and us in considerable danger. Additionally, I have a strong suspicion that you have been drinking and it is quite obvious your dipshit buddies here are."

Alex had a bad feeling about where this was going and it did not get any better with the cop's next question.

"Maybe you can tell me one good reason why I shouldn't take you into jail right now?" he asked.

Not sure of the best response, Alex decided to stick with the truth this time. "Well, Officer, the fact is we are going to Vegas and we are kind of in a hurry."

He realized how dumb this sounded the second it left his mouth and wondered if the bad karma from lying to Blair and the outhouse incident had already come back to kick his ass. A quick vision of himself sharing a Barstow jail cell for the night with a large meth-head in a Hells Angels jacket ran through his head.

"Son, Vegas is open twenty-four hours a day, seven days a week," the cop responded. He ordered everyone to stay in the car and remain still and then the two officers retreated back to their vehicle. The guys used the opportunity to double check that the beer cans were fully out of view. Alex cursed several more times.

A few minutes later, the two cops re-approached the car in the same formation. Kent-cop went to the driver's side window while cop number two returned to Roger's rear window. In the back, cop number two handed back Roger's and Mike's driver's licenses. They didn't say a word.

Kent-cop, however, straightened his mustache and his hat and leaned in to ask Alex a few more questions. "Do you boys know anything about an incident at an outhouse at the Chevron a few miles back?" he asked in a tone that suggested a mutilated body had been found.

"An outhouse, sir?" Alex questioned, doing his best to sound incredulous.

Kent-cop stared at him for about thirty seconds without saying a word. It was really freaking Alex out, but he simply maintained eye contact without trying to look like he thought he was a tough-guy.

Finally, the moment of truth arrived and Kent-cop began to speak again. "Okay, son, here is what is going to happen. I am going to give you a ticket for going ninety-five. You are going to consider yourself very lucky. Also, you are going to slow down the rest of the way to Vegas. If I see you again tonight, or on your way back home, you will deeply regret it."

Although the ticket ended up costing $545 and required wasting a few hours on an online traffic school course, Alex did indeed feel lucky.

INTERLUDE NINE

Gary (25)

AUGUST 13TH, 1999 WAS A beautiful day at Jack Murphy Stadium in San Diego. The sun was out, it was seventy-two degrees, and the Padres were about to begin a double-header with the Giants. Gary's boss had given him sixth-row seats behind first base. He and Roger were trying to find said seats, each carrying the maximum allowed sale of two large beers.

They found row F and headed inward. The ticket Roger held was for seat nine, while the ticket in Gary's pocket was seat eight. Even so, Roger led the way and sat in seat eight while Gary made himself and his beers comfortable in seat nine. It would prove to be a crucial detail.

The Village People were scheduled to perform after both games were over. Before game one, the Construction Worker came out to sing the national anthem. He stepped up to the microphone stationed near home plate and took off his yellow hard-hat, placing it over his heart. Gary and Roger rolled their eyes at each other, but both refrained from making any derogatory comments. In the end, they both admitted the guy did a pretty good job, though they were soon to be disappointed by the Military Man who came up five feet short on his attempt at the ceremonial first pitch.

Roger: "That was fucking weak. They should have gone with the Indian Chief."

Gary: "I don't know. That cowboy looks like he is hiding a pretty good fastball behind that mustache."

Either may have been more effective than the Padres starting pitcher. In the first inning, he walked the first two Giants hitters and then fell behind Barry Bonds three and one. The next pitch was a fastball. He was not the first and would not be the last pitcher to make the mistake of throwing Bonds a pitch over the middle of the plate. Bonds hitched his right elbow in, lightly lifted his right leg, and then almost unnoticeably opened his right hip and extended his arms in front of him in one fluid motion.

Roger was inserting a Kodiak at the time of contact, but the implication from the crack of the bat was unmistakable. He was able to look up in time to see the ball sailing out toward the right center field seats. It landed in the twelfth row. Shortly after the ball completed its flight path, Bonds slowly began to circle the bases. It was, for any baseball fan, truly a thing of beauty, almost a religious experience.

Gary, despite his appreciation for the talent, was a Padres fan and was not happy. "Retards. Why would you let Barry beat you in that situation?" he asked no one in particular.

Roger answered. "Oooohhh, I don't know, but it is helping my over."

The over came in easily, with the Padres ultimately losing 12-4. Roger was happy and, as it turned out, Gary would have something to be happy about as well. In the top of the third inning two young women carrying Mike's Hard Lemonades bounced down the aisle giddily. They turned into row F and made themselves at home in seats ten and eleven.

In seat ten was Blair Davis. She wore a green Marc Jacobs sundress with leather Gucci sandals she got at an outlet shop for ninety dollars. Her long brown hair flowed out of a pink Giants cap which clashed terribly with the sundress.

Gary thought she was gorgeous. It was not until the fifth inning, and another large beer later, that he worked up the courage to start talking to her. By now, the Giants were already ahead 6-1 so he was conciliatory and asked her how she became a Giants fan.

Blair explained her family was from Larkspur, across the Golden Gate Bridge from San Francisco, and she had grown up in a family of Giants fans. While accurate, the truth was she never cared for baseball whatsoever until, when she was twelve, Will Clark burst on to the scene as the Giants first baseman. Blair developed a huge crush on Mr. Clark, becoming a lifelong Giants fan in the process. She still remembered the day her family went to the game at Candlestick Park and she first saw Will. Her dad, who was a VP at Wells Fargo, had scored very good tickets and the family was seated four rows behind the Giants' dugout. Clark came to bat in the bottom of the first inning and the crowd erupted in cheers because he had hit a game-winning home run the night before. Of course he had a cute face, but it was something about the way he waved his bat around and wiggled his ass in the batter's box that really caught Blair's attention. A girl sitting across the field behind third base felt similarly. She was a blond in her early twenties wearing jean shorts and a white tank top that tightly gripped a pair of very large boobs. This girl stood up, yelled "Go Will," and held up a sign that read,

I'd Take the Pill
For a Thrill
With Will!!!

Blair did not know exactly what this meant, but she had a feeling she agreed. Her dad, Jim, also noticed the sign.

He did know what it meant and spent much of the game admiring its owner.

By 1999, J. T. Snow was the Giants' first baseman, but Blair was not interested in him at the moment. Like her first feelings for Will Clark, she had an instant crush on the person seated next to her in seat nine.

Gary remembered advice Alex had told him about how to pick up girls: always say something somewhat negative about them, but avoid actually being mean. At first Gary thought this was ridiculous, but after years of going out with Alex and seeing him repeat this procedure with tremendous success, he had learned to try to replicate it wherever possible.

"Are all Giants fans so color-coordinated?" he asked.

"What do you mean?" Blair wanted to know.

"Nothing, just the hat with the dress. It kind of looks like what a gay frog would wear to a wedding," was his reply. Somehow, he was never as good at this as Alex and immediately regretted the comment, wondering how something so stupid had come out of his mouth. He took another large sip of beer and averted his eyes back toward the game.

Blair thought this was a pretty stupid thing to say as well, but somehow she found herself a little bit more interested in continuing to talk to him anyway. Still, she was not about to let him get the upper hand in the conversation. "Interesting observation," she replied, adding, "It must take a gay Padres fan to notice such a thing. You know, queer eye for the yuppie baseball fan or something like that."

There was a brief awkward pause and then they both started laughing. Nearly twelve hours later, he kissed her goodnight outside of The Shack bar in La Jolla and programmed her number into his Motorola StarTAC phone.

Both had the very alive feeling you get when you meet someone you like and know that you will see them again. For Blair, it was the first time she had this sensation since meeting her last boyfriend, who ultimately turned out to be married in another state. She had a feeling that Gary, unlike that scumbag, was at heart a really good guy. Gary was pretty sure he was going to get laid sometime in the next few weeks.

Gary hopped in a cab heading toward University City and Blair began the half-mile walk to her apartment in La Jolla. As they moved in different directions, neither fully appreciated that their lives had just merged onto the same path, that their future joys and pains would be shared, or that new life would be created as a result.

CHAPTER SIXTEEN

ZZYZX

8:05 p.m.

*"Man looks in the abyss, there's nothing
staring back at him. At that moment,
man finds his character. And that is what
keeps him out of the abyss."*
—Lou Mannheim, Wall Street

AFTER THE EVENTS OF THE previous hour, the BMW was now content to push forward at a more conservative seventy-seven miles per hour. Inside, a complete analysis of the encounter with the police had been concluded and the silence was broken only by the broadcast of the Stanford game, which Roger had lobbied for successfully.

With Stanford, a three-and-a-half-point underdog, now covering the spread by ten and a half points, and a fresh Kodiak resting in his lip, Roger was pleased with the world and his place in it. He could imagine nowhere he would rather be than cruising through the desert with his best friends. He pressed his forehead against the window to get a better look outside and was surprised at how cold the glass was against his skin, but this also was pleasing. In the desert, it was noticeably dark. Night was omnipresent. The view out the window revealed a world of blackness with no visible horizon. In contrast, by craning his neck upwards, Roger could see a sky filled with more stars than he could hope to comprehend. Though it was windy outside, the BMW muted everything from the external environment. The world appeared perfectly still from inside the car, as if frozen in time. Strangely, there were no other vehicles within a quarter of a mile in either direction. As if to take advantage of the clearing, a tumbleweed nearly the size of a small car blew across the freeway just two hundred feet in front of the oncoming BMW, but no one noticed it.

Roger leaned back and used the back of his hand to wipe away the steam his forehead had imparted on the window. When he was done, he saw the iconic street sign for Zzyzx Road fly by.

On their first trips to Vegas, this sign was always pointed out as some kind of important landmark. Once, on a previous trip, they exited the freeway here to see what this mysterious road was all about. Had they researched it, they would have learned that the name was coined in 1944 by Curtis Howe Springer who claimed it to be the last word in the English language. Mr. Springer opened a health spa and sold bottled water from nearby springs to desert travelers, but was eventually arrested for misuse of the land and alleged food and drug violations. As of 2006, the land surrounding Zzyzx was under control of the Bureau of Land Management, who allowed California State University to manage it and conduct desert studies. But as far as the guys in the BMW knew, there was nothing of interest on Zzyzx Road. In fact, the paved portion ended fairly quickly before an unpromising dirt road took its place. It was all kind of a tease unless you were the type of person who wanted to leave the conventional route and venture alone into the unknown vastness of the desert.

On this night, there was no comment made about the strangely named street. It too moved into the past.

INTERLUDE TEN

Roger (26)

IN THE SUMMER OF 2000, Roger worked two jobs. Wednesdays, Fridays and Saturdays, he bartended at Moose Mcgillicutty's in Pacific Beach, and Thursdays and Sundays he worked as a valet, parking cars for The Chart House in Del Mar. Monday and Tuesday were his days off, used primarily for surfing, golfing, sleeping and going to the Indian casinos. Between the two jobs, he was pulling in about $1,400 a week, very little of which was reported to the Internal Revenue Service. He lived with a roommate in a simple two-bedroom apartment in Pacific Beach and tended to date the kind of girls who were not expensive to date. Therefore, he had plenty of money for whatever he wanted to do. Due to Alex's relentless prodding, he even opened checking and savings accounts at Wells Fargo and managed to sock away $5,000.

Roger felt relatively wealthy, but he noticed his new friend Wayne, a fellow parking valet, was really rolling in cash. In the last month, Wayne had taken his girlfriend on vacation to Australia, bought a Rolex, and bragged of winning three grand on a single straight bet on a recent Padres game. Wayne also took Roger and one of the other guys to dinner and drinks at Dakota Grill downtown and picked up the tab. It was that night, after several cocktails, that Roger learned where the cash was coming from. Apparently, the trip to Australia was arranged by one of the customers from The Chart House. On the last day of the trip, Wayne was instructed to meet a man at the beach who gave him a stuffed koala bear to take back to San Diego. Inside the cute and fuzzy bear were five kilograms of pure cocaine.

For taking the return trip with the koala, Wayne was paid $15,000 plus his expenses for the trip. Wayne told Roger he could arrange for him to take the same trip next month and would cover his valet shifts. Then Wayne would go again the following month. He pointed out that his boss in the arrangement preferred to have a rotation rather than just one person. Wayne was very convincing about how easy the whole thing was, and about how nice the cash was. Additionally, he pointed out that Roger could probably talk Andrea, one of the bartenders, into taking the trip with him. Roger had a crush on Andrea all summer but couldn't get past the simple flirting stage. Wayne painted an enticing picture of the two of them enjoying the Sydney beaches, which he assured Roger were even more appealing than those in San Diego.

The whole idea was very tempting. Roger told Wayne he would probably do it but wanted a day to think about it. As fortune would have it, Roger was scheduled to play golf the next day with Gary. He brought up the idea during the sixth hole of the Torrey Pines North course, a downhill par three with an unbeatable view of the Pacific.

Gary, who already had his ball teed up, suddenly lost interest in golf and the beauty of the surroundings. He stepped away from the tee-box and offered his opinion.

Gary: "Roger, no fucking way. Do not do this under any circumstances."

Roger: "It sounds pretty easy."

Gary: "It doesn't matter. You do not want to be a drug-dealer. This could fuck up your whole life. Listen to me. Do not do it."

That was the end of the conversation for the moment. Gary, flustered, duck-hooked his six iron into the brush and ended up with a triple-bogey. Roger stuck the green and made par to take three skins and six dollars.

Roger finished with an eighty-six and Gary, as always it seemed, shot a ninety-two. This earned Roger $18, and he bought beers after the round. Halfway through his Budweiser, Gary once more told Roger to forget all about the Australia idea. Roger took his opinion seriously, but still thought he was more likely than not to carry through with it just one time. That night in the Chart House parking lot, however, he went with his final instinct and told Wayne he wasn't interested. Wayne said he understood but was sorry Roger was missing out on the opportunity.

Three weeks later, Wayne took a Qantas Airlines flight from Los Angeles International Airport to Sydney. When he got back to LAX, rather than returning to San Diego, he took a six-year detour to the Bay Area where he lodged at San Quentin California State Penitentiary.

CHAPTER SEVENTEEN

Final Score
8:11 p.m.

"How about that?!"
—Mel Allen, *This Week in Baseball*

IT TOOK ONLY ONE MINUTE to pass through Baker, California. The world's largest thermometer, a neon pink phallic symbol rising one hundred and thirty-four feet out of the desert to commemorate the hottest temperature ever recorded in the United States (134 degrees Farenheit in Death Valley in 1913), showed that it was now only forty-seven degrees.

While possessing over three thousand songs on his iPod, Alex had not updated it in over six months, and so he was already bored of the available selections. Also, he knew that if Stanford covered the spread, Roger would have cash for the weekend and he would not have to lend him money. Roger was always good for his debts, but Alex considered it tedious to have to deal with the situation. He greatly preferred a world where he owed no one anything, and no one owed him. For both of these reasons he was happy to turn off the music to listen to the end of the Stanford game. Really, with possession of the ball, less than two minutes left on the clock, and ten and a half points to give against the spread, it was more of a formality than anything. But Alex wanted everyone to be merry and was pleased to let Roger enjoy the moment. Then Roger announced that he was guaranteeing a Stanford victory.

This prompted Alex to reconsider the certainty of the outcome. Roger had a long and bloodied history of intra-game guarantees that somehow went impossibly sour. Gary had also been a witness to this strange phenomenon over the years.

Gary: "Rodge, you idiot. Why can't you keep your mouth shut for two minutes?"

Roger: "Don't worry. This one is done. No question about it. I am putting it in the fridge."

Washington was now out of timeouts so Stanford had elected to have their quarterback start taking a knee. Done properly two more times, this would run the clock down to thirty-eight seconds. A punt on fourth down, assuming it would not be returned all the way, would leave the Huskies with a maximum of one play to score a game-tying touchdown.

Remembering "The Play," in which the California Bears miraculously leveraged five lateral passes and the Stanford Band on a last-second kickoff return to win the 1982 Big Game, everyone in the car waited nervously for the ensuing punt. During the next snap, the announcer was also recounting the famous Big Game history when suddenly his voice rose mid-sentence and he became very excited. "Oh my Goodness! I think he dropped the ball! It looks like the quarterback has fumbled the snap. There is a big pile around the line of scrimmage. Yes! Yes! Washington has recovered."

Gary: "Oh, no."

Roger: "No problem. They still have to score a touch-down and then win by four in overtime to cover the spread."

Despite Roger's confidence, he was now chewing his fingernails. No one was surprised when Washington completed a forty-three yard pass for a touchdown on the first play from scrimmage. Stanford received the kickoff and chose to run out the clock and take their chances in overtime. After a commercial break in which no one in the car said a word, Stanford took the ball first in overtime. On the first play, they ran a simple screen to the right.

Announcer: "The Stanford quarterback drops back. He quickly looks right and fires a short pass out to Jones. Jones is hit immediately but shakes the tackle. He advances up to the twenty and cuts inside. He is really turning nothing into something. Oh, wait, Jones has lost the ball at the fifteen and Washington has recovered. That is a devastating turn of events. It is as if somehow a curse was placed on Stanford in the last few minutes of this game. I am not sure if I can ever remember a team falling apart so quickly."

Mike couldn't help but laugh. Roger did not think the situation was humorous.

Roger began shouting: "Ball-licking madness! This has got to be some kind of joke. What the fuck is wrong with these fucking sperm-seekers?"

Mike: "Still guaranteeing a win?"

Roger: "Shut your damn pie hole."

Alex: "Don't worry. Most likely Washington will settle for a field goal and you will still cover."

Roger: "Maybe if Stanford can pull their heads out of each others' asses for ten seconds to run a play."

Alex proved prophetic in his belief that Washington would be conservative. Following the college rules, they began their overtime possession on the twenty-five yard line. Washington ran the ball three straight times to start their possession, gaining exactly four yards on each carry and earning a fresh set of downs. Roger approved of their game plan and assumed they would kick when they got inside the fifteen. On first down they again ran the ball up the middle. Had the group been watching the game on TV, they would scarcely have believed how the Stanford defense could have missed so many opportunities to tackle a running back who was concentrating more on holding on to the football than gaining any serious yardage. Nevertheless, head down, he ran in a straight line all the way through the defense and into the end zone.

Roger was too defeated to yell. It was not the first time he had lost a bet on what seemed like extremely unlikely circumstances. He expressed his displeasure in a matter-of-fact tone, "Those too-smart for their own good monkey-fuckers fucked me right in the ass."

Alex was about to switch the music back on when the announcer indicated there was a flag on the play. It was holding on the offense and the touchdown was called back. Three plays later, Washington successfully kicked a thirty-two yard field goal for a three-point win, and a $1,400 swing for Roger's parlay.

Roger, though quite pleased with this second turn of events, felt a bit foolish about his previous outbursts and remained calm. "Huh. How about that?" was his only comment.

Alex switched the stereo back to the auxiliary setting and Gary scrolled to *All I Wanna Do (Is Have Some Fun)* by Sheryl Crow. She was not the only one.

INTERLUDE ELEVEN

Mike (27)

BY THE AGE OF TWENTY-SEVEN, fully burdened with the responsibilities of a standard corporate job, Mike had developed a sincere appreciation for the simple pleasures of day-drinking. So when Alex called to suggest a trip up to Hermosa Beach for Labor Day weekend, Mike was more than happy to cancel his Saturday plans with Jennifer Gates. Jennifer was his girlfriend of about a year, but Mike already knew he would break up with her at some point before the winter holidays. Somewhere around the July 4th weekend, she stopped trying to make him happy and shifted the focus of the relationship to her concerns. Usually, these were little complaints that the apartment was too cold or her food wasn't right or they never watched the movies she wanted or they never hung out anymore on Saturday night, or, or, or. On top of this, Mike was pretty sure Jennifer had gained some weight. Like most guys, however, Mike was awful at ending relationships. Actually, he had never officially done it. Of the three girls he had dated for more than six months, two had dumped him with little or no warning. With the third, Mike had slowly stopped being affectionate and basically stopped calling her altogether, though he generally continued to show up when she planned things. Eventually she got the hint and broke up with him.

Alex's silver 328i BMW was filled with conversation the entire one-and-a-half hour drive from San Diego to Hermosa Beach, but not once did a mention of Jennifer surface.

The destination was a house occupied by James, a high school friend of Alex's, and his roommate Julian. Julian never seemed to be in L.A., and pretty much everyone assumed was a mid-level drug dealer, though no one knew for sure. The interior of the house was dark, cramped and not very impressive. But the location was perfect, right on the beach and just a few hundred yards north of the Hermosa Pier. Also, it had a roof deck providing a panorama of the beach and ocean from the pier all the way to Manhattan Beach farther north. Just as important, directly in front of the house were four permanent beach volleyball courts. On any given afternoon it was more likely than not that at least one of the courts would be occupied by bikini-clad, decent-looking or better chicks.

By 2:30 p.m., Mike was in the best mood he could remember in a long time. He, Alex and James had enjoyed a tasty lunch at Amigos Tacos, washed down with Pacificos and lime. The three now sat in beach chairs on the roof terrace. Four chicks, three of them hot, were playing volleyball on the second court. Mike had bet Alex $10 on the team on the right and they were already winning 10-4. To top it all off, he took the last sip of his second Bud Light and noticed the definitive start of a soft day buzz. Mike was reaching into the cooler for another Bud Light when Gary opened the door leading to the rooftop.

Alex: "G-Balls! Good to see you, glad you could make it."

Gary: "Yo! Whattup? Of course. I wouldn't miss it. I just had to go in for a few hours this morning to finish up for the case I have been working on. How's it going up here?"

Mike: "Man, you work too hard."

Gary: "Tell me about it. Anyway, I am off until Monday so fuck it. Beer me."

Mike: "You don't have Labor Day off?"

Gary: "Let's not talk about it. Just give me a beer, please."

Mike reached into the cooler and threw Gary an ice-cold Bud Light. Gary opened it, took a sip with his left hand and wiped his mouth with the back of his right hand. "Fuckin' A," he decreed.

"Fuckin' A," Alex, Mike and James replied in unison.

James offered Gary a hit of weed from his pipe, which Gary declined. Instead he pulled up a beach chair and lined himself up so all four were facing the ocean. For the next two hours, the happy group did nothing but drink beer, pee, bet on beach volleyball, listen to the Yankees/Red Sox game on the radio, smoke pot (James and Alex only), eat Kettle Brand Salt and Pepper Potato Chips (James and Alex only), and discuss the pressing issues of the day. These began with an assessment of the relatively new President, George W. Bush, whom James disliked and considered an idiot but Alex, Mike and Gary supported fully. Each felt Al Gore was a disaster and all agreed with James that Clinton had been a good President, though Gary felt his foreign policy was weak. A consensus was also reached that a sitting President should never consider oral sex and cigar penetration with an intern in the Oval Office unless the girl is absolutely smoking hot. Other topics covered, in order and with summary conclusions in parenthesis where appropriate, included:

- If the 2000 election was fair (3 yes, 1 no)
- If the President was really controlled by secret businessmen (2 yes, 2 no)
- If the stock market would rebound (3 yes, 1 no)

- If WebVan would survive (4 yes)
- Whether San Diego or Los Angeles was better (3 San Diego, 1 Los Angeles)
- Why all hot chicks are dumb (God is fair)
- Why Bud Light is a great beer in the sun (smooth taste, God is generous sometimes)
- Why they should have partied more and studied less in college
- Whether law school is worth the time and cost (3 no, 1 not sure)
- How it would be pretty cool to be a mailman
- Why drinking in the day is more fun than at night (no good theories)
- Which of the girls playing volleyball on court two was the hottest (4 for one in the red on the right side)
- If all points should count in volleyball or only when a team has the serve (2 only on serve, 2 all)
- Why the American League should get rid of the designated hitter
- How stupid the college football playoff system is
- Why there should be more three-day weekends
- Why the holiday for Martin Luther King Day should keep the same name but be moved back a week or two to coincide with the Monday after Super Bowl Sunday
- How to interpret the effectiveness of condoms and birth control pills. Does 99% effective mean for each incident, for each year, or for life? (4 unsure)

These important subjects took just over two hours to cover. Now after four o'clock in the afternoon, the sun started a slow decent toward the Pacific, its rays dancing on the water and sparkling in mesmerizing patterns. Mike, who was rarely visibly upbeat, offered a positive review of the situation. "Man, we are really lucky," he said before getting up to go downstairs to pee and find a hat to protect his face, which was starting to redden.

He returned two minutes later wearing a baseball cap advertising Comdex 1999, opened a new beer and slowly settled himself back into his beach chair. His mood had not soured.

Mike: "You know, sometimes when I am at work, it is difficult to figure out what the point is because, you know, I certainly don't give a fuck about that place, but then sometimes you are reminded that life is pretty good."

James: "Fuckin' A."

Gary: "Yeah, we are lucky, but even work isn't that bad. I mean it would be nice to do a bit less of it, but work does allow for all of this and also I think we would get bored without it."

Alex: "I don't know. I mean, I am grateful for the cash, but otherwise I think I could live without it."

Gary: "So what would you do all day?"

Alex: "Get my handicap down to single digits, travel, get better at cooking and chase chicks."

Mike: "That doesn't sound like it would get boring too soon."

Gary: "It doesn't sound like it, but I bet it would after a while."

James: "You could also smoke a lot of shit, man."

James offered his comment with enthusiasm, but it was largely ignored.

Gary and Mike subtly glanced at each other and rolled their eyes. Alex completely disregarded it and moved on, simultaneously shaking his Bud Light can to see if there was enough left for a last sip.

Alex: "Well, I wouldn't mind finding out. Also, someday it would be cool to try to do the whole thing over again. Differently. Better somehow. What I do now is too commoditized."

Gary: "In that case, don't become a lawyer. We really do nothing. But we do a lot of it and at least we get paid."

Alex: "It is all about transferring big numbers around electronically and simply removing a small piece along the way. Intangibility is better."

James: "That's true, man. Nothing ever really happens."

James was missing the point of the conversation but Alex, Gary, and Mike, who usually paid only courtesy attention to him, let this comment sink in for a few seconds.

Mike: "That is kind of true. I mean I am twenty-six and jack-shit has happened in my life."

Alex: "Dude, you are so negative. That isn't true at all. Think about all the shit we have done. A million Vegas trips, the Mexico trips, LA, Miami, San Fran, Europe, all the nights out in San Diego, all the ping-pong and golf and poker days."

Gary: "Don't forget the no-hitter in Little League."

Mike: "Very funny. Yeah, but that's not what I mean. I mean nothing significant ever happens. We just...kind of...float."

Gary: "I don't buy that either. I mean I met Blair and that was a huge thing in my life."

This time it was James, Mike and Alex's turn to roll their eyes. But Mike was intrigued by the conversation as a whole and carried it on, the beer allowing him to produce a stream of consciousness longer than he would normally have felt comfortable with.

Mike: "Yes, Casanova, and that's great. Really. But I mean, don't you think it is weird that all of us just got here without really planning it? Basically you were born and then you went to school and then you went to college because your parents told you that you have to. And then you got a job because you were supposed to. Probably getting a job was a bit of a bitch at the time, but in retrospect it just happened and now you work and get paid and live your life and get drunk on the weekends and if you are Alex you nail a lot of chicks. But doesn't it all seem pre-ordained? I mean I never thought about any of this shit. It just happened, and really, it didn't require much effort on my part. Maybe it would have been better to join the Army, or move to Hawaii and rent out jet-skis on the beach, or something instead of just being a little ant marching along with everyone else."

Alex: "Most ants don't make a hundred grand at twenty-six like you do."

Mike: "Yeah, yeah. I am not complaining, I am just saying it is weird. And you know what? Because it is America and because we are from the families we are from, we are going to probably end up making more money, getting married somewhere along the way, and then buying a house somewhere in the suburbs, and then buying a dog and then having two point five kids. What if we want to do something different? You can't. You can't because society forces it on us. It is an overwhelming current that you can't escape."

Alex: "I guess so, Sport. And you know what else? You are going to have to drop two months of that fat salary on an engagement ring even though that makes no fucking sense at all, just because society wants you to. But you are living in a society and the society happens to favor people like you, so try to be a bit grateful."

Gary: "And you can get away with like five or six weeks salary on the ring. The two months thing is just propaganda from the diamond companies."

Alex: "You know you could have been born in South Central, or in Ethiopia or something, so make sure you don't complain."

Gary: "Also, you would be surprised. At first you think the diamond thing is stupid, but after you buy it, you find that you don't mind having spent the money. It is worth it to make the girl happy and you will be glad."

Alex: "Dude, enough about the diamond ring already. That isn't really what we are talking about."

Gary: "I am just saying."

Mike: "Yeah, I get all that. And I am not complaining. But still it is just interesting how we float through life and it kind of ends up the same no matter what."

James: "No man, I don't think that's true. I mean a bunch of my buddies got fucked up on drugs and their lives are totally messed now. Also, you can do real good shit, too. This dude Ken from high school that Alex and I used to hang with started trading options and made like fifteen mil. No offense to you guys, I love hanging with you, but you guys are sort of out of a Gap commercial where everyone is the same. But that is because it is the way you make it, not the way it is. Not real life."

The guys once again paused in mild surprise about the wisdom from James, laughing lightly at the Gap reference which was true enough to be funny.

Alex: "James is totally right. Also, I think the older you get, the more dispersion there is and that is all because of your own actions. It is true that basically everyone's lives are the same until at least the end of high school except maybe one person is a bit more popular or something. Then some people go to college and some don't. Assuming you go to a decent college, everyone gets out and gets some kind of job and you make between thirty and fifty K. When you get in your late twenties some people make a bit more and some are married but things still look pretty much the same. I think it is only when you get into your thirties that shit starts to look real different. Some of the dudes I work with who are in their thirties make seven figures and others are struggling not to get let go. Also, some are happily married with kids and others are divorced. Plus, you start to see a lot more drug and alcohol problems surface in the thirties. What is all just fun and games now starts to become a big problem for some people later. So I guess, Mike, in some ways you are right, but I think the way you position yourself now has a lot to do with how things turn out. It is just hard to see the differences at the moment."

Mike: "Sweet. Hopefully I will be the guy with the alcohol problem."

Alex: "I think you have a good chance if you keep working at it hard enough. I know what you are saying, though. I frequently have this dream where I have to go back to high school or college because it turns out I missed one or two classes that I needed to graduate. Then I realize it has been more than five years and they are not going to stop paying me now either way, so who gives a fuck if I really graduated or not? Anyway, I think it means somehow I feel I don't quite deserve what I have. But who knows?"

Gary: "It probably just means you feel guilty because you cheated your way through school."

Alex: "No. I hardly cheated at all, at least in college."

Gary: "You know what is kind of strange though? Sort of in line with what Mike was saying, is that it does seem that in our generation nothing ever really happens in the world either. I mean, there is a lot of progress with technology and such but there really have not been any defining moments."

Mike: "Like what?"

Gary: "Well our grandparents would have had the Great Depression and World War Two. Hiroshima and all that shit. Before that were World War One and the Spanish Flu. Our parents had Vietnam, the JFK assassination, the Cuban Missile Crisis, and whatever else. I mean, like, what have we had? What big events do you remember where you were for?"

Alex: "I remember the Space Shuttle blowing up."

Mike: "I remember where I was when Princess Di died."

James: "Didn't Reagan get shot?"

Alex: "Yeah. Also we had the Iraq War."

Gary: "That barely counted."

Mike: "There were a few big earthquakes."

James: "There was the Monica Lewinsky situation."

Mike: "I remember where I was when Joe Carter hit that homerun off of Mitch Williams in the World Series."

Gary: "I don't think sports moments should count for this. See what I mean? There isn't much."

Mike: "The Berlin Wall."

Alex: "The dot-com bubble. Who knows? We may still get our own Great Depression the way the market is going."

Gary: "Yeah. Anyway, it still sort of seems to me like nothing happens anymore."

Alex: "Maybe. I guess so."

At Fenway Park in Boston, as the guys listened on the radio, Mike Mussina nearly made history that day, retiring the first twenty-six Boston batters before yielding a two out pinch-hit single to Carl Everett in the ninth inning.

CHAPTER EIGHTEEN

Swingers
8:29 p.m.

*"I think you're all fucked in the head. We're
ten hours from the fucking fun park and you
want to bail out. Well I'll tell you something.
This is no longer a vacation. It's a quest.
It's a quest for fun. I'm gonna have fun and
you're gonna have fun. We're all gonna have
so much fucking fun we'll need plastic
surgery to remove our god-damn smiles.
You'll be whistling "Zip-A-Dee Doo-Dah"
out of your assholes! I gotta be crazy!
I'm on a pilgrimage to see a moose.
Praise Marty Moose! Holy Shit!"*
—Clark Griswold, *Vacation*

OTHER THAN ROGER'S OUTBURST toward the conclusion of the
Stanford game, things remained noticeably quiet in the car
ever since the encounter with California's finest. It had now

been about an hour since they had been pulled over, so Gary decided it was safe to crack another beer. He offered fresh ones to the back seat as well, which were readily accepted. Alex, who was maintaining a constant seventy-eight miles per hour, asked for a Diet Coke, which Gary also provided.

Alex had a better ability than most to move on from bad news, especially if it was the result of something he could not control. With regards to the speeding ticket, he reasoned that while he was largely at fault, these things sometimes happened and could not be completely avoided. Though not happy about the large fine he knew he would face, he increasingly considered the outcome of the whole event to be generally positive given the potential for much worse scenarios. Driving though the darkness, with the rest of the group quiet, it didn't take long for Alex's mind to wander from the unfortunate issue with the police to other items.

Alex: "Do you think Smurfette let a lot of the other Smurfs fuck her?"

Gary: "I really like to think not. I kind of had a crush on her as a kid. That would sort of ruin it somehow. She seems so sweet. Anyway, it didn't seem like the Smurfs were very sexual creatures."

Alex: "Yeah, but they always seemed so happy all the time. You know, except for that one that was always upset about something. I mean, especially considering they lived in mushrooms and had to provide for everything they had. They must have had to work pretty hard. It wasn't like they lived in an oil-rich emirate or anything. Plus, they always had watch out for Gargamel and that cat. It sounds like a pretty tough life. They must have been getting laid to be that cheerful."

Gary: "I don't think so. With only one chick, if they were fucking her, it would have bred too much jealousy and resentment. I think the fact that they were so happy is evidence that they were asexual."

Alex: "That is logical. But what about Baby-Smurf? Maybe someone slipped one past the goalie?"

Gary: "Smurfette never looked pregnant. There had to be some other way of reproduction. They were always making potions and stuff. It's the only thing that makes sense."

Alex: "Sometimes I wonder if the Russians created the Smurfs as some kind of communist propaganda to influence American kids."

Gary: "How is that?"

Alex: "Well, the Smurfs basically had a communist society. Remember how they were always all helping out to build something or accomplish some common goal? Plus there were no rich Smurfs. Clearly Handy Smurf could have made a killing if it was a free market. And Papa Smurf kind of had a role similar to a Soviet Premier."

Gary: "Are you calling Papa Smurf Stalin? I don't remember him sending any Smurfs to the gulag."

Alex: "Of course not. They wouldn't want to show that part. He did have that red hat, though. Anyway, think about it. The show was at its peak in the early eighties at the height of the Cold War, right? Also, it is consistent with Smurfette's role as the sexless beauty. One of the main reasons to make more money than your peers is to attract pussy. Having only one woman, who didn't or couldn't put out, is sort of the perfect scenario for communism to thrive."

Gary: "Well, I watched every Saturday and I didn't turn out to be a commie."

Alex: "I guess so. But I still don't trust those Russians."

Roger: "I bet Smurfette took it in every hole. She probably tied that blonde hair up into a pony tail, got down on her knees and took one little blue Smurf cock in her mouth while another one gave it to her from behind. Meanwhile, Papa Smurf was sitting in the corner with his red pants around his ankles punching clown and videotaping the whole thing."

Alex: "I think you are right, Rodge. The thing that bothers me the most is we will probably never know for sure."

Roger: "That dirty little slut!"

Alex continued to ponder the sexual habits of the Smurfs as he maneuvered the car through a slight curve to the left. A few miles to the south of the peak of Clark Mountain, Highway 15 northbound reached its own summit, revealing a view of an expansive valley of darkness and dirt below. Two straight, thin lines of red and white car lights divided the nothingness. They acted as feeder streams, emptying into a larger body of illumination at the border where the first Nevada casinos beckoned.

"Vegas, Baby! Vegas!" Roger exclaimed excitedly from the back seat.

Alex: "Keep your pants on. This whole thing seems way too much like Swingers already for my comfort level."

Gary: "Anyway, it isn't even Vegas, it's just Whiskey Pete's."

Roger: "Ah, quit being such pube-lice. Once in a while you all should quit worrying about the minutia and enjoy the moment. Vegas, Baby!"

Alex (26)

IN THE FALL OF 2001, ALEX made it a point to be in the office before the New York Stock Exchange opened at 6:30 a.m., West Coast time. On this particular Tuesday morning, he was running a few minutes late. During dinner at Elephant Bar the previous night, after a few gin and tonics, Roger had talked him into going to Viejas where he found a 4-8 Texas Hold 'em poker table with some very loose and stupid players. The result was he only got four hours of sleep, but he felt fresh anyway, invigorated by the crisp, clean morning and the extra $625 in his wallet.

Anyways, he was already on Interstate 5 and just a few minutes away from the turnoff for La Jolla, so he would be just ten minutes late at worst. One of Alex's pet peeves in life was the fact that no radio stations played much music in the morning. Instead, they preferred to let a bunch of dorks who tried to appeal to soccer moms and imitate Howard Stern at the same time babble on about whatever came to mind. The San Diego market seemed among the worst to him. Even so, for some reason Alex was too cheap to buy XM or Sirius so he usually spent his commute flipping endlessly between the preset channels of his silver BMW.

At 5:49 a.m., one of these channels finished playing *White Wedding* by Billy Idol, a song Alex always enjoyed.

Naturally, the disk jockeys began talking in that same peppy tone that suggested hunger, poverty and disease had somehow been cured overnight.

"Well Maria, get a load of this," one of them began, "there are reports that a small plane has crashed into the World Trade Center in New York."

"Sounds like someone needed a second cup of coffee before starting their commute," Maria replied cheerfully. She continued, "Speaking of coffee and work, we are going to go to work for you. That's right, its morning commute collection time! Just be the seventh caller right now and we will put you to work, giving you $101 for each of the last seven songs we have played that you can correctly name!"

"Whoooohoo, Maria! That sounds like the start of a great day!" her co-host added lamely. Alex was about to change the channel when, remarkably, they played another song. This time it was *Every Rose Has It's Thorn* by Poison. Alex had never been a big Poison fan, but he figured this was his best bet and left the tuner untouched. The radio version was less than three minutes long and ended with the male co-host returning to the air. "Well Maria, it looks like everyone in New York could use a cup of coffee! Now we are hearing a second plane has crashed into the other tower."

Maria concurred, "There must be something in the air today with those crazy New Yorkers," she said, laughing. "And I thought the traffic was bad on the 5/805 merge," she added. At this her co-host let out a peppier-than-usual howl. "Whooo-ha, you're right about that, Maria!"

"What the fuck is with these people?" Alex asked himself in the car a bit louder than he intended. His annoyance at this point was with their dorkyness rather than their stupidity, as he also had not yet grasped the situation. However, two planes crashing in New York sounded strange enough to him to switch the radio to one of the AM news channels.

He listened in silence for the next sixty seconds before again speaking aloud in the otherwise empty car, this time in a much more solemn and controlled voice. "Jesus Christ."

It took Alex another fourteen minutes to get to his parking space, where he remained in his car with the radio on for another twelve minutes. During this time, there were reports of another plane crashing into the Pentagon, light weapons fire inside the Pentagon, explosions at the Capitol building in Washington DC, explosions in Chicago, and reports of several additional missing planes.

Alex scanned the skies above La Jolla. Seeing nothing unusual, he opened the door and ran to his office, something he never did, even when it was raining. When he arrived, the usual buzz in the building was dead. Everyone stood completely still, eyes glued to one of the many TV sets. Usually they would have been tuned to Bloomberg TV or CNBC, but all eyes were now on CNN. On the screens, two iconic towers stood, giants peering down at a city of dreams. They emitted plumes of dark grey smoke into the pale blue sky of an otherwise still world. "Jesus Christ," Alex muttered for the second of many times that day.

Alex walked with purpose to his office (really more of a cubicle at that time), put down his briefcase and went to find a Bloomberg news terminal. Surprisingly, as he was leaving the cube, the phone rang. Alex wondered which of his clients would be the one to call him first in such a situation. When he looked at the caller ID, however, he realized it was not a client at all. It was Taylor, a friend of his who was a bond trader at Cantor Fitzgerald. "Holy shit," Alex thought, realizing that the Cantor offices were at the top of towers.

The trader, trapped above the flames, was professional, but there was clearly fear and terror in his voice. He was unable to reach anyone in New York and was checking to see if Alex had any information on the emergency response to the towers. Alex told him that he was unable to filter out any truth from rumor and couldn't offer any help. He said good-bye and thought back to the fun times he and Taylor had in Manhattan and also remembered that Taylor had once helped him reverse a bad trade where Alex had accidentally entered an extra zero, saving Alex from personally having to cover a meaningful loss. He had always respected Taylor, professionally and personally, and would never forget that phone call. In the future, he would refer to it to remind himself not to be lazy, and to take pride in anything he put his name on. But at the moment, he had the same zombie look as everyone else in the office and wasn't thinking about much that made sense. He quickly walked to a Bloomberg terminal.

News updates were arriving every few seconds, though it was tough to know what to believe. There were reports of explosions at the White House, another plane crashed into the ground in Indiana, and Russian intelligence, which apparently tracked these things, counted eleven planes unaccounted for. Major buildings throughout the US were being evacuated. A consensus began to develop that Islamic fundamentalists were to blame.

At around 6:45 a.m., the news flow on the Bloomberg terminal abruptly cut off. This was no doubt an order from the government. Alex returned to watching CNN with everyone else. The first tower fell fourteen minutes later.

Alex stayed at work until after six in the evening that day, despite the fact that not one client called him. He left work and drove home under the still-bright San Diego sky wondering what would happen next. Only when he was home alone in his kitchen, drinking a beer, again watching CNN, still largely in shock, did he realize how mad he was. For most of that night he was pretty sure he was going to quit his job and join the military, which of course never really came close to happening.

Like many Americans that day, Alex lost a sense of innocence but gained a greater feeling of love and pride in his country, the greatest ever known in the brief history of our small planet. A battle was lost, but a war that was really already underway was a long way from decided. Alex knew with certainty that eventually it would be won. Alex had never believed there was any particular meaning to his life. Nevertheless, from that day on he felt a patriotic duty to engage in all pursuits in life more aggressively.

To be more present.

CHAPTER NINETEEN

Viva Las Vegas
9:15 p.m.

"Take me down to the Paradise City,
where the grass is green and the
girls are pretty."
—*Paradise City*, Guns N' Roses

THIRTY-EIGHT MILES FROM the state line, the Mandalay Bay Hotel, for all practical purposes, marks the beginning of the Las Vegas strip. The black BMW approached stealthily, now only four miles from the Mandalay. *The Ruler's Back* by Jay-Z was playing on the iPod, and Gary turned the volume up a few notches. Due to the light from the strip, the sky was visibly transitioning from black to whitish-grey, like some kind of alien sunrise. Alex checked the clock on the dashboard of the car and was pleased to see it was still well before ten o'clock despite the In-N-Out stop, Mike's poo problems, and the little business with the police.

Alex never ceased to be amazed by Vegas. His relationship with the city was that of a man who falls in love with a prostitute. Vegas had given him some of his best memories.

It had also beaten the shit out of him a few times. But no matter what, he always maintained passion and respect for the city. It made him feel alive. He knew Vegas was far from monogamous, but in his heart he felt the city reciprocated his amorous feelings.

The tidal wave of new construction and the success of the city fascinated him. When he first started coming to Vegas during freshman year in college, the strip looked nothing like it did now. There was no Luxor, Mandalay Bay, New York New York, Treasure Island, Venetian, Monte Carlo, Bellagio, and on and on. Probably more important, the Hard Rock was still under construction and Palms had not even been conceptualized.

Also, back in those days, restaurants were entirely focused on quantity over quality and there was essentially nothing to do except gamble, drink by the pool, or go to strip clubs. The only nightclub he could recall from the college days was The Beach and it was off the strip. It was decent enough, but really just as well could have been in some shitty Mexican beach resort rather than Vegas. Now the restaurants were among the best in the world and the clubs were like cathedrals. At least in his mind, they were better than what Los Angeles, New York or Miami had to offer.

To Alex, Vegas demonstrated proof that the human spirit could accomplish nearly anything if given the proper incentive. It was also proof that civilization was getting better despite all the negativity still thriving in the world. If in most of the world progress happened slowly so you couldn't feel it, here the change occurred with a vengeance you couldn't avoid. It not only touched you but grabbed you and threw you like a pair of dice. Alex maintained nostalgia for the old classics like the The Freemont, The Sands and The Riviera, but the new stuff was undoubtedly better, whatever the old-timers would tell you. Whether you loved it or hated it, he felt the city truly was a wonder of the world. Alex did not dwell much on the underside of Vegas, with all its worms and maggots, and pimps, junkies and other assorted lowlifes, because he never had to face it.

For those who see the positive in Vegas, one of the highlights is arriving, whether by car or plane. Each of the passengers in Alex's car felt increasingly awake as the strip grew larger through the front windshield. Roger seemed to have a physical as well as mental reaction, and he subconsciously began to rub his hands together like an excited little kid told he is getting a new toy.

Mike expressed admiration for the city in his own way. First he ripped a loud fart and then said, "Just think about how many hot chicks in that city right now want to get fucked."

Gary: "Maybe if you can get control of your bodily functions for ten minutes you might have a chance with one of them."

Alex: "Basically, I am just pumped to be here with you guys, regardless of what chicks are here or not."

Mike: "So what, you are not going to try to hook up?"

Alex: "I am just saying that isn't the first priority."

Roger: "My first priority is winning some cash-money."

Alex: "Just try not to lose all your football winnings in the first hour."

Roger: "Don't worry, I will be under control."

Gary: "Sure, that would be consistent."

Mike: "You guys make me laugh. Of course it will be great to drink and gamble, but if Vegas was a dudes-only down, we wouldn't even be here right now."

Gary: "This isn't Riyadh, dude. America doesn't have dudes-only towns."

Mike: "Have you ever been to San Jose? Anyway, we will have them for real if those crazy fundamentalist rag-headed fucks have their way."

Gary: "Whatever. I am married and I am still pumped up to be here."

Mike: "Seriously, though, think about it. If there were no chicks, would we still be coming here? Basically, if you really think about it, everything we do is because of bitches. Think about where we usually go to dinner. Not where the best food is or who has the best price. We go where we are most likely to see the hottest chicks. I mean sure, N9NE has good steaks, but is that really why we go there? How do we choose where we drink on weekends in San Diego?"

At this point it was clear to everyone there was no point participating in the conversation so they let him elaborate.

Mike: "Like Alex said, why, even, do we work? Okay, we need to eat, so you would still have some job, but if there were no chicks would you really care if you made fifty grand or five hundred? The only point of making five hundred is to attract hotter chicks. Why do you need a great house with a view of the ocean if you can't have a chick over to see it and then play your skin flute? All I would need is a one bedroom with a microwave and enough money for PlayStation and beers."

Alex: "So you agree the Smurfs are a propaganda tool?"

Mike: "Will you let it go with the damned Smurfs? No, this isn't a political point. I am only noting that we think men dominate society. But the truth is that all we are is slaves to our swords. Basically everything we do is on some level because we want to get laid, even if we don't realize it. Really, we are controlled by women."

Gary: "So, when we played golf together last weekend, was that so one of us could get laid?"

Mike: "Okay, so it isn't literally everything, but the point is the same. If there were no chicks, we would not be driving into Vegas right now. We would be at one of our places playing cards and drinking beers."

Roger: "He kind of has a point. If there were no girls, all I would do would be drink and gamble."

Alex: "That's pretty much all you do anyway, Rodge."

Roger: "Hmmm. Maybe. But I am still the only one who had sex last night."

Mike: "I don't know why it is so hard for you all to accept the truth and admit your dicks control you. The more I think about it, the more I think we would be better off if there were no hoes corrupting everything."

Alex (sarcastically): "Mike is right. Maybe we would be better off without our dicks."

Gary: "This is a retarded conversation. We are in Vegas, gentlemen. So try to get over your bitterness and have some fun. Anyway, if there were no women, none of us would exist in the first place, so of course we would not be here."

Gary's logic was indisputable, so the four drove on in silence. The back side of the heart of the Vegas strip was now passing by on the right, dousing the car in white light. Between the Monte Carlo and the Bellagio was a vast span of relative darkness occupied only by several huge semi-lit cranes. A large sign explained that this was the future site of Project City Center. Alex knew from research at work that this was an MGM Mirage endeavor funded largely by Dubai World. It was estimated to have a cost of $8 billion, which was to be recouped in large part by selling luxury condominiums. With several other luxury condo buildings sprouting up all around the perimeter of the strip like weeds, Alex wondered where the demand was going to come from. Still, he appreciated the grandeur of the effort and was jealous that the people behind the project were operating on such a larger scale than he was.

Alex began maneuvering the car into the right-hand lane of the freeway in order to exit onto West Flamingo Road. From this exit, the Bellagio and Caesars Palace were immediately available one minute to the right, and the Rio and Palms were about two minutes to the left.

Although its location was awful, the rooms were small and expensive, and the service average, for the last few years Alex usually chose to stay at the Palms when in Vegas. When questioned about this choice, Alex could point out that he loved the restaurant there, had a good relationship with the VIP host, liked Ghostbar, and had decent luck at the tables. While all this was true, the fact was that the Palms tended to have the hottest chicks around.

The BMW slowly lost speed as it climbed the long off-ramp. It settled to a stop, first in line at the left-hand turn lane waiting for the red light to change. A woman with ratty clothes and a crumpled-up, stained face stood about five feet away on the dirt area just above the curb. The wind had picked up and Mike noticed the woman struggling to keep her cardboard sign properly aligned. A thin layer of dust and dirt blew by her ankles in the same direction traffic was moving on the freeway below. Her sign read:

Hungry.
Anything Helps.
Good Luck and
God Bless!

The woman was trying to make eye contact with Alex in the driver's seat, but only Mike read the sign. "Bummer," he said with no emotion and to no one in particular.

To his right, Roger had reached over the front seat and was shaking Gary's shoulders with both hands, trying to generate additional enthusiasm for the weekend. In front, Gary was evading Roger's annoying grasp while leaning forward to organize his Bag O' Tricks. He neatly stacked the remaining beers, tobacco products, and the Slim Jims on top of the porn magazine, whose cover was now significantly creased. This vexed Gary and he tried unsuccessfully to iron it out with his hand. Meanwhile, Alex was impatiently fidgeting with the wheel of the iPod, hoping to play *Wanna B a Baller* by Lil' Troy as the last song of the journey, but he scrolled too fast and ended up pushing play on Jennifer Lopez's *Jenny from the Block* instead. The light changed before he had time to fix it, and the BMW sped off eagerly toward the Palms.

INTERLUDE THIRTEEN

Gary (28)

GARY WAS AT A WATERSLIDE park. He didn't know why he was there, and really wasn't all that enthusiastic about it. Nevertheless, after walking up the hill to where the slides began he remembered that waterslides could be pretty fun and began to feel more positive about the situation. It was a bright, cloudless day accentuated by the faint smell of blueberry muffins. He stood on a cement waiting area. The entrance to one slide was to his left, while another one was on the right, requiring an additional climb of about twenty yards further up the hill.

Gary decided the one to the left would be sufficient and he walked over to the entrance. Strangely, there was no attendant at the top, so he just jumped in and began moving down the slide feet first. There were a few turns and he tried to shift his weight in an effort to make his body move up the sides of the slide, but he wasn't going fast enough to get the momentum required.

Then, after just three turns, he entered a straightaway and saw the pool at the end of the ride just ahead. Though he was not going that fast, he hit the pool and was immediately submerged. His body was caught in a current and he flipped around head over heels a few times. Just as he was starting to panic about not being able to breathe, his head popped above the surface.

The fear subsided immediately and he looked back up at the slide in disappointment. It was the shortest, least fun waterslide he could remember having been on. Gary wondered if this really was a lame waterslide or if he just had inaccurate memories from childhood. He had not been to a waterslide park in probably fifteen years and it was quite possible that he was much smaller then and they just seemed a lot bigger and cooler.

He walked out of the warm water of the shallow pool and onto a small grassy hill. In front of him were some trees, similar to eucalyptus trees, but taller and thinner. They created a nice shady patch and he thought about going to sit in it for a while. Then, to his left he saw something quite unlike anything he had ever seen before.

There was a sea, stretching all the way out to the horizon. It reminded him of the sea off the coast of Dubai, although he had never been there. A few miles out, jutting up from the sea was the coolest looking waterslide he had ever seen. It was not built on a hill, obviously, but instead was held up by massive stilts coming out of the water. It was huge, perhaps a thousand feet high. The only way to get to the starting point was to climb a ladder at one end. Though the construction appeared very solid, it looked dangerous even to make the ascent. The slide came down at a sharp angle with several steep and twisting turns. Water rushed down it at an unnaturally eager pace and spilled over the sides at the sharper curves. At one point, about halfway down, there was a twenty-five foot gap in the slide where the rider would be airborne, required to jump the space before landing on the second half of the slide. The gap was still about a hundred yards up above the sea. If one did not have sufficient speed to make it across, it would be a fatal plunge downward. All told, the slide appeared to be almost two miles in length.

Gary was not sure if he wanted to try it. Certainly it was dangerous, but it looked like the most fun ride he had ever seen. Also, he wasn't sure how to get out there. Maybe there was a boat service? He walked closer to the sea and instead noticed a one-lane land bridge with a paved road. He could drive. A car was right next to him. It was a convertible sedan, kind of like a three series BMW, but there was no brand name on it. It was dark green. While he was still not sure if he would actually climb up and ride the slide, he knew he wanted to check it out. He got in the car and started driving on the land bridge toward the slide. The sun sparkled off the sea.

There were a few sharp turns in the land bridge. Some of them snuck up on him and he almost lost control of the car and crashed into the sea. Gary realized he should probably slow down, but he wanted to go faster to get to the slide. He accelerated further, the car fishtailing around curves, the slide getting closer. He was pulled toward it by an unknown force.

Then, his cell phone rang. He was curious who could be calling. He stopped the car on the land bridge and answered the phone. It was his boss at work, Jim, one of the partners. Jim informed Gary that he had forgot to submit his STS report last week. Usually, whenever anyone mentioned the STS reports, there was an obligatory joking reference to *Office Space*, but Jim was not joking. He was quite serious about the problem with the STS report. Gary knew that if he wanted to avoid big trouble at work he would have to go take care of the report immediately. He was hit by a wave of sadness and literally felt heavier than before. It was hard to move. He would not get to ride the crazy-looking waterslide after all.

Gary arrived at the office almost instantaneously. He had substituted the bathing suit he was wearing for work clothes. Even though almost no time had passed to get to the office, when he arrived it had completely burnt down. The fire was already extinguished and there was no smell of smoke. All that remained were blackened fragments of the support structures of the building and piles of ash. Jim was there, explaining what had happened.

Gary looked around the scene. The office where he spent most of his days was gone. He felt nothing. He wondered if his favorite tie burned up in his desk.

Two hours later, over coffee and egg-white croissant sandwiches for breakfast, he told Blair about the dream. It was not until he said it out loud that he realized how obvious it all was. He took a sip of coffee.

Maybe if he didn't have the mortgage payments. Maybe if he wasn't married. Maybe if he didn't have a little daughter. But he did. He thought back to the dream and wondered if he would have made it up the ladder, and if he had, if he would have survived the gap.

CHAPTER TWENTY

Primping + Taxi Ride
9:22 p.m.

*"I see you wear braces . . .
I wear braces too."*
—Butt-head, *Beavis and Butt-head do America*

ALEX SELF-PARKED THE BMW in the garage in order to save
the valet fee. He popped the trunk and all four doors opened
simultaneously. Everyone stood up and stretched. All were
happy to be out of the car, though they remained bonded by
a shared sense of anticipation. Roger rolled his latest spitter,
a twenty-ounce Sprite bottle, under the blue Ford pickup
truck parked immediately to the right. The truck, with
Nevada plates, had a bumper sticker that read, "I Love
Animals. They're Delicious!"

Gary reached into the trunk and distributed the four sim-
ilar-looking black duffle bags inside to their respective own-
ers. He unzipped his briefly to insert the Bag O' Tricks and
the group moved toward the entrance of the hotel.

In the next sixty-seven minutes, much was accomplished:

- Alex checked into a standard room with two queen beds
- They stopped in the sundries store and bought eight Heinekens, four Dasani waters, one pack of Big Red cinnamon gum, one pack of Orbitz mint gum, one pack of Marlboro Lights, one pack of Dunhill Milds, and two sticks of cherry flavored Chapstick
- Each showered
- Alex shaved his chest and armpits
- Roger sent five hundred dollars from his online sports book account to Alex's PayPal account in exchange for five hundred-dollar bills
- Gary stepped out of the room into the hallway and had a six-minute phone conversation with Blair
- Roger ordered twenty-four hours' worth of continuous porn on pay-per-view
- Each dressed
- Seven Heinekens were consumed
- Gary won $12 from Roger playing $1 hands of black-jack on the bed

Highly satisfied with themselves, the group left the room and took the elevator down to the main floor. Each wore similar variations of modestly faded jeans with black shoes, though Mike's were half-boots while Alex donned pointy-toed Salvatore Ferragamo loafers with no socks. Mike had on a white button-up shirt with small red vertical stripes, successfully completing the default outfit for all twenty-five- to thirty-five-year-old males in Vegas in 2006. Gary donned a bright red satin button-up shirt with large blue buttons and small blue vertical stripes in the front. The back featured a large image of Papa Smurf, who was giving a thumbs-up signal and had a big smile under his white beard. Gary bought this particular shirt on Melrose in Los Angeles a year before he met Blair. He had only worn it three times, all in Vegas. Based on the earlier conversation in the car, it provided a round of laughs when he emerged from the bathroom wearing it. Alex had selected a patternless, canary-yellow Prada cashmere sweater he purchased a few weeks ago at Saks while visiting New York. The Elvis sunglasses were back on his face. Roger wore a shiny black-collared short-sleeved shirt that he used for most occasions requiring something more formal than a tee shirt.

Inside the elevator, Sheryl Crow informed them that love is a windy road. The walls in the elevator were mirrored, giving the group a final chance to check their look before heading out for the evening. They approved of themselves wholly, though Alex slightly modified his hair. At the ground floor, before the doors had fully parted, Roger slipped out and was quickly two paces ahead of the group, heading directly toward the $25 blackjack pit. Gary ran to catch up and subtly steered him away from the tables, convincing him of the merits of waiting until they got to the Hard Rock before gambling.

Alex, who rarely smoked outside of Vegas, lit a Dunhill and then walked briskly to join the group. The four headed toward the main exit of the casino side by side. Had anyone been watching from the door they may have been reminded of a softer, yuppie version of the walking scene from *Reservoir Dogs*.

Outside, the air was considerably cooler than in the casino, but just as smoky. Taxis and limousines, half of them bright lime green with the Palms logo on the side, swarmed around like bees outside a nest. High-heeled twenty-something girls in miniskirts and small dresses walked speedily in every direction. An even larger number of men, nearly all wearing jeans and light colored button-up shirts, also milled about but somehow seemed more stationary.

A mixture of people of all ages formed a taxi line that snaked to the left for about eighty feet. Alex quickly estimated it would take at least fifteen minutes to secure a cab in this fashion. He found this to be an unacceptable solution. Without saying a word to anyone, he dropped his cigarette, cut his way through the line, and walked briskly away from it toward the direction most cabs were approaching. Ninety seconds later, after guaranteeing the driver a twenty-dollar tip to skip the normal taxi line, Alex returned to the main entrance in the back of a yellow cab, waving the others in.

Gary hopped into the front seat and Roger and Mike joined Alex in the back, with Roger in the middle. The cab reeked of cheap perfume. Roger, Mike and Gary simultaneously took a few seconds to appraise their new driver. She was attractive, in her early thirties with long dark hair featuring voluminous bangs supported by a lot of hair spray. She was quite obviously Russian. Gary confirmed this by checking her cab license which identified her as Svetlana Federova. She looked much better in person than in the picture. She became universally more attractive once she began to speak. "Sooo, boyszz, veer do vee go on dis night?" she asked slowly in a thick Russian accent, treating each word as if it were its own entity.

"Anywhere you want," Roger answered stupidly.

"Hard Rock please," Alex overruled.

"Has anyone ever told you that you look like the cab driver from *Pulp Fiction*?" Mike asked tentatively.

"Ahh, yez. Many times," she purred slowly. Continuing, she asked, "and, you, vat do you sink?"

"I think you are way hotter," Mike said.

"Tank you, tank you veeery much," she offered.

Sadly, no one had any ideas on how to spur additional conversation with their new friend. Instead, they sat in silence and awkwardly fastened their seatbelts while she navigated the taxi across Las Vegas Boulevard and into the entrance to the Venetian. This led to a back exit with direct access to Koval which quickly led to Paradise Drive. Ultimately, they began to discuss amongst themselves the details of the arrangements for the night and clarified who was covering which expenses. Alex instructed everyone to make sure they were together and ready to go into the club no later than midnight.

Two minutes before arrival at the Hard Rock, their sexy escort began to speak again. "So, boyzz...do zou know vaaht Teeeger Voods and Meeekel Jagzzon haaav in couwmmon?" she asked, again nearly purring.

It took everyone a second to realize she wanted to tell a joke. Gary, being in the front seat, felt obliged to act as spokesman. He remembered this joke and recalled that the punch line would be that they both liked to play with little white balls. "No. What is it?" he asked anyway.

"Zey are both neeeegers," she said even more slowly, her accent deepening. She took a few seconds to let the answer sink in, then coyly looked around the cab for a reaction. A childish smile crept onto her mouth and into her eyes.

There was a moment of stunned silence followed by a simultaneous eruption of laughter. "No fucking way," Alex said to no one in particular, though he turned his face toward Roger, eyes wide, and began elbowing him lightly in the ribs.

One minute later, the cab came to a rest immediately in front of the main entrance to the Hard Rock Hotel and Casino. Alex, who had finished laughing but was still smiling stupidly, handed the driver two twenties for the eighteen-dollar fare. Three doors opened and the four exited the vehicle. Roger, still chuckling lightly, was the last to get out of the cab.

Inside the hotel, *Fly Away* by Lenny Kravitz was playing loudly, overshadowing the buzz of the crowd and the incessant jingle of slot machines.

INTERLUDE FOURTEEN

Alex (29)

THE DANCE-FLOOR AT JIMMY Love's in downtown San Diego was packed. Alex was surprised to find himself on it for two reasons. First, he really didn't like dancing. He only did it if he felt it would significantly increase his chances of hooking up. Second, it was almost midnight on a Friday night and, much to his surprise, he was completely sober.

Freddy Moyer, a college friend, had flown in that night from Phoenix. Freddy's flight was scheduled to arrive in San Diego at 9:00 p.m. The plan was that Alex would pick him up at the airport. Both would already be dressed and ready to go out. Alex would park his car downtown (he drove a black Cadillac Escalade at that time) and they would take a cab home so they could both drink freely. The plan went off track immediately. Due to thunder storms in Phoenix, Freddy's flight did not arrive until 10:45 p.m. The pair rushed downtown and made it into Jimmy Love's by 11:15 p.m., early enough to salvage the night.

Almost immediately after paying fifteen dollars each for cover charge and entering the bar, Freddy spotted a girl he used to date in college. Three minutes later, he took her downstairs to catch up and Alex found himself alone at the bar.

"Fucking perfect," he mumbled to no one in particular.

Now half an hour before midnight, Alex decided it wasn't worth having to pay for a cab and the overnight parking fee just to drink alone for two hours until the bar closed. Thus, this looked destined to become his first sober Friday in as long as he could remember. Still, that didn't mean he couldn't have a beer, so he ordered an Amstel Light.

The beer arrived and he grabbed it with his right hand while scooping up his change (a ten and five ones) with his left hand. He separated one dollar off of the pile with his left thumb and let it fall to the bar. As he shoved the rest of the money indiscriminately into the left pocket of his Seven for Mankind jeans, he felt someone rub up behind him and try to elbow their way up to the bar to his right. This caused annoyance until he spun around and saw the offending party.

If Amber Jones was a bit aggressive in trying to get to the bar, it was only because she was not used to getting any resistance from males for anything she did. With long light brown hair, big brown eyes and red lips, she could pass for a young version of Cindy Crawford if she wished – minus the signature mole of course.

"Excuse you," Alex said to her in a half-rude, half-flirtatious manner.

It had the desired effect.

"Oh, I'm sorry," Amber replied and smiled while batting her eyelashes. While barely twenty-one, Amber knew how to spot an opportunity for a free drink.

"Well, just this one time I will forgive you," Alex said, then added, "and not only do I forgive you, if you apologize for being so clumsy, I'll let you buy me a drink. What are you having?"

Predictably, she wanted a cosmopolitan. Predictably, she assumed correctly that Alex would actually be the one paying. Alex gave her order to the same bartender who gave him the Amstel Light. Instead of using the money crumpled into his pocket, he set his beer down on the bar and pulled out his wallet. When the beverage was prepared, he exchanged a crisp green hundred dollar bill for one shiny red cosmopolitan. This time he left a two dollar tip out of the ninety-two he got back. He shoved the other ninety dollars into his pocket. He handed Amber her drink, carefully holding the glass by its stem, and took a step back to get a better look at her body. It was nice. She had a slim stomach and even better tits than he first expected. They were nicely displayed in a black half-shirt from Bebe covered by a thin white jacket (also from Bebe). The jacket ended just above a pair of tight, light-blue Guess jeans that curved around her hips perfectly. Alex noted that she dressed well, at least for her age. This meant she came from a family with some money, so he would be better served trying to impress her with charm than wealth. Also, it meant she would respond better to subtle insults than flattery.

Within five minutes, Alex realized he had developed a crush. Despite her looks, Amber was surprisingly smart and interesting. If it turned out she could cook and liked to clean, Alex thought jokingly to himself that he may have to revisit his views on marriage. He had already overruled as frivolous his previous idea that she was "too young for him." Two minutes later, however, she uttered the two words proving she was not perfect.

"Let's dance," she demanded with the same level of confidence Alex projected on his side of the conversation.

"Ah, of course," Alex thought to himself.

Alex wrapped his hand around the side of her stomach: "Dance? Maybe, but with who?"

Amber laughed: "Me, silly guy."

Alex: "Well, in that case, okay. But next time you should wear something sexy."

Amber was confused at his comment but she grabbed his hand and moved closer to him.

Alex had never fully fathomed the point of dancing. Basically you moved your body around in unnatural jerky motions, accomplishing nothing. Not only that, you couldn't keep score, or win, or have a conversation, or drink as much while you were doing it.

His aversion to dancing began around sophomore year in high school at the winter Sadies dance (Wizard of Oz theme) which Leah Brandt took him to. Leah was a junior, a cheerleader, hot and popular. Alex had hoped to make out during the dance and maybe even ask her to "go out." However, she ended up dancing with her girlfriends the whole time while Alex, dressed as a scarecrow, lamely shuffled his feet on the side of the gym with a few of his buddies who faced a similar predicament. As high school moved into college, dancing gained a whole new importance, perhaps even more important than sports. Now, people danced at nearly every party. While the ready availability of alcohol made this bearable, it remained far from optimal. Alex's brain extrapolated this troublesome trend to assume that as life advanced, dancing would become the central focus of being. This turned out to be sort of true, especially in his early twenties at clubs and during his mid-twenties when it felt like there was a wedding nearly every few weeks. Luckily, by his late twenties the trend began to reverse.

In any case, Alex never came to understood people's desire to dance. Still, he was a highly adaptable creature and learned to make lemons into lemonade. As it turned out, if you could get a girl to dance with you, it became much easier to get her to go to bed with you. Meaningful physical contact is one of the primary barriers to sex, and dancing allowed for significant contact. Therefore, dancing was a useful tool and Alex came to embrace it. He also learned that if you wanted to attract a girl in a club, dancing with other male friends in as obnoxious a way as possible was usually quite successful. His "Monkey Dance," which consisted solely of bending over to put one fist on the ground while shaking his ass around and making "ooh-ooh-ahh-ahh" monkey noises was particularly successful. On tamer nights, he stuck to some decent robot moves that always got laughs.

Alex did not plan to do the monkey dance or the robot for Amber, but led her by the hand to the center of the dance floor, elbowing his way through the crowd. He always felt if you are going to dance, you should take the girl to the middle of the floor no matter how crowded it was. When they arrived, *Naughty Girl* by Beyonce was playing. Alex wrapped his arm around Amber's waist and held the small of her back with an open hand while moving the rest of his body appropriately. After a moment he backed off to see if she would reinitiate contact. Five seconds later she danced her way over to him and pressed her body into his, halfway wrapping her legs around one of his.

He knew he had Amber hooked, but he couldn't resist toying with her a bit more. He leaned into her right ear and reinitiated conversation.

Alex: "How long did you spend getting ready tonight?"

Amber: "I don't know. Half an hour maybe. Why?"

Alex: "You have lint between your toes."

Amber: "What?"

Alex: "Your toes. There is lint stuck between your toes. Or it could be something else, but it looks like lint. You really should keep them cleaner."

Amber stopped dancing and looked down at her feet for about five seconds. Not finding any problems, she looked up to see Alex suppressing a smile. She put her arms around his head and jumped into him, kissing him deeply. She tasted very good.

One Britney Spears, one Prince, and one Nine Inch Nails song later, Alex heard the beginnings of one of the few songs he genuinely did like to dance to. Some of the best guitar chords ever combined poured out of the club's sound system. "Dun-na-na-Na...Dun-na-na-Na...Dun-na-na-nun-na-na-nun-na-na-nun-na-na..."

"Oh, what is this crap?" Amber wanted to know, looking a bit confused.

Alex was shocked. "You don't know what this is?" he asked loudly enough to be heard over the music. He quickly answered his own question. "It's Guns N' Roses. *Welcome to the Jungle*. This is one of the greatest songs of all time."

Amber rolled her eyes before responding. "Duh...I know that...I have parents too, you know."

It took Alex a moment to realize what she meant and that she was serious. He had enough of a sense of humor to laugh about it, but he suddenly felt too old to be on the dance floor. "Let's get out of here," he suggested.

Ninety minutes, a thirty-five dollar cab ride, four Amstel Lights, and two of Alex's best attempts at making a cosmopolitan later, Alex was lifting Amber's black Bebe shirt over her head and moving down to suck on her breasts. With Freddy passed out on the living room couch and the bedroom door closed and locked, Alex climbed on top of Amber who was now fully naked. A moment later he rolled off her and ran to the closet to grab a condom. He tore it open while walking back to the bed and began applying it immediately. Speed was of the essence at this point. A lost erection was most likely not an impossible obstacle to overcome, but after six beers he did not care to risk it. He pounced back on top of Amber. The condom covered the head of his cock but did not seem to want to acquire any more real estate. He pushed more forcefully but the effort was counter-productive. Alex had tried to roll it inside out.

"Son of a…God, I hate these things," he muttered more to himself than her. He ripped off the now useless piece of latex and flung it aimlessly across the room with a plan to go back to the closet for another one, his cock already starting to deflate.

Apparently, Amber felt a similar aversion to condoms. "Don't worry, just put it in me. I want to feel you in me," she moaned while reaching down and softly stroking Alex's balls with her fingernails. "Come on, fill me up," she added for good measure.

Alex was sold. Her words reversed any softening trend the condom mishap created, and he slid into her easily. She was tight, but very wet, and Alex felt pure bliss in a way he could never describe. His dick felt like it was at the center of the universe. Even better, for the first few moments it felt like it was the whole universe and that a second big bang might originate from his trusty little meat-puppet right there in his bedroom. As the intensity subsided, he opened his eyes to look down at Amber's perfectly proportioned body and tight skin. He wrapped one arm around her neck and reached down with the other one and wedged his hand between the bed and her ass, his open palm feeling her flesh. He decided twenty-one definitely was not too young. He looked at her face. Amber's eyes were closed, but she reached around him to grab his ass and pull him deeper inside of her. She moaned softly with pleasure, clearly in another place.

Minutes later, they rolled over so Amber was on top. Without him coming out of her, she got into a squatting position and began to bounce up and down on him. The feeling was incredible and Alex felt his balls start to tighten. Not knowing if Amber used any kind of birth control, he told her that he was going to come soon. She sat up and scooted back between his legs.

Years of watching porn had Alex nearly convinced that it was nature's intended course of events for sex to end with the man ejaculating onto the woman's open-mouthed face. Still, he found this to be somewhat demeaning. Alex considered himself to be a gentleman and, therefore, preferred to come on a girl's tits – unless of course he actually disliked the girl. He began focusing on Amber's chest, but she had other ideas. She popped onto her knees and began sucking on him vigorously. Four seconds later, Alex came into her mouth while she continued sucking him and rubbing his balls. It was one of the most riveting orgasms he could remember in a long time. She swallowed as much as possible and then crawled up his chest and wrapped her arms around him, thankfully showing no interest in kissing. Two minutes of cuddling and a three-minute shower later, Alex closed his eyes and fell asleep a very happy man.

The glow began to fade about two days later. While taking a piss before getting ready for work on Monday, he felt a slightly uncomfortable feeling in his dick. Though it was unusual, he did not think much of it. However, the sensation grew worse over the next few days until Alex knew he couldn't ignore it.

By Friday, the situation demanded action. Since he did not have a regular doctor, and had in fact not even been to a doctor in more than seven years, on Friday afternoon Alex called the local Save-On pharmacy and asked for a recommendation for one. They gave him the number of a Dr. Katz, and he made an appointment for early Saturday morning.

Dr. Katz's office was downtown, in the heart the Gaslamp district and ironically only a few blocks from Jimmy Love's. Alex was surprised to find the doctor meet him in the lobby personally. There was no secretary. Dr. Katz was a bit on the short side, about forty years old, and had his hair shaved close to his head, though it was obvious he wouldn't have had much hair on top either way. He was charismatic and Alex felt comfortable with him immediately. On the walls were pictures of the doctor with all sorts of celebrities. Alec Baldwin, Yasmine Bleeth, Joe Montana, Roberto Alomar, Pamela Anderson and Junior Seau were among the few Alex recognized immediately.

They walked into a back office where the doctor directed him to sit on a table covered in butcher paper. He got right to the point.

"So who'd you fuck?" he asked.

Alex couldn't help but smile despite the fact that he found the whole situation anything but comedic.

Alex: "No one important. Especially now."

Dr. Katz: "So can you describe the symptoms?"

Alex: "Basically it just feels uncomfortable every time I piss. Sort of like there is a little more that needs to come out, but it won't."

Dr. Katz: "I see. So is it actually painful or just annoying?"

Alex: "More annoying I guess. It doesn't really hurt, but it doesn't feel right either."

Dr. Katz: "Any discharge?"

Alex: "Nope."

Dr. Katz: "I take it you were not real safe with this girl. Do you have any reason to believe she had any special risk factors?"

Alex: "No, I was stupid. I don't know, I mean she didn't seem like the type to sleep around, but then again, she seemed to know what she was doing."

Dr. Katz: "When was it?"

Alex: "A week ago."

Dr. Katz: "Believe it or not, Sport, a girl who is quick to jump into bed with you may very well do the same with other people. Anyway, let's take a look, but my guess is you may want to withhold judgment for a bit."

The doctor put on a pair of gloves as Alex pulled down his shorts and boxers, promising himself he would be smarter in the future, something along the "never again" routine which had taken place in his mind many times before. Dr. Katz lifted up Alex's penis, took a five-second look, dropped it and then asked Alex to turn around and lean over the table. As he did so, he turned around and applied a small amount of lubrication to the index finger of his right hand.

Alex was immediately confused and concerned. It seemed his celebrity doctor may have had a second agenda. "Whoa Doc, the problem is definitely on this side," he said firmly while pointing emphatically at his crotch. Dr. Katz agreed but told him that most likely what he had was not an STD but a simple infection in the prostate. The only way to tell for sure was to check it out. Alex had never heard of this and was very skeptical, but he was not in a position to argue. He turned around, bent over the table, closed his eyes and tried to think about work. Instead, all he could think was that he was not going to sleep with random chicks anymore.

In conversation with friends, Alex had learned that a lot of guys enjoyed having a girl stick a finger up their ass, but he had never understood this and had rejected it the few times someone had tried. As such, he really had no idea what to expect and feared the worst, but it turned out the docs finger entered him quite easily and didn't cause any significant discomfort. He was trying to relax when he felt a sudden and massively sharp pain in the head of his penis. For about three seconds it felt like a medium-sized iguana was trying to claw its way out his urethra. It came as such a surprise that he actually screamed and looked down to see if his dick was still in one piece. Just as quickly, the doctor withdrew his finger and the pain completely subsided.

He quickly turned around and fought back an instinct to take a swing at the doc, instead grabbing his penis with both hands and bending over slightly. Dr. Katz chose this moment to deliver the first good news of the day. "My guess is you don't have any kind of STD, but just a normal infection. Still, just to be sure, we will take a quick sample and have it sent to the lab."

This made Alex feel better, but only for a second. Before he knew what was going on, the doc had a q-tip in one hand and was grabbing Alex's dick with the other. "Just need to get this in there for a second," he said, still calm as ever. For the second time in less than five minutes Alex had part of his body penetrated for the first time. This go-around was no less unpleasant. It seemed the iguana wanted back in and was being quite violent about it. Alex groaned though clenched teeth. The q-tip came out just as quickly as the doc's finger, but this time the pain took longer to subside.

Alex was very happy to pull his pants up, though he was still partially immobilized from the pain. After regaining his composure, he asked the doctor what the next step was. Dr. Katz reiterated that he felt most likely this was a naturally occurring infection but that he could call in for the results of the test in three days. Until then, he advised not to hold anything against the girl in question. He also wrote a prescription for an antibiotic and told Alex to make sure to finish all of the pills even if the symptoms went away first.

Alex was gathering his things to leave, but the doc had a few other words of advice. "In addition to taking the antibiotics, it would be a good idea to try and drink a fair amount of cranberry juice and also to make sure you have an orgasm at least every two days to keep things flowing in there. Think you can handle that, Sport?" he asked with a wink that Alex found partially charismatic and partially creepy.

"Yeah, I'm pretty sure I can figure that one out," Alex replied.

Dr. Katz told Alex he didn't take insurance for weekend visits and this was fine because Alex didn't know how to use his insurance anyway. Alex gave the doctor six hundred dollar bills and was informed that this would cover the lab fees as well.

"Great, take it easy then," Dr. Katz said and started heading out the door.

Just as they were about to exit the office together, a thought entered Alex's mind. "Hey Doc," he started, "if I did have some type of STD instead of what you think it is, would you have prescribed the same drug?"

Dr. Katz thought for a second and replied that, yes, it would have been the same remedy.

Alex was confused. "If that is the case, couldn't we have skipped the whole jelly finger and q-tip routine and just prescribed the pills?" he asked.

Dr. Katz pondered the question for a minute, tilting his head slightly to the right and narrowing his eyes. "Yeah, I guess we could have," he replied. After a short pause he added one more word – "Interesting." Then he gave Alex a quick military salute before spinning around and walking briskly away, leaving Alex standing alone in the morning sun.

CHAPTER TWENTY-ONE

The Casino Part I
10:57 p.m.

*"You think I like avoiding my wife and
kids to hang out with nineteen-year-old
girls every day?"*
—Beanie, *Old School*

SOMEWHERE IN LA JOLLA, three hundred and thirty-three miles in the past, the seagull that pooped on Alex's foot earlier that day, thereby unknowingly altering the fate of the entire weekend, of all eternity really, settled in and fell asleep for the night. In the middle of the Nevada desert, four men who began their day in San Diego felt as if they were just getting started.

Part of the magic of walking into the casino at the Las Vegas Hard Rock Hotel at any point before about midnight on a Friday or Saturday night was that it provided the rare sensation of entering a great party at exactly the right time. Each of the guys had heard the rumor that casinos pump extra oxygen into the air to keep people gambling longer, but none of them ever knew if it was true. Regardless, there was no doubt that the environment created an instant stimulus and provided a feeling of vitality similar to the effect of certain drugs that were most definitely being consumed by a fair number of the patrons.

Once inside, Mike and Roger found a ten-dollar minimum blackjack table while Gary and Alex chose to hang out in the Center Bar in the middle of the casino for a drink or two. Alex maneuvered his way to the crowded bar and found a spot to order between a twenty-something pretty-boy who looked disturbingly like a younger version of himself and a tall, mostly unattractive woman who was part of mostly unattractive bachelorette party. He had to wait four minutes before being allowed to exchange twelve dollars for two Heinekens. During this time he found out from the woman that the bachelorette party was from Minnesota, her younger sister was the one getting married, she was a logistics manager for Fed-Ex, her sister was a secretary at AIG, and that the group would be in Body English later if they wanted to meet up. Alex lied when asked if he had a condom for a scavenger hunt and also lied and said he did not know where he was going later in the night. Once he had the beers, Alex returned to the perimeter of the bar where Gary was waiting. Alex handed Gary one of the Heinekens and instinctively gave him a small hug, the second time he had done so since they entered the casino. Though only fifteen feet from the bar itself, it was refreshingly less crowded here and the two found a spot where they could rest their arms and beers on the ledge separating the bar from the casino. From this vantage, they could see everything going on in both areas.

Gary: "Thanks man."

Alex: "My pleasure. And I am sorry again about the thing earlier with Blair. Really, I think she is awesome and I want her to like me too. It is tough sometimes being single when all of your friends are getting married and settling down."

Gary: "Yeah, well I can't say I am not still a bit mad about it. That kind of shit is just not okay, Alex. But also I think I understand. It is strange, you know. When I was single I couldn't believe how people just disappeared when they got married. I never thought it would happen to me. But then somehow it does. In a way, people are all kind of the same. We all think we are different somehow, but really we are not. And the thing is, I still don't know how it works. It is just this weird function of marriage that I don't really understand. And then when you have a kid, well forget about it. But it is what it is. Anyway, you will probably have the two clowns we came up here with to yourself for a long time. I can't imagine either of them getting married anytime soon. Also, Doug will probably be divorced soon and maybe Tyler as well. So you should be fine. Anyway, you never know. One of these days you may find yourself ready also."

Alex: "Yeah, maybe. Anyway, it is really good to be out here with you."

Gary: "Hey, check out the hooker at the roulette table with the older dude!"

Alex: "Wow. And some people say money can't buy happiness."

Gary (laughing): "Yeah, seriously. And some people say fake tits are a bad idea."

Alex (now also laughing): "Well, those look like the best that money can buy. One thing I have never understood are these guys who pay for these girls and then take them out like it is a date or something. I mean, while I don't personally have any desire to pay for sex, I don't see anything wrong with it if others do, as long as it is a consensual transaction.

But why you would want to make a clown out of yourself by parading around town with a girl who is obviously only with you because you paid for it just seems strange to me."

Gary: "Maybe some people get more enjoyment out of the companionship of a beautiful girl than from actually banging one."

Alex: "Again, it seems strange to me."

Gary: "So, you have never paid for it?"

Alex: "No. I don't think I could enjoy it if I did. Anyway it's more fun to hunt for it. Not to mention, for some weird reason or another, lately I am super paranoid about diseases and shit, so it just wouldn't be good for me."

Gary: "Yeah, one thing that is nice about being married is you don't have to worry about that stuff anymore."

Alex: "I can appreciate that. Just keep one eye on the milk man."

Gary: "Hmm?"

Alex: "Never mind. So you never think about cheating?"

Gary: "Of course you think about it, but no, it isn't something I would do. Right now we have a good thing and it isn't worth risking it for twenty minutes of fun."

Alex: "The rumor in college was that you were only good for two or three minutes."

Gary (smiling): "Man, one bad performance and you get labeled for life. Anyway, if you were with Sylvia Towers you wouldn't have lasted more than a few minutes either."

Alex: "Yeah, she was incredible. But that is an interesting concept; just think about Bill Buckner."

Gary: "Yeah, something like that. Though I think the rest of his career was pretty darn good, while the rest of my college love life was pretty average."

Alex: "Don't sell yourself short. Two minutes with Sylvia is a decent career in itself."

Gary: "Anyway, I think the other thing about not cheating is that once you have a daughter it brings a tremendous amount of clarity to your life. It helps you understand what is important and also reminds you every single day that life is precious, which I think can be easy to forget otherwise."

Alex: "Yeah, it can be easy to forget. Very easy. That is cool, man."

Gary: "It is. Very."

Sweet Child O'Mine by Guns N' Roses started playing in the casino. Gary and Alex were both facing out toward the gaming tables and staring at the hooker's tits which were bouncing up and down in excitement. Apparently she had hit her number in roulette. The dealer slid a short stack of yellow five-hundred dollar chips in her direction. She took them and gave her date a hug and a peck on the cheek.

Alex, particularly pleased with the music selection, tried to light a cigarette but he had put the wrong end in his mouth and the flame uselessly surrounded the filter without catching. "Piece of shit. Cock and balls!" he cursed nonsensically to no one in particular and threw the now-useless cigarette to the ground, spitting out the tobacco grains which had stuck to his tongue. He pulled another one out of the pack, lit it correctly, took a deep drag, and then offered one to Gary, who declined. Gary then continued the conversation, which they both found more interesting than the significant array of stimuli occurring around them.

Gary: "Don't get me wrong though, it isn't easy. Sometimes you really feel you are missing out on something. That is the tough part. And honestly, coming here with you guys probably doesn't help much. For instance, there is a hot twenty-four-year-old first-year at work who just graduated from UCLA Law who has all but told me that she wants to fuck me even though she knows I am married. So, you see, this kind of thing can be extremely difficult to, um, to process."

Alex: "She wants to boff in the office?"

Gary: "Yeah, she pretty much hinted at that. Which would be incredible, but I can imagine it would be my luck to get caught and lose my job and my wife all at once."

Alex: "That's hot."

Gary: "That is one way to look at it, but really it just causes problems."

Alex: "Maybe you should tell this girl about your really cool buddy Alex."

Gary: "Yeah, no problem. I will mention it. Actually if she went out with you it might help her ease off on me."

Alex: "I would be happy to be of service."

Gary: "Okay, yeah, remind me when we get back. I could do without that kind of distraction. Not cheating is tough, though. In addition to wanting new things, you also start to miss things you used to get. I mean, I basically told you the gist of the situation earlier. But also, for example, even before the porn incident, Blair promised she would give me just as many blowjobs after the baby was born as before. But how many blowjobs do you think I get now?"

Alex: "One first thing in the morning and one as soon as you get home from work every day?"

Gary: "Ha. Ha. Very funny. Anyway you get the point."

Alex: "What about the money situation? Do you fight about it?"

Gary: "Why do you ask?"

Alex: "I am just trying to understand this whole marriage thing a bit more. Lately I sometimes feel I need to change my lifestyle somehow. Maybe become a bit more mature. But the marriage thing is just...confusing for me. It's like, I have everything basically in order and going pretty much the way I want it, and then I am supposed to just take it all and gamble the entirety of my happiness on one gigantic bet that some chick will stay cool. I am not even sure I can stay cool myself."

Gary: "The money thing isn't really a big deal. At first it is weird but you get used to it quickly. After that it is pretty easy to just think of all the money as a mutual asset."

Alex: "I think it would be hard for me to give up that control and not be able to do whatever I wanted with it."

Gary: "You can still basically do what you want, especially with your level of income. But you just have to consider anything big together."

Alex: "So, if you came out here and blew two grand at the tables, how much of a problem would that be?"

Gary: "That would be a pretty fucking big problem actually."

Alex: "Better or worse than the *Barely Legal*?"

Gary (laughing): "Man, you are just a big giant dick. Better I guess, but worse than *Huge Black Cocks*. Seriously, it wouldn't be good. She would probably be cool with losing a few hundred, but anything more than a grand would start to be an issue."

Alex: "And since you are working and she isn't right now, do you get any extra freedom about how the money is spent?"

Gary: "No, it doesn't work that way. Anyway, taking care of Sarah is probably harder than my job. Actually, I am a total hypocrite about it because it drives me crazy when she wants to spend a few hundred on new shoes or a new bag, but it seems totally rational for me to pay two hundred bucks for a round of golf or go to Vegas and blow some cash."

Alex: "I can imagine."

Gary: "Hey, here comes Mo and Curly."

Roger and Mike carved their way through the bar toward Gary and Alex, each with a half-finished Corona in hand. The four clinked bottles and each took a healthy swig. Gary looked back into his Heineken and noticed it was nearly finished. He lifted it up and finished it in two large swallows. "Everyone need another?" he asked and began moving back toward the bar.

"Did you see the fruit on the hook at the roulette table?" Roger asked, momentarily ignoring Gary. Everyone nodded enthusiastically, then confirmed to Gary that he should buy a full round of beers. Guns N' Roses smoothly transitioned to *Break on Through* by The Doors.

Alex: "How did the tables treat you?"

Roger: "Oooh, nicely. I am up about six bills. It was a grand but I bet two hundy on the last hand and had to double down and the bitch pulled a five card twenty-one to beat me."

Alex: "How about you Mikey?"

Mike: "I am down eighty bucks. It was bullshit. The table was super hot but I kept getting shit and busting before the dealer."

Alex: "Sucks. Are you guys ready to hit the club after one more beer?"

Both agreed and Roger started play-fighting with Alex, landing several soft blows to the stomach before Alex spun around behind him and put him in a headlock.

"Can I have a cigarette?" Mike asked Alex bitterly.

"Of course, big guy," Alex answered and released Roger to get out a smoke for Mike. Roger used the opportunity to begin slapping Mike in the face, bobbing and weaving like a featherweight boxer.

CHAPTER TWENTY-TWO

The Club
11:40 p.m.

"No Donny, these men are nihilists.
There's nothing to be afraid of."
—Walter Sobchak, *The Big Lebowski*

DESPITE HAVING A TABLE RESERVED, getting into Body English, the club at the Hard Rock, was no simple task. By the time the group made it across the casino from the Center Bar, a disorganized mass of people had grown in front of the entrance to the club. Because groups of attractive girls were ushered into the club like dust into a Hoover, what remained was a tightly packed group of mostly males with some less attractive girls scattered about.

Because he had a connection with the VIP host of the club, Alex led the group. He paused outside of the ever-increasing mass of hopeful entrants and looked for the best pathway to get to the front. He picked a line of attack that looked less densely concentrated and began to fight his way forward. It took about two minutes to reach the entry point. About halfway there, he noticed the tall girl from the bachelorette party but avoided making eye contact. The proverbial "velvet rope" in this case was simply a black plastic removable barrier like those used at the check-in counters and security lines at the airport. Behind this barrier was a well-lit waiting area occupied solely by the five security people who determined who was let into the club. The crew consisted of three medium-sized white men in their mid-twenties wearing black suits, carrying clipboards and wearing listening devices in their ears; one large black man who was about thirty and who was also wearing a black suit but with only a black tee shirt underneath his jacket; and a slightly older woman wearing a purple pantsuit with expensive looking eyeglasses and high heels. Alex quickly got the attention of one of the young men with the clipboards.

"Good evening," he shouted to the doorman. "I am Alex Reine. We have a table under my name, but I am a friend of Charlie's. Please let him know we are here."

The doorman referenced his clipboard. Once he located Alex's name on it, he smiled, told a group of younger guys to Alex's right to move aside, and waved Alex and his friends in. "How many in your group?" he asked.

"Just these three," Alex said motioning to Gary, Mike and Roger.

The doorman quickly returned the barrier to its place, then turned back to them. "Welcome, gentlemen, please wait here and I will tell Charlie you arrived," he said.

While they waited, Alex realized he had chatted with the black security guy earlier in the year but he could not remember his name. He approached the large man and offered his hand, "Hey, good to see you. How's it going?" Alex asked.

The bouncer shook his hand, engulfing it. "Yo, man, welcome back. Have fun tonight," he said before turning his attention back toward the crowd behind the divider.

Charlie, who was the main VIP host of the club, appeared seemingly out of nowhere. At six feet five inches tall, he had an instant presence. He looked to be roughly the same age as Alex, but he wore his hair slicked back so it was hard to tell. He had an infectious smile and always seemed to be in a hurry. Alex met Charlie a few years before when he came to Vegas with one of his co-workers who was a big gambler. In that case, the casino had sent Charlie up to their hotel suite to escort them into the club through a back entrance. Alex didn't get this kind of treatment on his own, but he maintained enough of a relationship to ensure he had no problems getting into any club in Vegas and he always got a good table when at the Hard Rock.

Charlie (smiling and extending his hand): "Alex! Great to see you, buddy."

Alex (shaking Charlie's hand and passing him a hundred-dollar bill): "Hey Charlie. How's it going?"

Charlie: "Fantastic man. Living the dream."

Alex: "Sweet, man. Good to hear that. You will make sure we have a nice spot inside?"

Charlie: "Always, my friend. Consider it done."

Charlie (to the young guy in the suit): "Patrick, these guys are friends of mine. Make sure they are taken care of."

Patrick: "Of course."

Charlie: "Okay, Alex, have a blast and let me know if you need anything else this weekend."

Alex (patting Charlie on the side of the shoulder): "Thanks, Charlie. Take care."

Patrick: "Gentlemen, please come with me."

With that, Charlie disappeared as if in a magic trick and Patrick led the way toward a hallway at the back of the waiting area. On the way there, he explained to the guys that there would be a crazy amount of hot chicks in the club on this night, but Alex knew from previous experience that the hosts always said this regardless of its accuracy.

The group stopped in front of an elevator and Patrick hit the call button. The elevator arrived promptly. Its doors slid apart to reveal a silver- and black-walled cabin bathed in purple light. Along the left-hand wall was a very attractive woman who appeared to be some blend of French and Persian with tastefully large fake breasts. She was wearing a violet silk evening gown and black high-heeled shoes. The purple lighting illuminated her, reflecting small pieces of glitter embedded in the exposed skin on her shoulders and neck. She looked elegant, slutty and exotic all at once.

Patrick informed the guys that the woman, Alexandra, would take them to their table. Then he turned to Alexandra and let her know that the group was friends with Charlie and would be at table number eleven for the evening. Alex slipped Patrick a ten-dollar bill and then tried to get into the elevator immediately next to Alexandra, but was already boxed out by Mike and Gary. "God, Vegas is great," Roger said to no one in particular.

Alex was still trying to figure out how to maneuver closer to Alexandra when he felt something poking him in his left buttock. Surprised, he looked down over his left shoulder to find a midget in a black tuxedo looking up at him with a disturbed expression. He had his right arm raised and was pointing up at Alex with one little finger, jabbing it angrily.

The midget's face was tightly wedged between Alex's ass and the back wall of the elevator, so Alex stepped away to give him some breathing room. "Sorry, buddy," he said, not sure if a more appropriate response was available.

The midget said nothing, so Alex returned to his previous preoccupation, but by then the doors on the far end of the elevator opened and Alexandra walked out, instructing the group to follow her. Gary led the way, followed by Mike and Roger. It was darker inside the club and it was difficult for everyone to see while their eyes adjusted.

Alex: "Did you see the midget?"

Mike: "Yeah. They are quite trendy right now."

Alex: "Oh."

Alexandra led them through a smallish room which was filled mostly with girls standing around talking with one another while drinking out of champagne glasses. There was a bar on the right-hand side. This led to another, larger room with a bar on the left. The second room opened up to the main part of the club, which consisted of a sunken dance floor about the size of half of a basketball court. The dance floor was surrounded by circular black leather couches which wrapped around black tables. Overhead, a number of white chandeliers hung from the ceiling.

The group continued up to the left and reached another roped-off area, again using the plastic dividers found at the airport. A medium-sized black man in a black suit stood behind the divider. Alexandra said something to him and he opened the divider and smiled, revealing a steady white set of teeth that glowed in the black light permeating the club. Alex recognized him and stepped up to say hello.

Alex: "Hey Randy, good to see you again."

Randy: "All right, my man. Good evening. I am working security in this area so if there is anything at all you need, just let me know."

Alex: "Thanks. I'm Alex, we have met a few times before. As always, we would be happy to hook you up if you introduce someone we may want to talk to."

Randy: "Cool, man. Do you like blondes, brunettes or Asians?"

Alex: "Anything very high quality. Otherwise we are equal opportunity."

Randy (smiling): "Yeah. Yeah. Of course. You got it."

Randy and Alexandra led the group past a few tables set against the wall and directed them into a mezzanine-level booth overlooking the center of the dance floor. Two semicircular black leather couches surrounded a medium-sized black table, creating an oval-shaped sitting area. The benefits of this layout were several. Primarily, the space was distinguished from the main passageway of the VIP area, but only by the height of the couches. This meant it was easy to see everyone in the space and invite them in, but otherwise it was difficult for people to enter. Secondly, there was ample room to sit on the couches for conversation, or to stand in front of the balcony to dance or simply watch the action below.

Alex, who was getting sick of having to tip everyone himself, asked Gary if he could give Alexandra a twenty. Gary, happy to oblige, fished out his wallet and pulled out the bill to give to her. With that, Alexandra let them know that Yvonne, their server, would be with them shortly; then she left with Randy following.

Below, the dance floor was about half full, but the population seemed to be visibly intensifying. Roger and Alex sat on the left side of the booth and Mike and Gary sat on the right side. Alex lit another Dunhill and offered one to Roger. Roger shook his head and informed Alex that he was going to have a Kodiak instead but was dissuaded by Alex's request that they attempt to appear to be somewhat classy for at least another hour or two. He accepted the cigarette and grabbed Alex's out of his hand to use to light his own. Once it was lit, he put it in his mouth with his left hand and used his right to try and mess up Alex's hair. Alex successfully fought off the attack and called Roger a sword-swallower, laughing as he said it and in very good spirits.

On the other side of the booth, Gary and Mike were also in a positive frame of mind. Mike grabbed the drink menu off of the table and perused it quickly, even though he knew in advance what they would be ordering. He noticed the prices were slightly higher than he remembered from the last time he was at the club just over a year or so ago. Bottles of Stolichnaya, which for no particular reason had always been the vodka of choice for the group, were $350 each. Mike noticed that Grey Goose was $425, and a bottle of Cristal champagne could be purchased for $600. Small type at the bottom of the menu informed the reader that a twenty percent service charge would be added automatically.

The music in the club was loud, but not such that you couldn't have a full conversation with the people immediately around you. While Mike was looking at the menu the DJ seamlessly mixed Prince's *Raspberry Beret* into AC/DC's *You Shook Me All Night Long*. Mike was satisfied with the music selection but was slightly annoyed that the songs seemed to switch after only about forty-five seconds each.

Mike: "I think the fucking DJ has ADD or something."

Gary: "Yeah, but at least it isn't all techno. I hate that shit."

Mike: "Totally. Man, you know what, they are not shy here about charging for a cocktail."

Gary: "How much are the bottles?"

Mike: "Stoli is $350 plus twenty percent."

Gary: "Hmm, you aren't kidding. Do you think we will go through two or three?"

Mike: "It depends how much we give away to bitches, but probably three given the way Alex and The Rodge drink."

Gary: "Probably, yeah. Oh well, no one said Vegas was cheap. But I have to give it to Alex, he seems to do quite well at having a good time."

Mike: "No doubt. Yeah, I am pretty fucking happy to be here also. It really is cool that we could all make it out together. We used to have a lot of good times out here, remember?"

Gary: "Yeah, it was a lot of fun, though we sure as hell were not blowing a grand on a few bottles of vodka back in those days."

Mike: "Fuck no. I used to bring two hundy for the whole weekend. It was all about the five-dollar blackjack tables and cramming a bunch of guys into the cheapest hotel room we could find."

Gary: "If we even got a room. Do you remember when I slept in the bathtub at the Imperial Palace?"

Mike: "Yep. I ended up sharing a bed with Fat Freddy that night."

Gary: "Ouch. I am not sure which is worse. Good old Fat Freddy."

Mike: "Was that the trip Alex hooked up with the jouster chick from the show at Excalibur?"

Gary: "I think so. Classic. Of all the showgirls, how do you end up with a jouster? At least she must be good with a pole. Yeah man, those were some good times. This is fun too, though. It is just crazy how things have changed."

Mike: "Totally. We are getting old, dude."

Gary: "Well, yeah, that, but I mean also the way the city is now. Anyway, it is good we have some cash now. I mean if you are in college now, coming to Vegas must be frustrating because you can't really afford anything."

Mike: "I think if you are still in college, you don't even know what you are missing. Anyway, you would basically come to the same club but instead of sitting VIP you would still be waiting in that line outside."

Gary: "God, that would suck."

Mike: "Yep. Anyway, have you talked to Blair yet since we left?"

Gary: "Yeah, I called her while you were in the shower. I told her you are not really getting married but that it is kind of a long story and I would tell her about it when I get back. She didn't sound too happy, but was generally okay. Basically, I am using a lot of political capital on this one, but it will blow over."

Mike: "That's good. I think your lady is pretty cool."

Gary: "She is. I think we both realize you have to let the other person live their own life sometimes. We may not like what the other person wants to do on their own, but as long as they stay respectful of the relationship it should be okay."

Mike: "Cool. It is hard to find a chick that is rational enough to think that way."

Gary: "I know. Anyway, don't get me wrong, I will still get a lot of hell for this, and she probably will use the money I spend as an excuse to either buy a new bag or not let me buy the steak knives I want."

Mike (wondering why steak knives were so important): "Oh."

Gary: "Anyway, enough about home. We're in Vegas. How do I not have a drink yet?"

As if on cue, Yvonne arrived. She was nearly six feet tall, with long brown hair that went about halfway down her back. She had a very nice, thin, tanned body with a flat stomach that was largely visible between a black tied-up shirt and a black skirt. Her face was pretty, but in a Midwestern cute way, with pudgy cheeks that didn't seem to fit her body. Though well suited for her figure, her rather small breasts seemed notable in their contrast with all of the silicone competition present. Nevertheless, she had a genuine smile and everyone immediately approved of her.

She sat on the couch next to Gary, who was on the outside of their section, and put her hand on his knee. Then, careful to make eye contact with everyone, she said, "Welcome to the club, gentlemen. My name is Yvonne and it is my job to make sure you all have a great time tonight. So, is anyone here planning to drink anything this evening?"

This got a laugh from everyone. Gary ordered two bottles of Stolichnaya vodka and asked for sides of cranberry juice, orange juice and soda water. Alex then asked her to also bring six sugar-free Red Bulls which Yvonne informed them would cost an extra six dollars each. Yvonne then asked who would be giving her a credit card to secure the tab. No one moved for a few moments, so Alex dug into his pocket and pulled out his wallet and handed Yvonne his Platinum American Express card.

Yvonne grabbed the card and stood up, flashing her smile again. "Thanks guys, I will be back in a minute," she said, then spun around and disappeared. Instantly replacing her was a short Mexican man who brought over a large silver tray containing ten tumbler-sized plastic glasses, two medium-sized buckets of ice and one slightly larger bucket with a scooper in it. Within two minutes, a different Mexican man arrived with a tray containing six sugar-free Red Bulls and one large carafe each of cranberry juice, orange juice and soda water. The carafes were placed on the table next to the glasses and the buckets of ice. The music changed from 2Pac's *California Love* to Beyonce and Sean Paul's *Baby Boy*. Yvonne returned carrying two opened bottles of Stolichnaya. She bent down in a fluid motion and jammed one of the bottles into one of the medium-sized buckets of ice. Then she sat down next to Alex, her legs set apart just enough to be sexy without ruining her elegant image. Without saying a word, she grabbed four glasses from the tray, set them upright, and filled them about two-thirds full with ice from the larger bucket. Once completed, she asked who wanted a drink. Roger spoke up first, requesting a vodka-cranberry, heavy on the vodka. Yvonne poured similar drinks for the other three and said cheers to everyone.

Once she was gone, Gary stood up and raised his glass toward the middle of the group. "Cheers, dudes," he said. The other three stood and all clinked plastic glasses. Nothing else was said, so they began to drink. A thirty-four second version of *Cowboy* by Kid Rock provided the backdrop. Mike chose to finish his entire glass, so he reached for the now-two-thirds-full bottle of Stolichnaya and began to pour himself a new one.

The boys spent the next forty minutes mingling mostly with each other. One group of three ambitious, but not cute, girls forced their way into their area and sat down. Gary poured them drinks, light on vodka. Mike commented to Roger that "they are basically Fours", and would feel somewhat guilty the next morning when he couldn't remember if he had said it loud enough that they may have overheard. Alex found a way to escort them out of section before they could pour themselves a second round. Alone again, the guys alternated between sitting on the couch and standing against the rail over the dance floor, which was now completely packed. The first bottle was finished.

At half past midnight, a stunningly sexy blonde wearing a pink silk mini-dress which very well may have originally sold as lingerie strolled into the booth on unusually high-heeled black shoes. She immediately raised a long, creamy leg and lowered it between Alex's legs, then sat down on his lap, though really it was more like only his right thigh. She swiveled so both her legs were between his, placing her left arm around his neck and pressing her large left breast against Alex's right shoulder. She introduced herself as Mariah and asked if she could have a drink. Alex asked Roger, who was again sitting next to him, to do him a favor and fix her a nice cocktail. Roger complied.

Across the booth, Mike and Gary ended whatever conversation they were having and did little but stare at this new arrival into their little world. Mike leaned toward Gary and said, "Jumping Jesus, look at that."

Gary: "Ladies and gentlemen, I think we have our first Ten of the night."

Mike: "She looks a bit slutty."

Gary: "What is your point?"

Mike: "Yeah, I guess you are right. Alex is amazing. I don't know how he does it."

Gary: "Fuckin' A."

Mike: "I have to say, sometimes it pisses me off."

Gary: "Jealousy is a female trait, my friend. Be happy for him."

Mike: "Yeah, I guess so...But still. Wow, she is unbelievable."

Gary: "Fuckin' A."

Meanwhile, Alex was getting to know Mariah.

Alex: "How did I get to be so lucky?"

Mariah (lifting one leg up to show her shoes, revealing the entirety of her upper thigh): "Well, my feet were getting tired in these shoes so I needed a place to sit down. Then I saw you and I just really wanted to sit on you."

Alex: "Well, I want you to know I am quite particular about who I let sit on me, so you should feel honored."

Mariah (looking directly at him with large blue eyes): "I do. I think I could sit on you all night if you wanted me to."

Alex: "Don't you think you might start to get a little heavy?"

Mariah: "Well, maybe we could switch and you could be on top for a while."

Alex: "It might look funny to people if I was sitting on your lap."

Mariah: "You're silly. I like you."

Alex: "You are silly too."

Mariah: "You have a nice body, honey."

Alex: "Thanks. I used to be in a Bow-Flex infomercial."

Mariah: "You are an actor?"

Alex: "No, never mind. It was kind of a joke."

Mariah: "So, what do you do for money?"

Alex: "I am a carpenter."

Mariah: "Seriously?"

Alex: "Yeah, you know, just like the Big Guy."

Mariah: "Who?"

Alex: "You know...Jesus."

Mariah (touching his nose with her right index finger): "You're silly."

Alex: "No, I am just kidding, I work in finance."

Mariah: "So are you some kind of agent?"

Alex: "Umm…Something like that."

Mariah (nodding to the rest of the group with her head): "That's really cool. And are these your buddies?"

Alex: "Yeah, these are my best friends, mostly from college. What about you, are you here alone?"

Mariah: "No, I am with you."

Alex: "Good point."

Mariah: "So, what plans do you and your buddies have for the rest of the night?"

Alex: "Nothing too defined. Party here for a while and then see what sounds good."

Mariah: "Well, I have an idea for you. I am going to be at Spearmint Rhino later. You should definitely come see me."

Alex: "You are working there?"

Mariah: "Yep. I will be there until five. I really hope you can join me."

Alex (rapidly losing interest): "So you are a stripper?"

Mariah: "Yes, sweetheart."

Alex (sitting up to raise her off of him): "Okay, I'll keep it in mind, thanks."

Mariah stood up and straightened her outfit, then gave Alex a kiss on the cheek and waved to the other guys before walking toward the exit. Alex, who along with the rest of the group was now more than a little buzzed, noticed she entered one of the other booths across the walkway and sat on someone's lap.

Gary: "What was that all about?"

Alex: "It turns out she is a stripper. She said she wants me to meet her at the club later, but I think she just comes here to get a few free drinks and try to get people who look like they can spend some money to go over and buy dances from her later."

Gary: "Interesting strategy."

Mike: "Which club?"

Alex: "The Rhino."

Mike: "Maybe we should go there after this."

Alex: "Nah, I have no desire to go to a strip club tonight, so whatever. But you are right, it probably is a good strategy. You can't blame someone for doing some marketing."

Gary: "Yeah, whatever. But damn, she was fucking hot."

Alex: "No doubt about that. That's one interesting thing about Vegas. It keeps getting better and better, but at the same time it is changing in a weird way."

Gary: "How do you mean?"

Alex: "Well, just think about when we used to come out here. First of all, look around at what the chicks are wearing now. Also, think about it; I just had a stripper sit down in my lap in our booth at the club. That's a bit strange, right? I don't think it would have happened even a few years ago."

Don't Cha by the Pussycat Dolls began to play.

Alex (waving his hand around at nothing): "Here is another great example. Basically the Pussycat Dolls are the next generation of the Spice Girls, right? But the Spice Girls were kind of cute and nice while the Pussycat Dolls are simply in your face about sex and money."

Gary: "I don't know if that's true. What did the Spice Girl's song say? If you want to be my lover, you've got to get with my friends. I mean, that's pretty hard core, don't cha think?"

Alex: "I don't think they literally meant you had to boff their friends before they would sleep with you."

Mike: "That is what it sounded like to me."

Alex: "I don't think so, dude."

Everyone took a moment to contemplate this while listening to the song.

"See, I don't care, but I don't think she's gonna want to share ...

Oooohh. Don't cha wish your girlfriend was hot like me?

Don't cha wish your girlfriend was a freak like me?"

Gary: "I liked that blonde Spice Girl."

Roger (to Gary): "You are weird."

Roger (to Alex): "So, the new chicks are hotter. Big deal. Why are you complaining about it?"

Because it was too loud for all four of them to hold a conversation together, Roger moved back to the railing overlooking the dance floor without waiting for an answer.

Alex: "I am not complaining about it, but it is interesting. Everything is more material now than it used to be. Everything centers on money and sex. I mean think about the fact that we are buying four-hundred-dollar bottles of vodka. For that, they send a hot girl over to serve it to us and then the chicks in the club know you have money so they want to drink with you."

Gary: "I think they come to drink with us because they know we will give them free drinks, not because they necessarily want to fuck you."

Mike: "Ninety-nine percent of girls are whores in one way or another. Don't ever forget that."

With that, Mike stepped away to the table to add a top-per of vodka to his half-full drink and then joined Roger on the railing.

Gary: "Actually, this city is set up well for girls. They can pretty much drink for free off of chumps like us who are paying a fortune. Then, if they do want to go home with someone, they can pick whatever guy they want as long as they are decent looking themselves. Meanwhile, we are paying hundreds of dollars and will probably go home alone."

Alex: "I thought you weren't interested."

Gary: "That isn't what I meant. I am just trying to make a point."

Alex: "Anyway, Chief, you aren't going home alone because either Roger or I will likely be sharing a bed with you."

Gary: "Oh yeah. Sweet, I almost forgot."

Alex (laughing): "Anyway, you are starting to sound like Mike."

Gary: "Yeah, maybe. Sorry."

Alex: "My original point was just that society is becoming more materialistic than it was. Have you noticed almost every other table here bought Grey Goose? There is just no way a bottle of Grey Goose can be worth fifty dollars or whatever more than Stoli. I would argue it isn't even as good at the same price, but aside from that, the only reason to buy it is to show that you are a baller and have money. People don't even buy houses now based on where they want to live; they'll choose one they think will appreciate more, or even just to flip. Also, look at shit like that Sweet Sixteen show on MTV. It's fucking disgusting, but these kids are all about how much cash you have. I saw one where this high school chick had a VIP section at her own birthday party."

Gary: "Yeah, I happened to see that one. Sarah likes that show. That was gross."

Alex: "You let Sarah watch MTV?"

Gary: "Yeah, just not the dating shows like *Next* or *Date My Mom*. But even those she tries to TiVo."

Alex: "Your three-year-old knows how to TiVo?"

Gary: "Yeah, they are smart little fuckers. You have to watch them all the time."

Alex: "Also, basically every rap song is about how much money the person has and how many chicks he is nailing. Since there really isn't any new rock music anymore, rap is now the main pop culture. I am the whitest guy around and ninety percent of the songs I download lately are rap or hip-hop."

Gary: "I think rappers have always been singing about how much money they have and how many chicks they are nailing. Rock was basically the same thing if you really think about it."

Alex: "It's worse now. Maybe it's all cyclical and this is what it was like in the eighties. Probably it will reverse again at some point, but I just feel everything is moving in a direction of the idea that money is the only important thing."

Gary: "Kind of a scary idea when you have a small daughter."

Alex: "Totally. It is something I have been thinking about a lot lately. In my mind I call it the Paris Hilton effect. Sometimes I think Paris fucked up society."

Gary: "How's that?"

Alex: "She is probably the biggest celebrity in America right now, right? But the thing is, she doesn't actually do anything that adds any value. She isn't a movie star. She isn't an athlete. She isn't really even a model. Basically she is the

daughter of rich people with a recognizable last name who
parties a lot. But she has become bigger than all those people
who do something just by making herself synonymous with
the image of glamour and money."

Gary: "That's hot!"

Alex: "Exactly."

Gary: "Didn't she just release an album?"

Alex: "Do you know anyone who bought it?"

Gary: "Good point. Well, she is sort of a movie star if you
think about it."

Alex (laughing quickly, then becoming serious again):
"Okay, true. Even that supports the point though. She has
become even more famous because it turns out she is something of a slut. But more than anything, she made it fashionable for money and sex to be what people respect and strive
for above all else. The money *itself* is the only goal now, not
how you get it."

Gary: "I thought you always believed in the free market
and that people should earn what they were worth based on
the demand?"

Alex: "Yeah, I do. And this really confuses me. On one
hand, I think she is the biggest genius there is. I mean, she
gets millions of dollars just for partying and showing up at
places. Basically she has turned herself into a brand. So I give
her credit for that, and she deserves every penny she makes.
But maybe we should question where our society is headed if
this is what we idolize. Money is and should be great, but not
just to show off how much you have. I think part of it is also
due to all these new Russian billionaires who are so in your
face about how much money they have. I think previous rich
people used to be more discrete about it, at least from main-
stream society. Anyway, I think it will continue to get worse

until we have a major recession, but it doesn't seem that will happen anytime soon."

Gary: "I don't believe that you, of all people, are worried that there is too much materialism. I thought you believed greed was the root of progress."

Alex: "I still do. Maybe there just needs to be something else that goes along with it."

Gary: "Maybe you are just getting drunk."

Alex: "Maybe. I think we are going to need another bottle."

When one o'clock arrived, each of the guys, high on a mixture of Red Bull, vodka, and nicotine and feeding from the energy of the club, found themselves armed with a strong sense of optimism and a high level of alertness.

At 1:05 a.m., Alex poured himself a new drink and informed the group that he was going to take a lap around the club. Roger decided to join, leaving Mike and Gary alone in the booth. With Roger and Alex gone, the space seemed awkwardly empty when compared to the packed surroundings of the rest of the club. Even the VIP area was now relatively full with people. Regardless, within a few minutes, Randy arrived with two girls and suggested to Mike and Gary that they may want to meet them.

The girls, both with medium-length blonde hair, looked to be around thirty years old, but were still attractive. Both wore designer jeans and expensive-looking shirts, in contrast to the more naked approach most of the younger girls in the club favored.

One sat next to Mike and the other stepped over Gary's legs to sit on the other side of him, closer to where she could look down on the dance floor. Gary asked the girls what they wanted to drink. At their request, he poured each a vodka-cranberry with a splash of Red Bull, leaving about three inches of liquid remaining in the second bottle. Mike, suddenly feeling a lot less cheap, waved Yvonne down and ordered a third bottle of Stolichnaya and three more Red Bulls.

Their inhibitions drowned by alcohol, each of the newly introduced couples rapidly engaged in conversation. It took Mike about three minutes to develop a crush on the one he was paired up with, Kristen. He found out from her that both of the girls were thirty-two, lived in LA, and were college friends from the University of Arizona. Kristen was a pharmaceutical sales representative and Ashley, her friend, was an elementary school teacher. They were in town for a quick girl's weekend and were staying at the Venetian.

Mike recounted some of the humorous anecdotes from the drive out, though he swapped Roger into his own role for the outhouse story. He was pleased to get several laughs, especially from his imitation of the Jeff Kent cop, and he was impressed that Kristen knew who Jeff Kent was. She also seemed genuinely interested to hear about the house he was buying in Del Mar, which Mike greatly enjoyed talking about. Happy that Alex had instigated the trip, Mike took inventory of how drunk he was. He decided he could afford to down another few drinks but realized he needed to be a bit careful. He poured himself a rather weak version of what Kristen was drinking and also made her a new one.

Gary also took the opportunity to fix fresh drinks for Ashley and himself. Yvonne returned with a new bottle of Stolichnaya and a new bucket of ice. One of the Mexicans followed her and swapped out several of the dirty glasses for fresh ones and also brought a new carafe of cranberry juice.

Yvonne sat down briefly next to Gary and asked how everything was going. Mike and Gary assured her things were very well and she sensed her presence was not desired at the table at the moment so she got up to leave. Before she did, she looked down to the dance floor and said, "It looks like your buddies are having a good time also."

Gary, Mike, Kristen and Ashley all leaned toward the balcony and surveyed the scene. The dance floor was generally packed, but it did not take long to find Alex in his yellow sweater. There was a bit of space around him and he was doing his monkey dance, bent over, supporting himself with one fist on the floor, and waving his ass around wildly. Though it could not be heard at this distance, the puckered shape of Alex's lips suggested he was complementing the dance with "ooh-ooh, aah-aah" monkey noises. Behind him, an attractive girl in a green mini-dress was trying to rub against him, but was struggling to follow because his butt was moving about unpredictably. In front of him, Roger was engaging in an aggressive version of the white-man's shuffle, pausing periodically to grind against a slightly overweight Asian girl who was obviously drunk. The Asian girl was so engaged with Roger that she appeared oblivious to Alex's antics, which were the main attraction for everyone else within ten feet of them.

Gary turned towards Mike and Kristen with a large grin on his face. "I haven't seen the monkey dance in years. Alex must be wasted," he shouted across the booth. Then, he and Ashley repositioned themselves so they could more comfortably watch the action below.

The next time Gary looked at his watch, he couldn't believe it was already 2:30 in the morning. It turned out he had a lot in common with Ashley, including being married and having a three-year-old daughter. Ashley also was concerned about getting her daughter into the best pre-school and how to pay for the twenty thousand or so in tuition once kindergarten and elementary school started. Her descriptions about the politics within the public school she taught at were genuinely interesting to Gary who was still a believer in public schools over private. Additionally, Ashley's husband was also a lawyer so she understood the demands of his job.

Gary realized it was the first time he had had a decent conversation alone with a woman other than his wife in over a year and probably the first time he had spent this much time alone with another woman while drinking since his wedding. He was bemused to realize he genuinely liked this person he just met in a club in Vegas, of all places. He had no ambitions of cheating on Blair when he learned he was going to Vegas, and now he found himself wondering if he wanted to now. Ashley had not given any direct signs she would be interested, but she was very flirtatious and demonstrated several of what Alex annoyingly and repeatedly referred to as "Indications of Interest." Clearly there was some connection. Perhaps because of the alcohol, he also began to see her as sexier than when she first arrived. It seemed her shirt had been repositioned to reveal more of the top of her breasts than before.

It took about ten minutes after the idea first came into his mind for Gary to realize that as much as he liked this new woman, and as much as he was physically attracted to her, he did not want to sleep with her and had absolutely no interest in attempting any kind of actual relationship. Still involved in their conversation, and still very much enjoying it, Gary did not have time to think much about his realization, but somewhere he registered an initial feeling of disappointment and regret. Happily, it was fleeting and quickly began morphing into something like relief, but closer to satisfaction or pleasure.

It felt good not just to think, but to know, that he was secure in his marriage and still valued it as much or more than ever.

The notion was reinforced when he took a break from the conversation to check out the group at the table next to them. While the other table had been occupied since just after midnight, Gary had not even made the effort to acknowledge them until now. It consisted of two rather ugly-looking Persian men in their mid-thirties and six attractive white girls in their early twenties. On the table were the remnants of one bottle of Grey Goose and four bottles of Cristal. Three of the girls were sitting by the guys and looked utterly bored. The other three were dancing against the railing and were, seemingly, thoroughly enjoying themselves. Somehow in Gary's mind it all looked quite pathetic.

He wondered, given the miscommunications of the weekend, what the chances were of Blair still allowing him to buy the steak knives he had his eye on. He had a feeling there was a new Gucci bag in her future. But, despite these petty desires, he knew he had something beautiful and something real and felt good about it. He refilled his glass with ice and poured two ounces of Stolichnaya into it, his eyes happily lingering on the ass of one of the dancing girls in the next booth.

Out on the dance floor there was no longer any sign of Alex or Roger. Gary excused himself from Ashley for a moment and repositioned himself to the other side of the booth next to Mike. He put his arm around Mike and said hello again to Kristen.

Gary: "How is it going over here?"

Mike: "Great. She is super-cool. How about you?"

Gary: "Really good, man. I am having a lot of fun. It is a bummer for you that these two are married."

Mike: "What are you talking about?"

Gary: "Check the rings, dude. You didn't notice?"

Mike quickly turned his head back toward Kristen and
checked out her left hand which was holding a plastic glass
filled with vodka and cranberry juice. She started to talk to
Ashley who had moved to her other side.

Mike: "Holy shit-show! You have got to be fucking
kidding me."

Gary: "You didn't realize it?"

Mike: "No. I guess I didn't even think to look.
Unfuckingbelievable. I really thought I was getting somewhere."

Gary: "Sorry, dude."

Mike turned back toward the girls: "So Kristen, how long
have you been married?" he asked loudly.

Kristen: "Um…I guess it has been about four years."

There was a brief silence filled only by the loudness of
the club and *Milkshake* by Kelis. Then Mike said that he
needed to use the bathroom and stood and left the booth.
Kristen and Ashley conferred for a minute while Gary sat
awkwardly. Then Ashley let Gary know that they needed to
get going and told him she had really enjoyed meeting him.
He stood and gave her a hug and she kissed his cheek. Then
they were gone. He sat again, now alone. Unsure what to do
and surprised with the sudden turn the night had taken, he
reached to the table and stole a Dunhill out of the pack Alex
had left there. He checked his watch, lit the cigarette, and
then checked on the Persian's table where Yvonne was bringing yet another bottle of Cristal. It was quickly consumed by
the girls who clearly were in no shape to tell the difference
between quality French champagne and Martinelli's sparkling
apple cider. Gary laughed to himself, took a drag, sat back,
exhaled and crossed his legs contentedly. A smile lingered on
his face.

It turned out he was not alone long. By the time he finished his smoke, Alex and Roger came bouncing into the booth, both dancing along to Duran Duran's *Reflex*. Gary's smile widened as it was clear his two buddies were quite drunk and it appeared likely that Alex, who immediately began eyeing the girls in the Persian's booth, might break into some of his robot moves at any moment. Instead he sat next to Gary, reached to the table for one of his Dunhills, lit it, and put his arm around Gary.

Alex: "Where is Mr. Happy Face?"

Gary: "He got a bit bent out of shape when he realized the girl he was ramping all night is married."

Alex: "Ah, bummer. I hate it when that happens. Where did he go?"

Gary: "He said to the bathroom but he went the wrong way. Where were you two?"

Alex: "At another table on the other side. Funny story. I will tell you later."

Roger leaned in, slurring his words heavily: "Alex was ramping the super hot blonde in the green dress and I was getting sloppy with some Asian chick."

Gary: "Yeah, I noticed that. I think the whole club did. So where are they? Do you want to bring them over here?"

Alex: "Nah, it is not important. I'd rather hang with you for the rest of the night."

Gary: "Another bottle of booze?"

Alex: "No. Fuck it, dudes. Let's go roll some dice."

CHAPTER TWENTY-THREE

The Casino Part II
3:05 a.m.

*"I'm not only legitimate, but running
a casino. And that's like selling people
dreams for cash."*
—Ace Rothstein, *Casino*

ONCE THE DECISION HAD BEEN made to gamble, there seemed little reason to spend even a minute longer in the club. Gary and Roger took an unsuccessful lap looking for Mike, and Alex asked Yvonne to bring a check. Alex left the charge on his Platinum Amex, signing away $1,324 for the beverages consumed and service charge. There was a quick debate about the acceptability of leaving without finding Mike first, but everyone agreed he was a big boy and he should be able to find them easily in the casino. To ease his conscience, Alex sent a text to Mike's mobile phone that read, "Craps. Hard rock. Join us. Btw, u r a little jizz mopper."

Alex had hoped to apologize to the midget on the way out for his previous behavior, which he now sensed was somehow inappropriate, but the little guy was nowhere to be found.

Because of the relative hassle entering the club, the exit was surprisingly immediate, and the three found themselves thrust back into the perimeter of the casino. Although music was playing, currently *Living on a Prayer* by Bon Jovi, it was decisively quieter outside of the club. Each of the three noticed a slight echoing sensation inside their heads, as if they were in a cave and a water pump was active somewhere in the distance. It was also a lot lighter. The small group gave themselves about thirty seconds to adjust before advancing further to find a suitable craps table. Gary, who somewhere in the last thirty minutes had crossed over the threshold from drunk to very drunk, failed to notice the one step down into the casino, lost his balance and fell to the floor, his head narrowly missing the side of a Wheel of Fortune slot machine. He popped himself back up and held a pose like Mary Lou Retton after her famous vault. Alex and Roger clapped for him. Then Roger jumped on his back and gave him a bear hug.

The population of the casino was notably thinner than earlier in the night, but there was still a good crowd, and the energy level remained high enough to motivate them. The Red Bull probably helped.

The first craps table they encountered looked appealing. It was about two-thirds full and seemed to have good energy as the participants were applauding the previous roll enthusiastically. Alex leaned in and noticed it was a $10 minimum table, which was good because he knew this was what Gary preferred to bet. Also, there was a space on the corner big enough for the three of them to squeeze in. Alex stepped toward the opening and had his wallet halfway out of his pants when he noticed another table on the other side of the pit. This one had only six players, two middle-aged Italian-looking men on one side and four girls who Alex remembered vaguely from the dance floor in the club on the other

side. Both of the Italian guys were wearing white pants with
white shoes and designer shirts complemented by gold
watches and gold cross chains. Each of the girls wore high
heels and short brightly colored dresses. One was slightly
overweight, but all were highly attractive.

Alex instinctively veered right and began making his way
toward the other table. Roger and Gary followed, none of
them managing to walk in exactly a straight line. When they
arrived, Alex saw it was a $25 minimum. He checked the
chip racks on the table and noted with interest that each of
the girls had well over a thousand dollars worth of chips in
front of them. This was quite rare, especially as they appeared
to be in their mid-twenties. He was intrigued.

Roger and Gary caught up. Alex immediately began selling the wisdom of playing at this table to Gary, expecting it
to be difficult to persuade him to play for higher stakes.
Perhaps because of the alcohol, it was not. Before Alex could
really get started, Gary patted him on the shoulder, walked
past him, and sidled up next to the girl at the end of the row.
Gary removed his wallet from his pants and offered four hundred-dollar bills to the dealer to exchange for chips. Roger
and Alex exchanged glances and shrugged their shoulders,
a bemused grin on both of their faces. By the time they could
join him at the table, Gary already had $25 on the pass line,
had his arm around one of the girl's shoulders, and had said
something funny enough to get all of them laughing.

Alex moved to stand next to Gary, and Roger positioned
himself next to Alex. Both took out $500 and bought twenty
$25 chips. Unlike every other casino, which used green for
the $25 chips, the Hard Rock used purple. Alex inspected his
and noticed the one on top was a commemorative chip featuring Madonna. He put it in his pocket for good luck and
placed the remaining chips in the rack in front of him. While

doing so, Gary introduced his friends to the girls who all smiled and offered their names. From left to right, they were Gina, Kelly, Natasha and Berlin. Alex repeated the names several times in his mind, hoping to remember them for future use, then patted Gary on the back, remembering how good of a wingman he had been back in his single days. He was quite pleased to see his friend having so much fun.

During the introductions, one of the Italians rolled the dice and hit his point. The girls all raised their hands above their heads in appreciation and began clapping as the dealer paid out their bets as well as Gary's. Gary moved behind them to offer each a high five, which the girls reciprocated while laughing.

Gary returned to his spot and placed another chip on the pass line. Each of the girls bet two chips, as did Alex and Roger. The Italian rolled again and everyone watched as the dice tumbled toward their side of the table. The dealer announced, "Eleven. Pay the line."

The stickman collected the dice to slide back to the Italian and the other dealer paid out the pass line bets. Everyone placed the same bet.

Hoping to establish more of a connection with the girls, Alex decided this was an opportune time to tell his standard ice-breaking joke. He motioned for the girls to lean closer and began:

"So, there are two muffins in an oven . . .

One muffin turns to the other muffin and says, "Holy shit! It is hot in here!"

Then the other muffin turns to the first one and says, "Holy shit!...A talking muffin!"

The two closest girls, Natasha and Berlin, laughed loudly. Berlin reached across Gary and patted Alex on the shoulder to tell him how funny he was. The other two, Gina and Kelly, found the joke to be stupid and looked at each other, exchanging the universal female "whatever" face. Gary, who had heard this joke many times before, had a similar reaction.

The moment was broken with another role of the dice, this time a seven and another winner. This made everyone happy. Gary stepped back to again slap hands with the girls.

Alex, watching Gary go through his high-five routine again, was again overcome with a surge of happiness. Having already had a very fun night, he felt certain that it would only get better. In recent months, Alex had begun to feel increasing anxiety about getting older, but at that moment he felt he would live forever, and live well at that. Convinced that his yellow sweater represented the height of fashion, he felt not only healthy but extremely attractive. As Gary returned to offer him a high five Alex realized he was beginning to tear up from joy and was at risk of crying. This was not the impression he wanted to make on the girls and he turned away from the table, pretending to cough as soon as he slapped Gary's hand.

The Italian hit one more point, and then crapped out. Each of the girls rolled with mediocre results. Alex managed to win $200 anyway because he had a superstition that you should always bet the most when the girl with the biggest tits at the table had the dice. It proved a successful strategy this time, as well-endowed Natasha hit two points, including a high-paying four.

Making things even better, by the time the dice got to Gary, the cocktail waitress returned with three glasses of Stolichnaya on ice for the boys and four cosmopolitans for the girls. Roger, a notorious over-tipper when he was winning, gave the waitress a purple chip and told her to return quickly.

Gary rolled a five to establish a point and everyone placed double odds behind their pass line bets. His next few rolls were meaningless and there was a lull in the conversation. "I wanna come!" Alex announced loudly, and he and Roger placed $25 come bets as well. The girls again had a split opinion on his humor and were content with their original bets, which Alex noticed had increased to $100 on the pass line with $200 odds.

Roger: "Where the fuck is Mike? I can't believe he is missing this."

Alex: "I don't know. It is disturbing. I mean, how often do we all get out here together and he goes and gets all morose just because some broad is married. I mean, what the fuck?"

Gary: "Take it easy on the guy. He has been cool, he just gets bummed out sometimes. Anyway, maybe he will meet up with us soon. Perhaps he just had another emergency run to the toilette. Maybe you can trap him in the shitter again, or do it to some poor innocent woman again."

Alex was concerned about how the girls would perceive Gary's drunken comments, but they appeared to be ignoring the whole conversation and were focused on the dice. Gary rolled again, this time a meaningless three. Alex checked his phone to see if there was any response from Mike. Indeed, there was a new text. It read, "Okay. Have fun. Don't w8 for me. C u at Palms." Alex flipped his phone shut and put it back in his pocket.

Alex: "Nope, he is done for the night. It is sad. Kind of pisses me off also."

Roger: "Relax, he will be with us all day and night tomorrow. Let's have some fun and hit some numbers."

Alex: "I guess so. I wonder if we pissed him off somehow. I can't see how."

Gary: "No, I was with him. He was just upset about the girl. He isn't like you who just ramps everyone in sight and then doesn't care if anything comes of it."

Alex again checked the girls, hoping his chances were not thoroughly destroyed by Gary's unfiltered lips, but they were still involved in their own conversation and not paying the least bit of attention until Gary picked up the dice again. When he did, he held them in his right hand and started performing a ridiculous dance to the music. Appropriately, the casino was now playing *Wannabe* by the Spice Girls.

Gary: "Check it out Alex, it's your song. Give me a quick monkey-noise."

Alex: "I don't think so, dude."

Gary: "Come on. Just do it. One time."

Alex looked at Gary, who was dancing alone while holding the one hand with the dice above the table to keep the dealers happy, and he broke out in a smile. He reminded himself that he came to have a good time with his buddies and shouldn't care what the girls thought. He put his hand on his head and began moving it back and forth like a pigeon, puckered his lips, then let out a loud, "Ooh-ooh, aah-aah!."

With that, Gary threw the dice to the far end of the table where the Italians were watching, entirely unamused with the antics of the shooter and his friend. The dice settled under the Italians, a three and a two. "Five, front line winner," the dealer announced.

With this, Alex did another "Ooh-ooh, aah-aah" and gave Gary a hug. Before turning to give Roger a high five, he glanced at the girls. To his satisfaction, all were smiling and two of them had a look in their eye that, despite his drunkenness, he understood well. Unfortunately, he could no longer remember any of their names. One of them might have been Moscow? But this wouldn't matter anyway. The dealer decided to start paying them with black $100 chips instead of the purple ones, and he scooped up his winnings.

Gary rolled a seven on the come-out role but couldn't hit his next point. Alex disappointed the group by making a six on his first roll and immediately crapping out. He apologized and then lit a cigarette to try and bring luck back to the table, another one of his stupid superstitions. It worked to some extent as Roger was able to hit two points before crapping out and the first Italian managed the same, including another four. The waitress returned with another round of Stolis. This time only two of the girls took new cosmos.

No matter how drunk he was, Alex had an uncanny ability to sum the value of a stack of casino chips very accurately and very quickly, earning him the nickname Rain Man some years ago. He scanned the racks and was pleased to see that he and Roger were now up over $700 and even Gary was up $525.

On the far side of the table, the Italians were conversing about something before the come out roll, and Alex noted that they increased their line bet to $500. Inspired, he and Roger increased theirs to $200. Gary, who already had a $50 bet placed, took a large pull of Stoli from his glass and added another six purple chips to his bet. The Italian rolled a nine.

Both of the Italians placed double odds, as did the girls. For some reason, Alex was intimidated by the nine and decided only to lay single odds. Gary, who historically rarely had more than $100 on the table, followed Alex's lead. Roger placed the full double odds.

"Let's get right back on that nine," Roger exclaimed, nearly shouting.

Alex looked to his right and saw Gary had his arm around the closest girl again, a silly nervous grin on his face. Alex began fumbling for a new cigarette when he realized everyone was waiting for him. Confused, he looked around trying to figure out what was the problem. One of the girls pointed to the other end of the table at the Italians.

The man with the dice in his hand said to Alex in heavily accented English, "Za monkey. Do za monkey, per favor."

Alex put the cigarettes back in his pocket and stepped back from the table. He put one fist down to the floor and wiggled his butt back and forth, emitting a loud "Ooohhh-oohh, aaahh-aaahh," in the process. For good measure, he stood back up, placed a hand on top of his head and issued a few more monkey noises.

The Italian threw the dice. No one was the least bit surprised when another nine appeared. "Atta boy! Right back on that nine," Roger exclaimed loudly. The girls were all high-fiving each other and two of them came over to give Alex a high five as well.

The Italians, in imitation of the girls, awkwardly gave each other a high five and one of them said to Alex, "Yes. The monkey. Bravo, Monkey-man! Very good American monkey!"

This proved enormously funny to the girls, and to Gary as well. Alex was unsure how to react, but remained in good spirits, especially when the dealer placed five black chips in front of him.

The second nine netted the Italians a $2,000 profit each. They conferred briefly with each other and decided to call it a night. Roger was miffed, considering it bad etiquette and bad luck to quit in the middle of a successful roll. He also did not appreciate the three-minute lull in the action which took place while the dealers counted up the Italians' chips and cashed them out for one-inch-tall stacks of yellow chips and some change. Roger was further vexed by the Italians' failure to leave any kind of tip for the dealers, but they happily scurried away from the table, lighting cigarettes and heading toward the cashier's cage. It was now just past 4:30 am.

The dice were passed to the girls, who reduced their opening bets back down to $100 and again managed mediocre results. The table managed to break about even during their rolls, except for Roger and Alex who lost a few hundred dollars on hard way bets made for themselves, the shooters and the dealers.

Alex did a quick scan of everyone's chips. He noted that Roger was up $950, he was up $1,100 and Gary was up $900. He did not know how much the girls had started with, but a summation of their chips showed they now each had over $3,500 in front of them.

Apparently the girls were also doing some mental accounting and were feeling content with their good fortune. Berlin told the guys that they were going to quit gambling for the night but hoped they would join them for a drink in the Center Bar, even offering to pay for the first round. Gary thought it was a good idea for two reasons. First, he was already beginning to understand that coming home with several hundred dollars in extra cash might help smooth things over with Blair. Second, he was having a very good time talking with the girls who seemed in tune with his sense of humor.

But neither Gary nor Berlin appreciated the impossibility of removing an intoxicated Alex and/or Roger from a dice table when they were doing well, at least not before sunrise. Alex attempted to persuade the girls to stay for at least Gary's roll by promising to do the monkey noise before every throw. The girls huddled quickly and decided even if they lost it would be worth the entertainment value alone to stick around for one more roll.

The stickman slid Gary the dice just as the cocktail waitress arrived with three more Stolis. Gary and Alex each exchanged a red $5 chip for theirs and Roger gave her another purple chip. Starting to feel the effects of the booze, Gary and Alex elected to switch the next order to grapefruit juice while Roger opted for a Bud Light. Alex used the opportunity to light another cigarette for good luck.

Gary's first roll was a three, prompting a groan from the table and incurring a $100 loss for all of its participants. He followed it up with a twelve, yielding the same result. Two of the girls, Natasha and Gina, began to urge the others to quit now. Alex assured them the best rolls often started this way and increased his pass line bet to $200 to show his confidence. The girls agreed to one more try and Gary rolled a five to establish a point.

Alex again backed his $200 bet with single odds and the rest of the table, beginning to lack confidence, did the same. Alex and Roger immediately began making $50 come bets with double odds and in no time had the lower half of the board covered with money on the four, five and six. As promised, Alex was providing a jungle soundtrack with every roll. One of the dealers made a derogatory comment about it, but the remaining dealers were encouraging, perhaps influenced by the few hundred dollars Alex and Roger had already tipped.

Between "ooh-ooh-aah-aahs," Gary proceeded to roll three tens in a row, a difficult feat which helped nobody. For Roger, it was painful to see the possible winnings left behind, and he placed a $50 ten for good measure.

The next roll was a four, netting Roger and Alex a quick $250, which they each immediately deposited back on $25 hard ways, including the six and eight for the dealers. Alex took the final drag of his Dunhill, then puffed up his cheeks and let out an enthusiastic "ooh-ooh-aah-aah." Gary responded with double threes and the dealer called out the six the hard way. "Ohhh yeah. That makes me hard!" Roger exclaimed, while Alex put one fist to the ground and waved his butt around in two concentric circles. "OOHH, OOHH, AHHH, AHHH, OOH, AHH!" he exclaimed while careful to hold onto his now extinguished cigarette, another superstition.

The dealers collected the $500 dollars for their hard way bets and paid Alex and Roger $225 each for their hard way and returned $320 each for their come bets on the six. They each promptly gave back $100 for place bets on the six and $50 to get the dealers back on the hard six.

The girls, while amused at the goings on, still found themselves down $200 on the roll with $200 more at risk. This changed promptly as Gary hit a five on the next throw, inciting applause and a round of high fives all the way around the table. One of the girls even tried to produce a monkey noise, but it came out poorly. From there, they left the primate imitations to Alex who was now nearly constantly bobbing his head even when not making the sounds.

Once Gary hit his first point, things started to happen fast. Gary rolled back-to-back eights, including a hard way on the second one. Everyone on the table increased their pass line bet to $200.

Natasha: "Gary, you are awesome."

Roger: "That's our man, G-Balls."

Natasha: "Sorry. My mistake. G-Balls, you are awesome."

Roger: "Come on, shooter. You are rolling until the sun comes up."

Alex: "Ooohhh, oohh, ahh, ahh, oooh, oooh."

Dealer: "Dice are out, coming out."

Stickman: "The role is eleven. Pay the front."

Berlin (her arm around Gary's waist): "We love you, G-Balls."

Alex (head bobbing wildly): "Oooh, ooh, aah, aah!"

Gary's next roll was an another eight, establishing a new point. After placing odds, Roger gave the dealer an extra $520 and told him to place five-twenty across, covering the table with bets. Alex did the same, switching his dead Dunhill from one hand to the other to do so.

The next rolls were: three, ten, ten, five, twelve, six, six and eight.

Once paid for his pass line bet, Alex paused from his monkey act to give Roger a quick glance which said without words, "Holy, shit, this is really good." Roger acknowledged by raising his eyebrows and reaching around to pinch Alex on the ass. Alex rotated his gaze to Gina who was bending down to organize her winnings, revealing most of her well-shaped breasts. For a moment, his vision started to blur from the alcohol and he saw four of the beautifully shaped mounds, but he was able to snap himself out of it and refocus.

Kelly, who had been the quietest of the group, bounced over to Gary and gave him a hug and a kiss on the cheek. Gary was all smiles, but switched his game face back on for the come out roll. He hit a seven, costing Roger and Alex a few small come bets but making a winner out of everyone else.

Alex, who paused to brush some cigarette ash off the sleeve of his sweater, remained uncontrollably happy, both with the few grand in winnings at the casino and with the good fun he was having with two of his best old friends and four new friends. After a quick "oooh-ooh, aaah, aah" and an "aaah, aah, ooooh, ooh" for good measure, he put his arm around Roger and watched as Gary rolled another five for a new point.

Roger remained confident in the shooter, who had now been rolling for eighteen minutes. He began reaching into Alex's rack of chips, a nearly full but disorganized array of white, red, purple, black and yellow. Heavily slurring, he said, "Gimme two yeeeelow ones."

Alex: "Dude, get your grimy paws off of my chips."

Roger: "Just gimme a grand. It'll be good. We'll split it."

Alex reluctantly pulled out two yellow chips and handed them to Roger, curious to see what his intentions were. Roger handed them, along with two of his own, to the dealer and asked for a $1,000 nine and a $1,000 ten. Gary, not wanting to be left out, threw down two black chips and bought a $100 nine and a $100 ten. Even Natasha and Kelly decided to throw in an extra $200 each to join in. Alex pressed the six and eight another $120 each. Roger followed suit.

Gary, who still had over $1,500 in his rack, suddenly began to feel a bit nervous and he could feel his heart beating faster. His jitters were somewhat relieved when he looked to his left to see Alex in the three-point position, trying to use his ass to knock Gary closer to Berlin. Gary let himself fall into her lightly, then fired the dice. Again, the results were nearly immediate. His first roll was a nine, igniting a shout of jubilation, a round of hugs, and more ass-grabbing from Roger. Roger and Alex pressed their nine up by $500, spent

$200 on new hard way bets and put the remaining $700 of the payout in a new rack of communal funds.

With the point still five, the next rolls were as follows: four, eight, eleven, two, four, ten, nine, four, ten, five.

The rowdy band of seven's enthusiasm for hitting this last point was so great that the casino manager wandered over from the blackjack pits to see what was so exciting. She was an attractive woman of about forty years of age with short straight brown hair, wearing a black suit with the skirt cut just above her knees. Her name tag identified her as Roxanne. Upon arrival at the table, she crossed her arms and watched with a combination of amusement and annoyance as Alex jumped up and down "oooh-ooh, aaah-aahing" like a gorilla in heat. She quickly scanned the chip racks to see what kind of damage was being done to the casino's finances. It took her only two seconds to identify the players as the type the casino wanted to attract, but no threat to the bottom line. She walked behind Alex and patted him firmly on his ass, shocking him back into humanity.

Roxanne: "Good morning. What is your name?"

Alex: "Alex."

Roxanne: "Okay, Alex. I am Roxanne. I am glad to see you guys are having a good time in here, but try to tone it down a bit, okay? This is a casino, not a zoo."

Alex, who for the last half an hour had been oblivious to anything except the craps table and its small group of participants, scanned the casino floor, surprised to see it was now nearly empty of patrons.

Two carpet-cleaning vehicles were silently maneuvering themselves around the slot machines, erasing the evidence of earlier activity with a soft hum. Outside, totally unknown to anyone in the casino, the sky over the eastern mountains surrounding Las Vegas began to brighten. It was a new dawn, announcing the imminent arrival of another day, in case there was any doubt. Perhaps the new day would be slightly different than the last. Perhaps it would build from its predecessor. Grow. Evolve. There was simply no way to know. The only certainty was that this night would soon become part of the past, irretrievable.

Alex agreed with Roxanne to behave and instinctively looked at the girls who were giggling like fourth-graders, which is pretty much what he felt like. Then he looked at his rack of chips and the piles of chips on the numbers on the table and ceased to care. Roxanne walked away and Alex leaned into Gary's ear and whispered, "Oooh, ooh, aaah, aah, motherfucker. Hit some more numbers."

Roger considered any type of interference from casino personnel to be a bad omen and considered pulling down the bets on the nine and ten, each of which were now two grand, but he decided not to.

Gary started a new roll and delivered a very well-timed seven, adding three more black chips to everyone's hoard. Roxanne was forgotten and the cheering and high fives commenced at an only slightly subdued level. These gains were given right back when Gary came out with a three, then replenished once again with an eleven. Finally, Gary made a new point, a six. Roger and Alex emptied out their communal treasury by placing $1,000 on the five and pressing the nine up to $3,000. Gary again imitated by placing $300 bets. Alex bobbed his head and did some monkey speak and Gary threw the dice. They bounced off the back wall. One fell into the middle of the table showing a six, but the other bounced strangely to the left and flew off the table leading to a round of cursing and concern. All three of the guys subscribed to the universal belief that it is extremely bad luck for any of the dice to leave the table.

Roger: "Oh, no. I don't like that one bit."

Alex: "Hmmm. It's okay. We just need to get through two rolls. G-Balls is our man."

Roger: "Okay. Let's go, shooter. Get back on that six. Numbers, numbers, numbers."

Alex: "Oooh, ooh, aah, aah, ooh, ooh, aah, aah."

Dealer: "Three, crap dice, three."

Alex: "Okay, no harm. Nice work."

Roger: "Let's go, shooter. All night."

Berlin: "Come on, G-Balls. Hit my spot."

Alex: "Oooh, ooh, ahh, aah, aah, aah, ooh, oh."

Dealer: "Four, the roll is a four. Duece, duece, four the hard way."

Alex: "OOOH, OOOH, AAAH, AAAAH, thataboy, G."

Roger: "Yes, G-Balls!"

Alex (quietly to Roger): "Have you ever seen anything like this?"

Roger: "Maybe once or twice, but it is very rare. Enjoy it while it lasts."

Kelly came back over to Gary and gave him another kiss on the cheek, her hand lingering on the small of his back. Alex decided to press up the four and the six by $2,000 each and also pressed the hard ways by $100 each and $10 more each for the dealers. He also made a $500 come bet. Roger and Gary had given up following Alex precisely but also added a number of black and yellow chips to their bets already on the table.

Dealer: "The dealers thank you kindly, sir."

Alex: "My pleasure. Let's make some more points."

Roger: "Numbers, numbers, numbers."

Alex (jumping up and down again): "OOOOH, OOOH, AAAH, AAAH, OOOH, OOOH, AAH, AAH!"

Natasha: "Let's go, shooter. Ooooohhh!"

Gary: "Here we go."

Dealer: "Eight. No field, eight. The hard ways fall. Pay the place bets."

Alex (bobbing his head rapidly): "OOOH, OOOH, AAAAH, AAAH"

Roger (to Alex): "Incredible."

Alex: "Yeah, that number is not as good as the others, but we will take it. Sir, give me $1,000 odds on the eight, take the place bet down and press the four by $500."

Roger (handing the dealer an assortment of black and purple chips): "Press my eight and press the four by $500."

Kelly: "Let's go, Gary. You are awesome."

Alex was so into the dice game that up until now he had largely ignored the fact that four very attractive girls were clearly extremely interested in him and his friends. He checked his watch, his left hand still holding the dead Dunhill, to see if there may be time left in the night to try and convince one of the girls to get a room with him. He pondered only a few seconds before deciding that even if the opportunity presented itself, he did not want to leave his friends. Also, he realized he was probably too tired and drunk to perform and should be satisfied if he could get a phone number, preferably from the one he now thought was named Krakow. He noted with amusement that the one in the pink was clearly infatuated with Gary despite the prominent wedding band on his left hand which he had been using to roll.

Finished with his reassessment of the girls, Alex quickly scanned the chip racks. While he, Roger and Gary each had one rack nearly full with chips, Alex was shocked to see how little actual money remained, as nearly all of the surviving chips were ones, fives and twenty-fives. Counting only the money in the racks, Roger was down to $875, Alex $790 and Gary $1,220. Only $500 remained in Alex and Roger's communal fund. The girls now had over $5,000 each. This didn't compute in his head until he scanned the table and realized he alone had over $6,500 on the board, with Roger nearly equal. He was a bit shocked as he couldn't ever remember having more than two grand on the table at any one time in his gambling history. "Rock n' Roll," he thought. Apparently, Roger had a similar observation.

Roger: "Dude, there's a lot of fucking money out there all of a sudden."

Alex: "I was just noticing that. Smoke 'em if you got 'em, I guess."

Dealer: "Dice are out."

Alex (beginning to bob his head): "Oooh, ooh, aaah, aaah."

Kelly: "Let's go, Gary."

Natasha: "Come on, shooter."

Roger: "Go, G-Balls. Numbers, numbers, numbers."

Alex (getting into the three-point stance and nearly humping the ground): "OOOH, OOOH , OOOH, OOOH, AAAH, AAAH, AAAH, AAAH!"

Berlin: "Come on, baby. Do it for us."

Roger slapped Alex on his ass: "Hey, over there, is that Mike? Check it out, walking by the sports book."

Alex stood up on his toes to get a better look over the slot machines: "Holy shit. It is. It's Sourpuss. Should we call him over here?"

Roger: "It looks like he is with someone."

Alex: "Yes. Hold on. Isn't that?...My God...It is. That's the biscuit from the In 'N Out burger. Tara."

Roger: "Damn, she is looking fine. You may need to rethink your fast food uniform fetish. She looks a hell of a lot better in a mini-dress."

Alex: "Fuckin' A. Absolutely incredible. She is indisputably the Queen of Vegas. At least for tonight."

Roger: "Makes you wonder how she ended up with Mike."

Alex: "All I can say is, Wow!"

Roger: "Yeah."

Alex: "Seriously. Wow!"

Roger: "From now on, I am eating every meal at In 'N Out."

Alex: "Yeah, those are good burgers. Jesus. Who is the big fucking winner in the casino now?"

Roger: "Mikey is."

Alex: "Yep. Mikey is."

As they watched, Mike and Tara stopped walking in front of the elevator bank that led to the guest rooms. They held hands, facing each other and staring into each other's eyes. They began to kiss, slowly at first; then it rapidly evolved into a sloppy make-out session with Mike's hands groping clumsily all over her ass.

Alex: "Check it out. Mikey, you sneaky little cooze-commando. You go, boy."

Roger: "Amazing."

Alex: "You see, I told you everything always works out."

Roger and Alex continued to be engaged by the romance of their friend and his beautiful companion, temporarily oblivious to the craps game. They watched quietly as Tara led him by the hand to the guest room elevators and hit the call button. One opened immediately and she dragged him inside. They started kissing again, her hand moving to the crotch area of his jeans. With that, the silver elevator doors slid shut. The next chapter would be their own.

Because he rolled it, Gary saw it first. "Ah, fuck," he mumbled.

Roger and Alex were still staring stupidly at the elevator door and didn't register what happened until they heard the dealer make the call, "Seven. Seven out. Line away." Alex's eyes immediately shifted back to the craps table, frantically searching for the dice. He saw a two at the far end of the table, and then, sure enough, located the other die leaning up against the dealer's stacks of chips. It came to rest at nearly a forty-five degree angle, but there was no doubt it was a five.

Their response was simultaneous.

Roger: "Thumper the God-damned Rumper Humper! Fuck me slowly."

Alex: "No. No. No. No. Schweddy, Schweddy Fucking Balls!"

~ THE END ~

Thanks very much for reading this book.

Any and all feedback is appreciated. Feel free to email to craig@333miles.com. I will try to respond in timely manner.

If you enjoyed it, someone you know might also. Remember, generous people are cool.

This book is independently published so every copy sold or read makes a meaningful difference in its success. I don't intend to make money with this book, but each order increases the chances it can be more widely distributed and read.

Additional copies can be purchased at:

www.333miles.com

or

www.amazon.com – search for 333 Miles.

Cheers.